I0693302

June 23

Dear Second,
Your words replay in my mind.
You called me to you, giving me
permission to pour my heart's
contents all over the floor. You've
offered to help me pick them up.

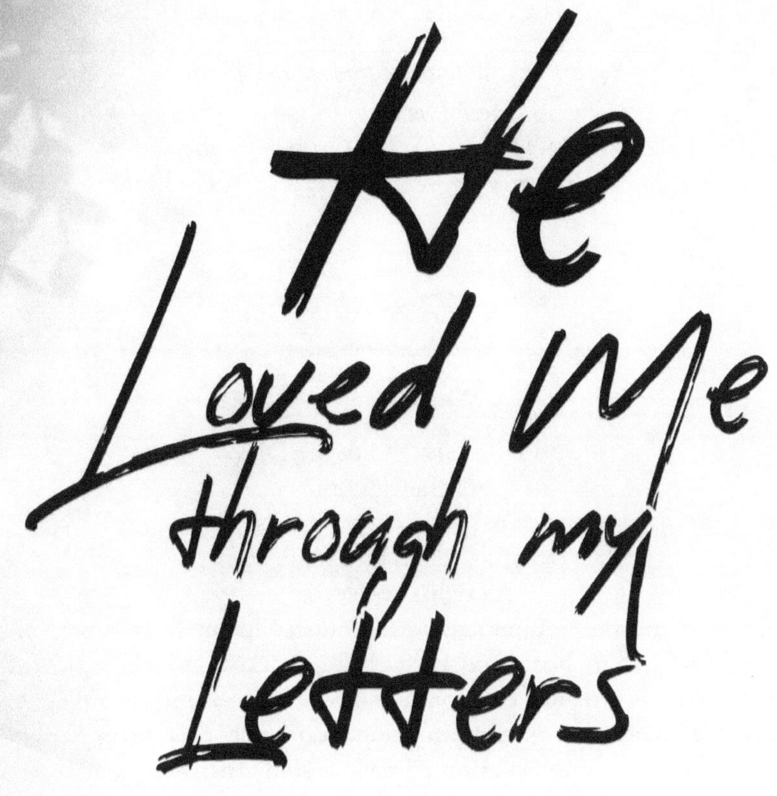

BOOK 2 OF THE WAITING TRILOGY

SARA FRANCIS

This one's for me.
To the girl who only wanted to see others happy.
To the teen who thought they were never enough.
To the woman who's stronger from all of it.

Three wrong words break a heart.
Five wrong words consume a soul.
Ten wrong words last eternity.

June 7

I've been waiting.

I've been waiting.

Days, months, years I've been waiting. My heart yearns for you. It cries for you. Please come and wipe my tears. Tell me everything will be okay.

Save me.

Please.

June 7

Hello Love,

I haven't had words to say lately. Life sucked the childlike enthusiasm out of me and replaced it with busy schedules, clients, and emails. I used to write letters to you every day. I would share stories of how I danced around the kitchen with my sisters, singing a song I hoped to share with you on our wedding day. I would tell you how many bulls-eyes my arrows struck in an hour. I would rant about work gossip with hopes that we could look back together and laugh.

Lately, my words are disconsolate. Pain drips from my pen as tears stream down my cheeks.

Why?

I have a secure job, a loving family, and I'm in a relationship.

And yet, why am I looking for ways to escape?

Why am I still writing to you?

Why am I still waiting for you?

Sincerely,

Violetta

June 8

Hello Love,

I don't know why I still write. Perhaps it's the prayer that I'll find you someday and share these letters with you.

A box overflowing with colorfully patterned notebooks and random scraps of paper hides in my closet. Almost a decade of letters, notes, and memories for you. My family doesn't know about this routine of mine. *He* certainly doesn't.

I know what you're thinking. Shouldn't I believe the man I'm dating will be the one these letters are for?

I thought so once. Three years ago when my heart was young and desperate. When life cracked my soul and I sought someone to patch me up.

But his repairs are messy. Sticky and unreliable. I'm falling apart bit by bit.

Soon, I'll shatter into a million pieces.

Ugh, Love, where are you? Everyone says "put yourself out there," or "he'll find you when it's time."

When is it time? How many pages do I need to go through? This summer's letters are scribbled across the pages of a new white leather notebook. One Aunt Margot gifted to me. One that belonged to her murdered sister. One she claimed would "save me" because it couldn't save Kayleigh.

Aunt Margot seems crazy, but I trust her. The stories of her witnessing her sister's murder are true. The part about Kayleigh seeing ghosts? I don't know.

My heart breaks for Aunt Margot. She told me they imprisoned her sister's murderer because of evidence left in a string of notebooks. Kayleigh didn't finish writing in this one before he killed her. Only three sentences scrawl across the first page.

Is that why I'm still writing to you? Am I afraid my current relationship will spiral and bleed?

Will I need evidence to prove I'm not crazy?

Maybe I'll start now and pray I won't need my sisters to turn my letters over to the police.

Yours frightened.
Violetta

June 10

Hello Love,

Today hurt.

An ache in my chest strangled my heart. He told me everything would be fine. He told me I should stop being paranoid.

A bright evening sun beat down on my forehead. Red spread across my face. My Irish freckled skin never did well in the heat. I surely burned, but he said it wasn't that bad. It was a cooler night than we've had.

"I'm happy we're finally alone," Bryce said as we walked. "It's been a little over a week since we've gone on a date. You're too busy for me now."

I shoved my hands deep into the pockets of my jean shorts. Sure, my job was tiring, but it kept me busy. No other event coordinator could develop run-of-shows, maintain complicated schedules, and manage day-long events without losing their sanity like I could. Would I be less busy if my co-worker actually did his job? Of course.

But honestly, the busier I was, the less I had to be with Bryce.

"I'm sorry," I apologized half-heartedly. "Don't forget you're busy, too."

He plucked a leaf off of a tree as we passed the park in town. "Don't turn this on me, Vi. You should request more time off."

A gust of wind blew through my hair. I wished I could be whisked away like the leaves tumbling around my feet. Taken far away from here.

Bryce grabbed my wrist and pulled it out of my pocket. He slid his fingers between mine.

A shudder went up my spine. His clammy hands squeezed my palm tightly, not to show affection, but to hold me close as if he knew I wanted the wind to blow me far away from him. I felt his nails dig into my skin. Rough, harsh. I prayed there wouldn't be blood today. I was running out of excuses for the scabs.

Years ago, I considered always staying by his side. The wide eyes he gave me across the room were like a puppy seeing a treat. It was innocent and sweet. The awkward moments exchanged in our high school hallway were endearing. His parent's house was a second home to my twin sisters. Whenever I would stop by the Kazanski's to pick up my sisters after an afternoon doing homework together, he always answered the door and chatted with me. After almost a year of being friends, he asked me out. It was a quirky date. We spent time at an abandoned train station, chatting about nothing. We sat in the grass, snacking on pretzels as the cargo trains rushed by. He wanted to make it official, so I gave him a chance, and it worked out.

Or so I thought.

The town filled the awkward silence between us. Cicadas chirped in the tall green trees. An upbeat melody from an acoustic band floated from a gazebo in the town park. Fireflies fluttered across our path.

Everything about this date was romantic. Strolling hand-in-hand through a lively village, watching a summer sunset.

But no love sparked between us. This was routine. We'd get chocolate and vanilla ice cream at Paula's Creamery, sit in the park to talk about our day, and then he'd walk me home. These weekly dates felt like regularly scheduled one-on-ones I'd have with my director at work. They were touch bases. Catch-ups. Any topics we didn't want to talk about, we'd "circle back" next time.

When we first got together, I suggested countless unique dates. I asked to go hiking, rock climbing, sailing, or something fun and exciting. The answers I always received cycled between "Well, you plan it," or "I can't give up a whole day," or "I don't want to do that, let's do this instead."

I never pushed back, so I stopped asking. I didn't want to fight. I wanted to make sure he was happy.

"Vi, you're always so quiet," Bryce commented.

I shrugged. "I've got a lot on my mind."

He rolled his eyes. "Yeah, so does everyone else. Why don't you want to talk to me?"

I shot him a look. "I never said—"

"Don't worry about it. I forgive you." He squeezed my hand even tighter; my knuckles turned white. "Just don't forget to call me later. We'll figure out time for another date–hopefully not over a week from now."

My fingers felt like static. I wanted to pull away but he'd get upset and think I didn't want his affection. I didn't want his nails to leave a mark. He craved attention and wasn't happy without it. I didn't want to push his buttons, but I prayed for the evening to end.

The red-door of my parents' home came into view. My heartbeat matched my pace. I wanted to get inside, shut the door, and sink to the floor.

"Don't forget, Trisha's party is this Friday." He smiled crookedly.

My stomach twisted. "Yes, I'll be late because I have to drive my sisters to their youth group. Like I do every Friday." I grumbled the last words under my breath.

"You're too nice, Vi. You should just make them pay someone to drive them." He waved his hand in front of his face. "Whatever, meet me there then. I want to show you off. Just don't wear that blue dress. Don't want the girls teasing you."

My neck reddened, matching the sunburn on my forehead. My favorite blue dress? The one I feel the most confident in? The one I *thought* he liked? First off, I would be twenty-three in September. Girls making fun of me for resembling Merida from that princess movie happened when we were in high school. The only reason why it still bothered me is because it bothered him. It didn't irk him because they mocked me with pointed fingers. It annoyed him because he hated that movie.

"That's my favorite dress," I mumbled.

He clicked his tongue. "Yeah, but it's not my favorite. I know what my friends like, trust me. That one won't go over well. Same with your fiery curls." He tugged on my hair. "Might want to get them under control."

Heat burned my cheeks. Did he know what I liked? Did he ever actually listen when I spoke? I loved my curly hair once, just like how I used to love that blue dress.

We walked the last stretch to the porch in silence before I asked, "Is Melissa going to be there?" I used to never care if his high school ex attended the same functions. But at the last gathering, I noticed the two talking a little too closely at the bar. If my best friend, Allura, and her boyfriend hadn't kept me company I would have sat in the corner anxiously waiting to be driven home.

I know what you're thinking, Love. Why didn't I call him out? I did on the ride home, but he brushed it aside and babbled about how amazing Melissa's new job is. His words only rattled my anxious mind.

He rolled his eyes. "Vi, you're so paranoid. There is nothing to worry about." His hand pressed to the small of my back. "Melissa is the past. You're my future." Thin lips kissed my forehead.

A chill shot down my spine. Every day, I asked myself if I used to believe it. I wondered if I ever thought if we were perfect together. I wondered if I ever thought his love would satisfy the hole in my heart.

But his lies were daggers digging into my heart's open wound, yanking downward until all the blood poured out.

I carefully wriggled out of his grasp. He didn't notice me squirming. "Thanks for the ice cream," I said as I hopped up my front steps.

He waved and I slid through the door, locking it behind me.

I exhaled a shaky breath. Sinking to the floor, I rested my back against the cool wood. I didn't have the energy to lean over and untie my high-tops. I stared into space, waiting for the sweet release of sleep.

"Are you back, Violetta?" A strong voice rumbled from the kitchen.

"No, I'm front." I groaned.

"I'll be left!" my sister, Eleora, shouted.

"Left behind is more like it," Aria quipped.

I heard a smack and a quiet curse.

I lazily reached for my shoelaces. "Does anyone who isn't left behind want to help me untie my shoes?"

"No," they shouted in unison.

"Love you, too." I forced myself to loosen my laces and kick the shoes off my feet. I crawled down the hallway, the gruff tiles scratching my palms. The sensation of Bryce's clammy hands scraped away.

The TV blasted the chaotic dialogue of one of my parents' favorite shows. We'd spend hours watching three robots hilariously comment on the dumbest movies. It brought us joy.

Peering into the room, I mapped out where all my family sat. Aria lay on the floor, eyes glued to the television. Sage curled up next to Felicity on the loveseat against the right wall. Eleora sat with my mom on the sofa against the back wall. Mom was closest to the doorframe. With a smirk, I pounced and shook her shoulders.

She didn't move an inch. Her side eye said it all.

"Ugh, c'mon, Mom." I rubbed her head. "Can't you pretend to be scared at least once?"

"She is the queen of jump scares," Eleora stated. "She scared the crap out of me when I came home last night. I didn't even know she was sneaking up behind me."

"That's six points for mom this week." Felicity signed in ASL. She tapped her face and her lips formed an *o*. "Oh, and four for me, don't forget."

"Yeah, yeah, we know, Felicity." Aria waved her hand. "You and Mom are the best."

Felicity arched an eyebrow and signed. "Oh, what was that? You know I can't hear. Please repeat that?" A smirk crossed her lips.

Aria grunted. "I saw you read my lips. I am not gracing you with another compliment."

Felicity chuckled and noted the points on her phone.

"What's the prize this week?" Dad asked.

"Laundry duty." Aria rolled her eyes. "Dad, your underwear is so gross."

Sage smacked her twin's arm. "Hey, you're no better."

Mom giggled and signed. "Aria's right, Sage. Try being married to him. All of him is gross."

My lips turned upward. My family always brought a sliver of light to the darkest of days. My Deaf mother and hearing father joined as one to give life to five unique girls. All multi-talented and a little crazy in their own ways.

"What did your mother say about me?" he shouted and stepped into the hall. A dish towel draped over his broad shoulder and the mug in his large hands looked like it belonged to my old doll's tea set. "I heard laughing."

"Nothing, Dad," we replied in unison.

My mom smiled and gently touched my arm. "How was your date with Bryce?"

The sliver of light dimmed as *he* came back into my mind. His tight hands, his passive comments. My fingertips gently rubbed the raw skin where his nails dug. Each memory tugged at the corners of my smile, dragging them downward.

My mom's brows furrowed. She knew something was wrong. She always did, but I never told her the whole truth. Her hands raised, but I gently clasped them.

"I'll be okay, Mom. Nothing to worry about," I lied.

Mom frowned and kissed my knuckles. Slowly and intentionally, she signed, "Just because I can't hear, doesn't mean I'm a bad listener."

My eyes softened. I knew that. I always did. But the dark truth about Bryce? That's one thing no one should have to listen to.

It's something I wanted to forget.

"I'm going to get changed." I jerked my head toward the staircase. "I'll see you guys later."

Fingertips brushed my shoulder, but I kept going. Tears burned my eyes. I couldn't let my family see me like that—especially not my sisters. I broke down too often in front of them. Their oldest sister, who was supposed to stand tall and pave a smooth path for her siblings, shuts down faster than a broken 90s computer.

I tossed my purse onto the floor, spilling the contents. I flopped onto my bed and buried my face into the pillows. I tried to hide myself in their soft blue plush, praying to empty my mind of anxiety and doubtful thoughts.

But the party on Friday occupied my mind and my heart ached.

Allura was still away with her family. I wouldn't have anyone to talk to. Bryce certainly wouldn't stay by my side.

I didn't hate my high school friend group. In better circumstances, I would have enjoyed their company. But when Bryce was there? It was like I didn't exist. He had an aura of fog that consumed me, making me invisible to everyone.

I lay for twenty minutes before I rolled over. Glow in the dark stars on my ceiling twinkle like I was looking at the open sky.

When I was a little girl, my dad told me those stickers were bits of magic to keep my darkness brighter. Bits of God's beauty splattered on my ceiling.

Miracle, magic, whatever *M* word, I prayed for it. I needed to add a little sparkle to my dimming life.

And that's why I keep writing these letters.

I write them with the hopes that you'll find me, Love.

I miss writing about my joys. I want to smile as my pen strokes the page. The water in my eyes should be from laughter, not tears.

I miss my old self. The little girl who thought her ceiling was magic or would run around with her sisters playing hide-and-seek. I want the teen who sang so loud it rattled the walls, no matter how bad she sounded. I want to become a woman who loves to adventure and explore without the fear of someone pushing her down into the mud.

I want the real Violetta to come back, not this depressed version you see between the pages of this white leather notebook.

But I need help bringing her home.

With sorrow.
Violetta

June 12

Hello Love,

Bryce is not the one. He never was. These letters were never for him.

Again, I say this. *Again*, I write this.

But I can't take it.

I hate the lies. The image of Bryce whispering in her ear while he watched me with a smirk is stuck to my eyes. I don't know why I go anywhere with him. I don't know why I am still with him.

Is it because our families are friends? Is it because of what happened last time I tried to leave?

I don't know what to do. I should be getting married soon. We've been together so long, everyone says we should just tie the knot.

But they don't see it. They don't see the glares. They don't hear the disappointed groans. They don't notice the tight grip on my hand while the other is reaching for someone else. I don't think he sees it, either.

I wore the dress he wanted. I did my hair how he wanted. I thought if I pleased him, he'd listen to me.

It's never enough.

When I told him I was leaving the party, he called me lame. He said I was being "too uptight." He said I was "overreacting." Melissa wasn't flirting. He said he didn't ignore me.

If that was true, then why did everyone I encounter ask, "Where is Bryce?"

The worst part? Tomorrow he won't be mad at me for dipping early. He'll flip it and convince me I was tired. He'll claim it was better that I went home and rested. No words will be shared about the woman he flirted with in the kitchen.

Gah. The mascara burns my eyes. Tears stain these pages. I am tired of these nights. Sorrowful, tear-filled, heartbroken. I want someone to take me away. How many times do I have to scream? How many times do I have to cry:

"I've been waiting."

"I've been waiting."

"I'VE BEEN WAITING."

You don't have to wait anymore.

???

What

Ummm

What is this?

Where did these words come from? Am I that exhausted that my hands wrote faster than my mind could think?

No, no, I'm not that crazy. Am I? Violetta, you're confused. That's not your handwriting. The real question I should be asking myself is "What is this?"

I am not sure. I've been hearing your voice over and over.

Okay, Violetta. Now it's official. You're going insane. Those words just appeared. And is that glitter sparkling on the page? It's gone now. Am I hallucinating?

I didn't drink tonight. I drove myself to the party. He didn't want to be late waiting for me to drop my sisters off at the youth group. For once, I'm happy I am a people pleaser. If I didn't say yes, I wouldn't have had my car. I would've been trapped there. I would've locked myself in the bathroom and cried.

Then, when I saw you, I had to say

something.

Okay, I'm officially freaking out. I'm trying to erase the words but they won't disappear. Every time text appears, there are sparkles like tiny fairy lights dancing on the paper. I try to erase them, but they won't disappear or even fade.

I shut my curtains. Is someone watching me? Why are they only responding to certain things I write? Or are they listening to me mutter to myself? What if I say out loud, "You can see me?"

Yes, I can see you, and I can hear you.

Panic time. I didn't say it out loud. I wrote it.

Can you see me?

No, no, no, I can't. I have no idea who you are.
I'm so confused.
Hello?
You're not responding to my flailing arms or screaming voice. You're not responding to these scribbles.
Silence fills my room as I listen. All I hear is the wind whipping against the house and my dad's wooden chimes singing from the front porch.
Looking back at this letter, maybe I should write grammatically? Maybe my response should be written in story form?
No, that's crazy. *I'm* crazy.
But still…
Eh, screw it.
"Only your words."

That's amazing.

No way, it worked. Can I have a conversation with this person?

"What is your name?"

They call me Second.

"Nickname, I presume. That's okay. I still don't understand what's going on. I've been doing this almost every day for years, but no one has ever replied to me."

It's only because I didn't hear you until now. But when you spoke to me for the first time, I haven't stopped thinking about you.

Hold up. Time out. This guy has heard me speak before? He's thinking about me?

These letters are meant for the man I've prayed for. The one my soul cries for every night. The one to whom I desire to say, "I've thought of you every day for ten years."

Could he *really* be replying through these letters?

This notebook belonged to Aunt Margot's deceased sister, Kayleigh. The girl who claimed to speak to a ghost right before her fiancé killed her.

Did that actually happen? Was the ghost real?

Is… is that happening to me?

I'm sorry to do this, but I need to go. I don't want to, but there are people who need me. Will you be back?

He needs to go? Where do ghosts wander off to?

No, Violetta. He's not a ghost.

But… Aunt Margot isn't crazy. She watched her sister die. There is truth to her claims. The real question is how much?

I guess it's time to find out.

"I haven't broken my routine in ten years. The question is will you speak to me again?"

Of course I will. You may get sick of me
by the end.

The end? The end of what?

"How can I be sick of someone I don't know yet? You'll have to explain yourself when you return. Until our next speaking, Second."

I need to talk to Aunt Margot.

After our conversation, I snatched my phone off the nightstand. My wrist smacked against my glass, splashing water all over the floor. I swore, jumped up, and ran out into the hall to grab a towel.

Aria flung open the bathroom door as I was about to yank on the handle. She squealed. "Geez, can you not try and get extra points so late at night?"

I shoved past her and flung open the closet door.

She grunted. "You okay? You look like you've seen a ghost."

"Interesting choice of words." I grumbled as I plucked a fluffy hand towel out of its disheveled pile.

"That's a weird thing to say." She dragged out the last few words. Water droplets flew off her bangs as she shook her head. "Whatever, you're pale. Get out sometime and see the sun instead of hiding in your room like a vampire."

"Can vampires and ghosts live in the same universe?" I forced a smile to hide the tears brimming at the corners of my eyes.

"I don't know, host a séance and ask Kaaaayleiiiigh." She sang the name of our aunt's dead sister like a phantom rising from the grave. Aria was always insensitive to our family's history. When I returned from my last visit with Aunt Margot, Aria asked if I saw dead people or if ghosts can make food so she can have a personal chef that won't eat her leftovers (the culprit is usually Eleora).

The towel prevented my nails from digging into my palms. "Will you stop picking on Aunt Margot?"

She threw her hands up. "Will you stop being a stick in the mud? It's a good story. I know it by heart. If you weren't so distant, you'd know that parapsychology is something I love to research." She gathered her phone and hairspray.

"I know you're a science nerd obsessed with the paranormal." I paused. "But do you believe Aunt Margot's story? Did a spirit she called 'Little Ghost' actually try to save her?"

She rolled her eyes and slipped through her bedroom door, leaving my question hanging in the silence. I returned to my room, cleaned the mess, and wrote down our exchange. I wondered if the ghost would hear our conversation, but he never responded. I suppose there are only certain phrases he'll reply to, so I guess I can continue these letters as I always do.

Aria never answered, but the more important question is for me. Do I even believe it?

Yours skeptical.
Violetta

June 13

Oh love,

Aunt Margot is not crazy. Aunt Margot is traumatized. Truth rang each word like a bell. Sadness pricked each syllable. Her heavy heart drowned in a sea of mortifying memories.

My family doesn't think she's crazy. My uncle knows his wife is sane. Despite winning the case to put away her sister's murderer, most of the world views her as a nutjob.

"He was horrible." Aunt Margot set a plate of fresh zucchini bread on the table. "Constantly making Kayleigh feel bad. Telling her it was her fault." The wooden chair creaked as she sat. "She deserved the world, and he took everything from her."

"Why didn't she leave him earlier?" I wrapped my hands around the warm mug of coffee, watching her slice the bread with a delicate precision.

She placed down the long blade and picked up a fork. "When you're in a situation, it's hard to tell its severity. Sometimes you feel alone or guilty." She raised her eyebrows. "Sound familiar?"

I humphed. Aunt Margot was one of the few people I talked to about Bryce. She and I grew closer over the past year. One of the first nights he left me crying in the parking lot, I ran to her house. I couldn't bring sadness to my home, and my best friend was out of town. So, I brought it to someone who knew what real pain was. Someone who could tell me if I was overreacting or if my hurt was real.

"I gave you Kayleigh's notebook for a reason." She speared a piece of zucchini bread and plopped it onto her white porcelain plate. "I know she's still here. She wants to help another girl escape the fate that befell her like Little Ghost tried to do for her."

There it was. The part of the story the world latched onto and twisted. Aunt Margot told this to my sisters and me several times to warn us. Kayleigh was abused by her fiancé. She wrote her evidence in notebooks. A ghost told her to break up with him. She tried to run away, but her fiancé killed her.

Each retelling followed the same plot. Nothing was out of place. Nothing changed. The ghost was *always* there. He tried to save her and failed.

I pressed the mug to my lips, breathing in the nutty chocolate aroma. "Why a ghost?"

She shrugged and lathered butter across her bread with a small spreader. "God grants gifts to certain people. Is it crazy? Yeah. I doubted Kayleigh at first, too. But the fear in her face. The conviction in her voice." The knife slipped out of her hand and clattered against the plate. She exhaled through her nose. "Violetta, why did you come here to ask me these things?"

Red flushed my cheeks. "I'm sorry. I didn't mean to bring up bad memories."

"Did Bryce make you cry again?" Anger flickered in her voice. "What did he do this time? He didn't hurt you, did he?"

I bit my lip. Tears welled in my eyes. I didn't want to tell her. I didn't want to tell anyone. I didn't want to show anyone the tiny bruises on my hands from his long fingers or reveal all the nights spent crying alone in my room. Those were my problems. Everyone struggled day-to-day. No one needed to carry my struggles, too.

"Violetta," she scolded, "I've told you a million times. This relationship is dangerous. You *have* to tell your parents."

"I can't!" I cried. My knuckles turned white as I clutched the pink ceramic mug. "They don't know anything about it, and I don't want them to. His siblings are friends with my sisters. I don't want to destroy their friendships. Besides, there is so much going on…"

"Yeah, like what?" She tore the bread into small pieces with such ferocity I thought it would crumble. "What is more important than your mental health? What is more important than saving your heart from being torn apart?"

My breath caught in my throat. I wanted nothing more than to be saved.

How? A ghost spoke into Kayleigh's mind for years before his voice became vivid, begging her to leave. How could I be saved?

If Second was real and not a figment of my anxious brain... is that what he would try to do for me?

Aunt Margot popped a piece of bread into her mouth. "I think I know why you're here," she mumbled with stuffed cheeks. "As sad as the situation is, I have a good feeling. It must be time." She swallowed, jumped up from the table, and disappeared into a dark living room.

Moments later, she returned with a wooden box. Its corners were tarnished, and its lock rusted. The delicate bronze vines along the edges turned green with age. She slid the bread aside and placed the box down. "I've never shown anyone this, but you need to know." She unclipped her necklace. A small silver key dangled from its chain. Inserting it into the lock, she clicked it open and said, "If I need anyone to believe me one *hundred* percent, it's you."

My heart raced as she removed the contents. Notebooks, letters, photographs, all from Kayleigh.

"These are only the books the police found unnecessary." Aunt Margot picked up a printed photo. "This, however, I kept for myself." She held it out.

I took it gingerly between my fingers. My stomach knotted when I saw *it*.

A woman with a heart-shaped face and a sad smile awkwardly stared down at the camera. The pixelated selfie looked like it was taken on an early 2000s cell phone. Kayleigh appeared different from the photos on Aunt Margot's walls. Different from the youthful smiling headshots that made Aunt Margot say, "She reminds me of you, Violetta."

Sure, we had similar hair textures, face shapes, and body types. But Kayleigh? She was beautiful no matter the photo. In the print between my fingers, fear filled her light eyes but they were distracted by something—someone—who stood behind her.

A transparent glowing figure of a rugged (albeit handsome) man peered over her shoulder. White eyes, white skin, white everything. His long hair floated above him as if he was frozen underwater. A kind expression covered his face.

A ghost. *The* ghost. The voice that Kayleigh called Little Ghost. The voice that turned out to be a man trying to repay his debt.

The man who tried to save her.

"I-is this real?" My fingers trembled and my stomach didn't want anything in it anymore.

Aunt Margot pursed her lips and nodded. "I never showed anyone this. Not your uncle, not your parents, not even the police. I promised Kayleigh I wouldn't tell anyone. I needed to protect her case. But you," she reached across the table and placed a hand on my arm, "you are hurting like she was. I've *seen* it."

I pinched my eyes shut. How was my pain comparable to Kayleigh's? The man abused her. He *killed* her. Sure, Bryce was bad…

"Your feelings are valid." Margot's eyes narrowed. "Stop trying to downplay your emotions."

My head shot up. "How did you know I was—?"

"That's the face Kayleigh made when debating if her situation was really that bad." Her expression softened. Warmth glowed in her eyes. "You so often remind me of Kayleigh." She let out a shaky exhale. "You need to take care of yourself. Listen to your heart. Listen to God's answer." Leaning forward, she whispered, "Listen to the ghost."

My beating heart raced faster and faster as the summer wind rattled the shutters. Goosebumps raised along my arms. It wasn't fear. It wasn't horror.

It was the thought of being freed.

With hope,

Violetta

June 14

Hello Love,

Sorry these letters are a mix between evidence and notes to you. I honestly don't know what to think about all this. After my conversation with Aunt Margot yesterday, I don't want to leave any details out. If I am going to speak to Second again, I need his words as evidence that I'm not crazy, even if it is only to convince myself.

Today, I spent the hour at Church praying about how to go about my situation with Bryce. How do I break up with a man who will convince everyone I'm the bad guy? How do I cut ties with someone so tightly knit to my family? How do I run away when his dark secret is tied around my waist, yanking me back to him?

I didn't have an answer. I couldn't decide everything in one day, so I needed to focus on one day at a time.

Tomorrow, work will be chaotic. I need to unwind, but I don't know how. I sit on the edge of my bed, staring at my hobbies spread across the room. I don't want to draw; the pictures have all been creepy. I don't want to sing; my sisters ask me to kill the dying cat whenever I try. The archery range is closed for maintenance, and I don't have the energy to hike to my favorite shooting spot.

I could stare at the ceiling and count the glowing stars, but they're starting to fade.

Honestly, Love, I want to talk to you. I want to know who you really are. You're not Bryce—you've never been.

So who are you? Are you *really* answering me?

Hey, I'm back.

My heart flutters. Words appear on the page with glittering sparkles, fading into view like revealing invisible ink. Slow, gradual, and magical.

This is the strangest thing I've ever encountered. I think I should be worried, but I want to *understand* what this is—who Second is. Is he really a ghost who needs to save me in order to move on?

"It's been a minute."

I spoke with you a few hours ago.

Is that why he hasn't reached out? What time is it for him?

"Nope. Days."

Does time go faster for you?

"Not sure. This is still weird for me."

Same, but it's kinda cool.

I appreciate how casual he is. Does he know he might be a ghost talking to me? Does he know that he's speaking through a notebook gifted to me from my aunt's dead sister?

Then again, I'm proud of myself for how relaxed I've been. I didn't drown the notebook in Holy Water or bring it to our priest for a blessing.

Wait, on second thought, maybe I should? I believe this is from Him, but what if it's not? If this starts to get really weird, maybe I will.

"So, Second. What did you do in the time we were apart?"

I did a crazy prank for some sticky buns.

Definitely not what I expected. Low-key adorable.

"Stop, that's hysterical. What did you do?"

Well, no judgment, okay? I work at an all
boys summer camp.

He *is* a guy. Thank God. I had assumed, but I'm glad I was right.

My co-worker, Anderson, is always getting
into trouble with the other Packs—what we
call cabins. So, we snuck around and tied
the other captain's clothes to a flagpole
and hoisted it up. Oh, Captain is a fancy
title for a counselor.

Seems like *almost* a harmless prank. In theory, I'd say I'd be in, but I would feel so bad the next day. I'm wishy-washy with large-scale pranks like that. I like to keep the jokes personal. I love teasing my sisters. I'm the oldest so it's in the job description. I only executed small annoying pranks. From little dolls I hid behind the towels in the closet to the time I told my sister I could turn invisible and hid from her the entire day. They were never thrilled, but I found it funny.

It fits the theme, though, because
everything is backwards at Camp Southpaw.
Breakfast is for dinner, the left-handed
outweigh the right, and we do practically
nothing inside.

Sounds like my household. My sisters' favorite dinner meal is waffles with a peanut butter spread and a side of french fries. Sweet syrup filled every square, thick peanut butter sticking to the roof of our mouths. My favorite meal after a rough day of cleaning hiking trails and maintaining grounds with my dad. My soul rejuvenates every time I dip my fries in the maple-sugary-goodness. A guilty pleasure that Bryce thinks is weird, so I haven't had it in a while.

Well, that's what life used to be like back in high school. Some things seemed much simpler then.

"Your job sounds like a lot of fun. The outdoors is more of my home than a house is thanks to my dad."

Your dad?

"He is a forest ranger. I've been outside since I knew how to walk. Bugs, dirt, none of it bother me."

Did anyone pick on you for being outdoorsy?

Easy answer, but not a fun one. Memories of "forest troll" being chanted in the girls' bathroom lingered in the back of my mind. Harsh words, sneers, rumors that there was nothing original about me whispered in my ears. Bryce's blank stares as they'd only speak to me in a butchered Scottish accent.

"Eh, they think I stole my personality from a cartoon princess. Meanwhile, I've been an archer and nature lover since way before the movie came out."

You're an archer?

That's a cute response. One I didn't know I wanted to hear— well, read. Excitement and curiosity rather than agreeing with those mocking high schoolers.

"I have been since I was little. It's something my family and I can all do together."

My father wanted a son, but he got five daughters instead. Each one is beautifully unique. Archery is something he encouraged us to do together. We only needed our eyes, a bow, and a quiver. I'll never forget the way the world melted around us as the arrows flew down range. In those moments, everything would be okay.

I miss those days.

I'm not so bad at archery myself.
Although, I'd rather be hiking or mountain
climbing.

Why is my heart racing? Why are my cheeks red and my mouth smiling? Bryce would never do anything outdoorsy with me. The fact that I'm an archer shocks him. I've wanted to go hiking with someone down the back trails of my dad's forest, but Bryce would never take me.

"You sound like a person I'd have fun with."

I mean it. Every word. In these brief conversations, I remember how joyful it is to talk to someone with similar interests. Something every basic friendship needs.

Something Bryce and I don't have.

So, is it okay if I ask for your name?

I almost jotted my name without a thought. I almost wrote it in cursive with a heart dotting the i. I want to tell him. Aunt Margot said to listen to the ghost, but how can I trust him?

"You can ask, but I'm not going to tell you. This mystery is more fun."

Ugh, but is it though? Not really. I want to know who he is. I want to know his name. I want to see him and understand what the heck is going on.

Okay, but can I try and guess?

Super cute, again. I have a love/hate relationship with how this is going.

"Sure, my real name starts with a V. You only have three guesses."

Uh, Vanessa?

Classic.
"Nope."

I actually don't know any other V names. I
feel really stupid right now.

He gave up easily. Maybe he didn't want to offend me? He seems genuine.

"Don't feel stupid, my name is pretty hard to guess—which is why I didn't mind you trying to figure it out."

That hardly seems fair. But I guess I can
say the same about mine.

"Oh?"

No, M. It starts with M. You have three
guesses.

I'm so glad he didn't say B.
"Michael."

Common guess. Nope.

"Okay, umm. Maxwell?"

One more guess.

"Mark. Final answer."

Sorry, no prize for you.

That's definitely something I would say, thanks to my dad. During long car-trips, we'd play 20 Questions. Every time we failed, he'd make a buzzer noise and claim we lost the cruise and cash.

"Ugh, now I know how it feels. Maybe just change your name to Mark for me."

Nope, too expensive.

I'm giggling. Why am I *giggling*? This is absurd. His dry wit makes my soul happy. This humor is a love language to my family. We only go two ways: over expressive or deadpan. There is no in-between.

"Fine, Captain Second. New question: will you tell me more about what you are like?"

Well, I don't know where to start.

This phrase masks insecurity. I know because it's one I've used frequently. A segue into another conversation rather than talking about myself. It's the opening line to an impressive story that I can never finish. Not only because I fear what others think of me, but because Bryce hates when I share anything about my life that doesn't involve him.

"Is it you don't know where to start or you're afraid to tell me?"

I know he is uncomfortable sharing, but I crave learning more. My soul needs to understand who this ghost is. Why is he talking to me, toying with my mind?

I'm sorry. I have to leave again.

Is he chickening out? Is something really calling him away? I don't know how ghosts work on this plane of existence. Do they travel between purgatory and here? Is this their purgatory, struggling to find someone to send them home?

"It's okay, I've accepted you can't stay long during our visits. But this means you'll come back, right?"

Absolutely.

Despite the questions swirling in my head, my heart is content for the evening.

"Well, then. I'll talk to you later, Second."

Yours questioning.
Violetta

June 15

Hello Love,

My sisters brought it up again. They mean well, but the way they go about it is entirely unhelpful.

I sat around the kitchen table with Felicity before we both headed off to work. She looked more put together than I felt that morning. Her natural makeup accentuated her cheekbones, and red hair curled beautifully around her round face. Felicity and I were the only sisters to have the Sparks's fiery mane, but she knew how to tame hers better than I ever could. Every morning, I'd crunch my curls with my favorite lavender and pine hair cream and say a prayer.

I placed a pink mug with her favorite cartoon character before her and poured her a cup of coffee.

"Thank you." She signed. Curiosity filled her dark eyes. Her fingers hesitated before she gathered the courage to bring up the question I've been avoiding. "What actually happened the other day? You stormed upstairs after Mom asked about Bryce?"

My heart thumped in my chest. Felicity didn't need to worry. She had her own struggles and trials. I never wanted to impose my burdens upon my little sisters. I know they're hardly little anymore, but I'll always be the protective older sister. I only want them to be happy and throwing my problems at them doesn't work towards that goal.

I waved dismissively. "Nothing you need to worry about. Just another date."

Even though she didn't speak, her arched eyebrow and crossed arms shouted louder than any word. She didn't believe me. Why should she?

I let out a long sigh. While I wanted them to be happy, I still needed to be honest. "It wasn't great. He was a jerk again." Another vague reply. "Mom didn't need to worry about me. She has enough going on with work and dealing with Aria and Sage's shenanigans." My tone attempted to be lighthearted, but the notes soured.

"Is that why you went to see Aunt Margot?" Her head cocked.

I looked down at my favorite bear mug. Ceramic black eyes stared into my soul as if to say "tell her." I took a deep breath. "Yes. She understands and now seems to think," I picked up my cup, "that there's a ghost following me." I whispered the last sentence into my coffee.

Felicity's eyes widened and her lips pursed. "Did I understand that right? A ghost?"

I opened the can of worms. They wriggled all over the floor and I wished I could shove them back in. "Yeah, remember how Kayleigh heard a voice she called Little Ghost?"

"I am well aware." She signed. "Even though I don't believe the ghost story nor that you're being haunted, Aunt Margot is right." Her brows furrowed. "You're crazy for not leaving Bryce, V. You talk to Mom about the dumbest things like when you stub your toe or eat something that makes your stomach hurt. Why don't you tell her about something so serious?"

"Am I crazy?" I replied, pouring more coffee into my bear's head. "Are you going to check me into the institute? Will they help my tummy aches?"

"I should. They'll finally accept you because of this ghost thing. I don't think stomach aches count, though." She rolled her eyes. "You're supposed to take care of yourself." She snatched the milk carton from my hand and splashed it into her coffee followed by three tablespoons of sugar. I know she doesn't *actually* like it, but her exhausting new job drove her to drink—thankfully just coffee.

I scoffed. "What is this strange phrase? Taking care of myself?"

"Vi, I can't see what Felicity is telling you, but yes, take care of yourself. I want your room," Eleora called from the hallway. "Be happy and just move out." She poked her head into the kitchen. "I'm tired of sharing with her. She's a slob." Her hair whipped as she spun back into the hallway.

Felicity's eyebrows furrowed and stuck out her tongue at Eleora. She signed a long string of insults.

I almost spat my coffee when she called her a "cheap-floral wearing-swamp ass." I coughed and smacked my chest, trying to regain my composure.

"I know she's talking about me!" Eleora ran into the room with only one shoe on. Her earth-green maxi dress fit Felicity's description perfectly. "What did you sign?"

Felicity looked away and sipped her coffee. She gagged and forced herself to sip again. The process would repeat until the cup emptied.

My watch vibrated. White letters scrolled down the small screen:

Bryce Kazanski: Hey, why aren't you answering me?

I let out a long breath and swiped the message away.

"Who was that, Vi?" Eleora asked.

"You know." Felicity signed. "Your turn to convince her."

She puffed out her cheeks as she exhaled. "Ugh, but she won't listen to me either." She flung open the pantry door, looked for something to eat, closed it and repeated the process with the fridge. "Do we need Jesus to come back from heaven and tell you, 'Violetta, break up with the man?'"

I groaned and pressed my head against the table. "That would be such an easy sign."

"But what other signs do you need?" Eleora snapped. The brown bun atop her head bounced with her attitude. "You cry during every rom-com we watch whining, 'Oh, why can't I have that?'"

Heat bloomed in my cheeks and a lump caught in my throat. The two of them always noticed my red puffy eyes after my date nights. They sensed the tension whenever he was over.

They knew we weren't meant to be. And yet, their words weren't enough to get me to leave. They didn't understand. They didn't know *him*. They didn't know what he'd do if I left.

Guilt tied me to him. Nothing was sharp enough to cut it and set me free.

"But what about Aria and Sage?" I said into the table. "I don't want to make things weird for them and their friends."

"Dude, they're teenagers." Eleora removed almond milk from the top shelf of the fridge. "They'll understand if their big sister breaks up with an asshole. Who cares if they're still friends with the family? You don't have to be."

She was right. *They* were right. They always were. They knew I wanted out. They've told me multiple times to leave *without* knowing any details. Nothing like what I've shared with Aunt Margot.

And yet I can't leave. I can't because I'm afraid Bryce will... I don't even want to think about it. I don't want to think about what happened last year again.

And yet it sits at the forefront of my mind, looming like a storm cloud. I am praying that it doesn't start raining.

"If you don't break up at some point, I'll do it for you," Eleora threatened.

I lifted my head and rubbed the sunburn above my eyebrow. "Tempting. I have to think about it."

Felicity furrowed her brows. "Stop thinking. Do it."

I pushed myself away from the table. I flung my purse over my shoulder. "Ehhhhhhhhh, no promises."

"If you're still with him by the time of our family camping trip, I'm hosting an intervention," Eleora threatened.

I waved her comment away as I slipped into the hall. As I bent down to put on my shoes, a glint of sunlight caught my eye from the living room. Bright rays bounced off the shiny gloss of the mahogany piano. My gaze lingered on the ivory keys. I ached to hear their melody and sing along. Memories of my dad playing our favorite songs floated in and out of my ears like a ghostly whisper.

I miss the joy and peace of listening and singing along to music without fear of judgment. I miss the evenings where my dad sat at the keys, playing with his eyes closed. I recall my mom pressing her hand against the top of the piano, feeling the song in her soul. My sisters and I danced around the room, singing off key without a care in the world.

But I don't sing anymore, love.

Long car rides with Bryce cut my voice box. Whenever I would start singing along to a song, he jammed the "power off" button. We'd sit in silence until he was ready to lecture me on his new obsession.

I never thought I was that bad of a singer. I participated in musical ensembles in high school and while I was never the best, I never thought my voice was nails on a chalkboard.

Now, my gut twists whenever my heart wants to sing. Lately I've tried to sing in the car by myself, but his side eyes and harsh words are etched into my memories.

I shook my head hard. My sisters' words stirred up in my mind as the memories receded to lay in the dark. Hundreds of scenarios flickered behind my eyes. If I broke up with Bryce, would Aria and Sage resent me cutting ties with their best friends' family? How would their friends respond?

More importantly, how would Bryce react?

Honestly, I'm scared to find out.

Yours discouraged,
Violetta

June 16

Hello Love,

I haven't heard from Second in a few days. He claimed time passes differently for him. I wonder what he's doing? Is he pulling a prank on another counselor? Is he hiking in the woods, drinking in the crisp mountain air?

Ugh, Violetta. He might be a ghost.

If he is, is he like Little Ghost who tried to save Kayleigh? Did Kayleigh become a ghost and send him to help me?

I have no idea why I'm not 100% freaked out by this. Maybe I'm so desperate I'll take any attention. Even if it's from a ghost.

Although, I have to be careful what I wish for. I definitely got way too much attention at work today.

"Violetta, where are we with the charity gala?" Kirk asked. He leaned back in the black office chair, tossing a ball into the air and catching it. "Boss wants a report. Jessica is on PTO so you need to do it."

Little did he know, Jessica wouldn't be back. We had lunch last week and she told me she was leaving after taking the rest of her days off. I'm going to miss her dearly and the reminder of her permanent absence from the workplace didn't improve my spirits.

I ignored him and furiously typed up the next event's run-of-show. My fingers clacked against the keys like a broken typewriter. Obnoxious and loud. Kirk was supposed to do this one. An over-the-top graduation party for a kid who most likely *barely* passed his classes. Kirk dropped the ball and the client grew agitated. I swooped in to save the day… again.

Why didn't I let him fail? Because even though the graduate may be a spoiled rotten brat, their bright smiles and happy memories are in our hands. I can't bear to see someone disappointed.

"I'll get it to him when I'm done," I snapped. I tried not to be angry in the workplace, but my mood had not improved from the previous day. It was the Mondayest Tuesday ever. Between Bryce sending passive-aggressive texts, my sisters' over-simplified advice, and Kirk's attitude, I was ready to explode.

Thankfully, the anticipation of the Sparks's yearly camping trip kept me sane. We leave this weekend.

"No need to get snippy," he sneered, running his fingers through his perfect blond hair. He spun in the chair, hopped up, and peered out the window at the bustling city. "Our job is to make Grandview Entertainment look good."

Heat rushed to my cheeks. I took a deep breath and took my eyes off the screen for a moment. A colorful vinyl of the company's mission statement spread across the paper white wall to my left. I focused on the words, reading over and over again.

"Grandview Entertainment lives for the details so you can live in the moment. Our mission is to ensure each client creates unforgettable memories at every event. Grandview Entertainment's goal is to provide exceptional planning services that exceed expectations and ensure every guest has a grand ol' time."

Don't get me wrong: I love my job. I'm detail-oriented and seeing the joy on client's faces is fulfilling. I'm happy with what I do… just not how *much* I do.

But I know the exhaustion and sleepless nights will be worth it. I have a review at the end of August. If all goes well, I'll get the promotion I've begged for. The one I deserve after three years of dedication, hard-work, and growth.

Once I get that, maybe life will be better. Maybe—just maybe—I'll be able to move out of my parents' house and start my life.

A life without Bryce.

I still need to figure the second part out.

Years ago, I had planned to move out with my best friend, Allura. She was the Ying to my Yang. The pepper to my salt. But she is in a serious relationship now. There is no point for her to move out when they'll be getting engaged soon.

A quiet sigh escaped my lips. My hand hovered over my phone. I hadn't texted her in a while. She and her family are on vacation, and I didn't like to bother her when she was away. Besides, I hated telling her about the Bryce drama. Her healthy relationship brought joy and hope. I never wanted to burden her and bring her life down.

My phone buzzed and Bryce's name appeared. I locked it and threw it in my bag.

Closing my eyes, I said a quick prayer, and went back to typing the rest of Kirk's project. I tried to ignore him as he stared out the window, rambling about a dog taking a dump on the sidewalk.

My mind shut-down as my fingers got into a flow. It felt good. A busy mind kept away discouraging thoughts.

But it didn't keep away the daydreams.

As I typed up a catering menu, I thought about Second, and wondered what he would have chosen first. From our previous conversation, he might have skipped the savory menu altogether and ran straight for dessert. He'd probably float toward the tower of cupcakes and cookies, ready to fight anyone who tried to stop him.

What would I do? Would I let him devour the cupcakes before the graduate?

Honestly, I'd tell him to stop and then sneak one with him. We'd pluck chocolate fudge cupcakes from the top of the display tower. I'd scrape off frosting and poke his cheek, leaving the sweetest mark and calling it an initiation for the cupcake club.

He'd probably smile and try to get back at me. We'd play fight until we were covered in chocolate. He'd wrap his arms around me and kiss the sweetness from my cheeks. My heart would race. I'd pull him closer and—

"Violetta, did you hear me?" Kirk's voice cut through the daydream.

I shook my head and looked up at him. His perfectly waxed eyebrows stuck to the top of his forehead.

"Why are you ignoring me? You were just staring."

"I was remembering the little details," I lied. "Our guests deserve the best down to the smallest thing."

Kirk rolled his eyes. "Yeah, whatever. I was just saying I got called in for a meeting with a client. Don't mess up while I'm gone."

"You don't mess up while you're gone," I mumbled when he was out of earshot. I took three deep breaths to calm my beating heart and returned to typing—and one or two more daydreams.

Oh, Love, I'm distracted. Why am I daydreaming about a ghost I've never met? A man who had a terrible fate befall him?

With chocolatey sweetness.
Violetta

June 17

Hello Love,

Bryce texted me all throughout work yesterday and finally called me today. I still haven't spoken to him since the party. Ignoring him is killing me. It's a poison sitting in my stomach that is slowly seeping into my brain. I'm wondering if I should answer and pretend like nothing happened.

But, how much longer can I play dumb? How much longer can I pretend like nothing is wrong?

And yet, the more I play pretend, the safer he'll be. The first time I tried to leave, he called me from the train tracks near where we had our first date. There was a hidden clearing in the forest where the locomotives zipped through. The sound of the wind whistling past the microphone and the blaring horn rang perpetually between my ears. The low voice threatening to walk in-front gripped my heart.

My heart hurts. I can't go through it again. But the responsibility and fear he may do *that* again weighs me down. Maybe I should just call him back. Maybe it'll be safer that way.

```
I hope I didn't keep you waiting too long.
```

Warmth blooms in my cold tired soul. I knew words were powerful. I knew they could stop wars, start families, and change lives.

I didn't know they could make my tarnished heart sparkle.

"It makes it that much sweeter when you return."

> You barely know me, but you look forward
> to my visits?

When I'm not daydreaming, he's a flickering image in the back of my mind. Now, his picture is clear. Aunt Margot says Kayleigh had a ghost try to save her. And I *see* him in that photo. It looks real. It *feels* real. My fingers tingle at its touch.

My sisters wouldn't believe me even if I showed them. I'm the crazy big sister in a toxic relationship. But my heart is telling me Second is real—ghost or no.

"You left me on a cliffhanger last time. You have to tell me what you're like."

> As you know, I love the outdoors—like you.
> In fact, I'm pretty well known around here
> for my feat of hiking the Vermont 5 in one
> day.

Bryce would never even attempt to hike a mole hill. The Vermont 5? In one day? Each peak is over four thousand feet. That requires dedication, incredible stamina, and lots of caffeine. He would've had to start at around one in the morning. It was possible, but I'd never thought anyone I'd meet would be crazy enough to do it.

Don't get me wrong, I love hiking. My dad took Felicity and me on our first overnight hike when I was seven. I was scared at first. I mean, who wouldn't be. A little girl out in the woods for two days without her mama is frightening.

Felicity was braver than I despite her being two years younger. I remember her wide eyes gawking in the sights. The smell of pine floating along the cool breeze. The crunching of leaves beneath our boots.

I'll never forget the first night. We sat around a campfire; its flames tickled the side of my fingers as we roasted hotdogs. Lemon-lime soda had never tasted so good.

The best part about these memories? Second relates to them. I love my friends, but none of them are woodsy. And Bryce? Whenever I reminisce about my childhood, he apologizes for us not having enough money to go on vacation.

Infuriating.

"Not to stroke your ego, but that is rather impressive."

Yeah, I'm just that good.

"Did you hike them on your own or with a group? Were you scared?"

Did it alone. Not really scared, just tired afterward.

Hiking alone is dangerous. My dad always said travel in pairs—at least. God forbid something happened.

Why did he go alone?

"I believe that! The Vermont 5 are high peaks. Does that mean you're from Vermont?"

No, I live a bit further south.

Super vague, Second. I'm further south, but so is Florida.

"Not gonna tell me where?"

Not yet, we're still strangers. I don't want you knowing where I live. You might try to kidnap me.

Lowkey wish I could. I'd run over to his house with trail snacks and hot chocolate. I'd ask him dozens of questions about his experience hiking the Vermont 5 and what he was running from.

But he's probably dead.

"Fine, then let's stop being strangers! How about life stuff? What do you do outside of camp?"

I've never been so bold. What is wrong with me? Is it because he's a ghost that I don't care how forward I am?

> I just graduated college with degrees in general education and a minor in creative writing. That was my life the past few years, so I'm not quite sure what I want to do now.

Sounds like a hipster. He probably drives a white four-door compact crossover SUV with bumper stickers of places he's been. I bet he has one sticker for each Vermont 5 peak. A notebook is definitely among his must-haves.

Which is *not* a bad thing. As long as he doesn't have a man bun.

"Understandable. Do you have any inkling as to what you want? Job or otherwise?"

> Kind of, but I don't think it's feasible.

"How do you know it's not feasible until you try?"

> You're right.

"Good, because your job needs to make you happy, otherwise why do it?"

A line I use often. As much as Kirk drives me nuts, my job is fun. Not many twenty-two-year-olds have a full-time job planning and executing entertainment events. If 75% of people enjoyed what they did, the world would be a happier place.

> You're right. I'll think about it more.

"As you should. Now, what about your appearance?"

> My appearance?

"Yes, please describe it."
Please don't have a man bun. Please don't have a man bun.

> Well, I'm a brunette. I have a beard—
> otherwise, I look like I'm twelve.

That's a cute reason to have a beard. Facial hair is rugged, handsome. Bryce couldn't grow a beard to save his life.

> I'm a six-foot tall white boy, but I tan
> like a true Italian.

Not British. My Irish grandmother would be thrilled.

> I wouldn't say I'm a gym junkie, but I
> take care of myself.

That's a modest way of saying he's probably fit. I wonder how thick his biceps are? Does he have a strong broad chest? I could imagine cold nights camping in the woods. Strong arms wrapped around me, pulling against him. I'd breathe in the scent of him and nestle my face into his chest. His warm skin against mine after—

Gah, VIOLETTA! You're writing letters to a guy who is either dead or in your head.

As my cheeks burn red, my mind realizes that if he just finished college… Did he die young?

Was *his* story like Kayleigh's?

"Gotta take care of yourself. Now what about the rest of your face? You say you minored in creative writing, so describe in detail."

> Uhh, well…

"No lying, I want to know!"
Oof, the exclamation point probably sounded desperate.
"What does your face look like?"
Maybe that was a good save?

> Well, you know I have a beard. Couple freckles here and there. My nose? Uh, arrow shaped. Not quite Roman, but I have a little bump.

Ah, he is a brunette with freckles? God exists and He's been listening to me.
"And your eyes?"
Please be green. Please be green.

> It's blue.

I'll take it. Blue is gorgeous too… but wait:
"It's? Does that mean something else?"

> I wear an eyepatch over the other. It shouldn't have happened. I was out with someone when they—

The words stopped appearing. What is he hiding?

> I lost it a few years ago.

Was it a hiking accident? Maybe someone nudged him too hard and he stumbled down a cliff side and hit a branch. Eleora cut her cheek once falling out of a tree. The twig just missed her eye.
And yet, my theory doesn't seem right. He completed the Vermont 5 in one day by himself. If that doesn't sound like running away, I don't know what does.

The question is, who did he run away from?

"How? What did they do? Who did that to you?"

She is long gone. I'm convinced I did it
to myself.

Cracks split across my soul. No. No. No. Those words are familiar. Not in the sense of walking into your childhood house and knowing where all the switches are or which cupboards held the dishes. This familiarity was a prison cell. Cold and filled with memories and regret.

"The pain you feel is justified. Sharing pain with someone who understands is the first step to mending a heart."

Does he know the pains of a broken relationship? Is his guilt and self-affliction like mine?

I never met someone who truly knew what I was going through. Aunt Margot was the closest person because she *knew* her sister. She read Kayleigh's entries. That's why she gave me this notebook. It wasn't just because I resembled her sister or I am the only one to treat her nicely. Aunt Margot wants me to be saved.

Is Second supposed to save me?

He hasn't replied. Maybe he doesn't know what to say.

"Well, I understand if you don't want to open up yet. We're still strangers after all. I won't press you."

I've talked about myself for a bit. It's
your turn.

"I guess if we have to. What do you want to know?"

Uh, I guess how old are you?

"I'll be twenty-three in September. I'm guessing you're about twenty-one?"

I'm older than you. I was held back from
college after my accident.

He suffered more than a hiking fall. Someone ripped out his heart when he lost his eye and took his soul. Why does he remain on earth? Why does he speak as if he's alive in the present? Did he fail to save someone like the ghost that haunted Kayleigh? Is he now a ghost reliving shadows of his life over and over until he fulfills his duty to move on?

I can't bring it up. I can't ask. Not yet. How could I? His vulnerability is something to cherish and protect. I cannot abuse it to satisfy my own curiosities—no matter how insane the situation of talking to a ghost is.

"That makes me feel better. I don't want to be a cougar."

I think I'd have to be a young camper's
age for you to be classified as a cougar.

"It was a joke, Second."

I promise I'm good at jokes. I mean, I
have a good sense of humor. Sarcasm is a
love language of mine.

"Glad we have that in common."

And just like that, we reverted to light hearted topics. We are alike and that worries me. Words hide us when pain tries to pull us forward.

I know everyone suffers. God puts us through trials to make us stronger. To build us up.

But why are *ours* so similar? Why did Second lose an eye and possibly his life to someone he probably used to care about?

I don't know. I need to find out, but not yet. This... is a lot. This ghost carries a painful secret from his past that may have tethered him to this life.

My heart clenches as my pen hovers above the page. I cannot say anything more right now. Words won't formulate properly and I'll end up saying something I might regret.

"Oh, boy, I'm fading fast. I'm so sorry, Second, but it's my turn to run away from you."

As long as you come running back?

Why is my throat dry? Why are my eyes burning and my cheeks damp? Never has a guy *asked* me to chase after him. Never has someone desired me to choose them out of free will. With Bryce there is always a motive. A threat. Some chain around my legs yanking me back despite the hurt.

"Like I said, I've been doing this for years. It's you who finally showed up. Have a good night, Captain Second."

I need more tissues. I've written letters to my future spouse for almost ten years. My heart spilled onto a page, coloring it blue, black, or graphite.

Why now? Why when I hope to leave Bryce and find the one that someone responds? Someone who is fun, creative, and caring. Someone I would love to talk with for hours while gazing upon the stars. Someone I think my parents would welcome with open arms.

Someone who is probably dead, and there is nothing I can do to help him.

Torn.

Violetta

June 19 – Day

Hey Love,

Today started out great, then it sucked.

Sunshine kissed my cheeks, gently waking me early this morning. I heard the footsteps of my mom puttering around the kitchen. A thumping bass from a speaker echoed up to my room. I freshened up and bounded down the stairs.

Mom glided around the kitchen as a classic 80s song bounced off the walls. She twirled like a queen in a ballroom, arms arched gracefully above her head.

Rhythmic thumps of the loud bass beat in my chest. My heart warmed at my mom's joy.

I mouthed the lyrics as I slid into the kitchen. Taking her hands, we shuffled to the beat across the tiles. As I danced to a song of love and hope, my mind trailed back to Second's words the night before.

The song ended and my mom smiled. "You seem in better spirits today."

"Only because I am going to my favorite coffee shop this morning." I grinned and threw my bag over my shoulder. "I deserve a second treat this week."

"You're definitely my daughter because you love your coffee," Mom signed. She pulled out her favorite green mug. On the front in 70s bubble lettering read "YOU NEVER REALIZE HOW WEIRD YOU ARE UNTIL YOU HAVE 5 JUST LIKE YOU."

"I take after the best." I winked and snatched my paisley lunchbox, threw an apple into it, and zipped it shut.

She laughed. "I hope you're getting breakfast today. I am not letting you leave the house with only fruit."

"If I'm getting coffee, I'm going all out," I replied. My mouth salivated just thinking about the breakfast sandwich. A thick fresh bagel, an over medium egg, a tower of bacon, oh, and ketchup. Yeah, I'm a BECSPK kind of gal. I hope to visit New York City and get a real one, but upstate wannabes will do.

My mom smiled ear to ear. "Your smile makes me happy."

My lips formed a straight line. I know it did. I never meant to cause her pain. She goes through so much being a mom of five and taking care of her students during the school year. So many lives to worry about.

She didn't need to worry about me, too.

"I'll see you later." I gave her a quick hug and ran outside.

My car beeped as it unlocked. I flung open the driver's side, slid inside, and chucked my bags onto the passenger floor. With a quick exhale, I shut the door behind me. I wouldn't let myself over think. I wouldn't spoil the day. Instead, I said my morning prayers on my drive to the coffee shop. My car-ride meditations were a routine I didn't like to break. My moment of peace before jumping into a crazy consuming day. Time to reset my mind and my soul. Bryce never liked to pray. I'd never force him, but I wish I didn't shake every time I wanted to pray before meals or thank God for the sunshine.

I timed it perfectly. My prayers ended as I parked in front of the coffee shop. "PEEK-A-BREWS" in a thick serif font spread across the dark windows. A white decal of a mirror behind it.

Bells rang over the door as I entered the shop. Its vintage charm and oddities gave an enchanting, creepy vibe. Mirrors line the walls, reminding you of how bad your hair looked no matter which direction you turned. Refurbished vanities became tables for the booths. It's the last standing local café in town, celebrating their 30th anniversary this year.

As I walked up to the counter, I thought someone stepped on my heels. I turned around, but no one stood behind me.

Shaking it off, I approached the barista. A handwritten chalkboard menu dangled above her. I knew what I wanted, but I read through the sugary offerings. My heart pulled my mind away as I wondered what

Second's favorite drink would be.

I imagined he'd choose the Stormy Night. Dark chocolate mocha with hazelnut. Mysterious, dramatic, but sweet. A drink so addictive you couldn't get enough.

The barista cleared her throat, "Welcome to Peek-a-Brews, what can our crew do for you?"

"A medium iced Stormy Night please." My heart betrayed me. Iced coffee with caramel was my usual. Not too sugary, but not too boring. "Oh, and the Bacon Care of Business on an everything bagel, please."

She took my payment, and I crossed the shop to wait.

I refused to pull out my phone, so I people-watched. Easy to do with the mirrors lining the cafe. As my eyes wandered, a shimmering light caught my attention. It gleamed off something on a vintage vanity across the room. Curious, I approached the table.

A silver-plated mirror rested on its back. A crack split the glass down the center, but the rest of the detail was immaculate.

I leaned over and looked at my reflection, except it wasn't a ginger with green irises staring back. For a split second, different eyes looked back at me. Bright. Glowing. Lifeless.

My heart skipped a beat and I jumped back. A gasp caught in my throat and my skin grew cold. Frozen in place, I stared until the barista called my name.

Shuffling to the counter, I grabbed my breakfast and ran out the door, not looking back.

Thoughts and questions consumed the rest of my car ride. I had no idea what to make of it. I thought maybe my imagination played tricks on me. But something tugged at the back of my mind. An explanation I wasn't sure I wanted to think about.

Was it a ghost?

I didn't want to look at my phone, but I forced myself to unlock it and head to messages.

Two unread from Bryce. Three unread from Aria. One meme from my dad.

Scrolling down, I tapped Aunt Margot's name. I sucked in a deep breath and sent her a message: ***"Good morning, sorry to bother*** *you. I know this is random-ish, but do you remember where Kayleigh first encountered her ghost?"*

I threw my phone into my backpack and hopped out of the car. Bryce's messages would remain unseen until I was ready to face it.

Going into the office, I plopped into my creaking blue swivel chair. Quietly, I ate breakfast while I worked on my tasks of the day, forcing my mind to focus on anything but the ghastly eyes from Peek-a-Brews.

Time flew like race cars down a highway. Productivity ran alongside me and I thrived. These were the days I remembered why I loved my job. Organized colorful sheets, happy replies from clients, and a completed checklist invigorated my creative mind. On top of my daily tasks, I submitted the graduation party's run-of-show on Kirk's behalf—even though he told me to send it back to him. Even better, I took my dad's advice and tagged our manager in the email. Bold? Yeah. But I want everyone to know that *I* finished his work. Not him. I wanted everyone to know that *I* took over the project because he couldn't complete it.

But once 4:30 pm hit, the overthinking came running. My bag grew heavier on my shoulder as I walked back to my car. Anxiety clawed at my ankles with every step away from the office.

Should I have openly said I completed the project for him? Would my boss say something? Would it be perceived negatively and impact my chance at the promotion? Bryce said I shouldn't brag about completing extra work. Always remain quiet and humble, he said.

There is a difference between humility and letting people walk all over you. But then again, I can't even stand up for myself.

My car beeped twice and I flung open the door. Thighs burned as they stuck to the hot leather seats. I started the engine, and my car rumbled to life. Rolling down the windows, I welcomed the cool evening breeze. My skin tingled from the quick change in temperature. It reminded me I was alive.

I wondered if Second sat in his car after a challenging college class. Did he sit in his front seat and write prose about the world around him?

Vibration rattled my phone against the cupholder, startling me.

Bryce Kazanski popped up on the car screen.

I leaned back against the headrest. Knots formed in my stomach and I wanted to throw up. Not uncommon these days.

A girl should *never* feel that way when her boyfriend calls. Her heart should flutter. Her hand should snatch the phone so fast she almost flings it across the room.

Like how I feel when Second's words appear…

Groaning, I rubbed my palms into my eyes. "Get it over with. Get it over with. Get it over with."

I jabbed the phone button on my steering wheel.

"Hey."

"Hey, are you okay?" he asked flatly. "I've been calling you for almost a week? You didn't show up on Thursday for our date."

He was worried about me? Did he feel bad? Would he apologize?

"I'm sorry. I've had the worst deadline since last I saw you."

He scoffed. "I understand. You always have something going on, it seems. I bet work is too overwhelming."

Aaaand there it was. Beating around the bush until the path was flat. Me ditching him at the party last week after he made me sob my eyes out? Never happened.

A few pounding heartbeats passed before he said, "Vi, why don't we go out tonight? My treat. You probably went over budget on mochas this week, so I'll cover."

I glanced at the crumpled Peek-a-Brews napkin on my seat. I treat myself to one coffee a week on Wednesdays. Maybe two if I treat myself or meet up with Allura, but she's been on vacation. So what if I wanted two this week without meeting up with anyone?

"Fine. What time?" I grumbled.

"Let's do 6 pm," he stated.

Fridays at 6 pm never work. He *knows* this. We even had this conversation before the party. I drive Aria and Sage to youth group. Since Felicity and Eleora are home from college they pick up, but I had been their ride for the past year.

I licked my dry lips. "I can't, I'm driving the girls."

"Ugh, never know how to say no to your family, do you?" Annoyance singed his voice. "I guess I can change things around tomorrow and we can go out then."

Pain shot through my palm as my fingernails dug into my skin. "Why don't we go out right after? It doesn't take long to drop them off? It's also one of their last meetups since school is out soon." I didn't really want to go out tonight, but I needed to know what he was up to.

His voice turned monotonous. "No, it's fine. You're probably tired after a busy work week anyway. I'll pick you up tomorrow morning. We'll do brunch. I gotta run. Talk later, bye."

The screen went black.

He hadn't asked if that time was good for me. He hadn't asked if I had plans. Clearly he didn't remember that this weekend is my annual family camping trip. I only reminded him a dozen times.

Blood boiling, I snatched my phone and slid to the messages. None unread. Aunt Margot hadn't replied.

My trembling fingers tapped Bryce's name. Distant and formal texts taunted me in blue and white bubbles. No cutesie flirty words. Not even emojis.

My fingers trembled as I sent: ***"I can't do it tomorrow morning. We're going camping. We could've done tonight if you wanted to."***

Three dots danced in a thought bubble.

"Whatev V. Tonite doesn't work for me anymore. Call me when you actually have time. if ever."

I gripped my phone so tightly it almost snapped. Jaw clenched, it took every fiber of my being to place it down before I flung it through the windshield.

Rolling up the windows, I locked the door and bent forward so nobody could hear me scream.

Yours spiraling,
Violetta

June 19 — Night

Hello Love,

I need to meet you. I need you to become the beast and scare away Gaston.

I can't believe I'm writing two letters in one night. I put burning memories to paper as soon as I got home. Bitter, depressing thoughts needed to leave my mind before I faced my family at dinner. My pain poured out through my pen so when they asked, the truth would be *closer* to "fine."

Four letters hid a thousand different feelings.

I wonder what Second would say? Would he have responded the same way? Would he see me as just a pain-in-the-ass girlfriend who is too busy being independent?

I wonder what his relationship with the girl who hurt him was like. I know he didn't explicitly say his relationship took his sight away. But even though I can only see his words, I sense the heartache behind the scrawl.

I wish he knew the time between our messages. My fingers twitch and my imagination wanders. Daydreams race through my mind. Images of him climbing mountains, racing around in a green forest, and sitting around campfires bring a small smile to my lips.

"I keep thinking about you. I wanted to talk to you and see if you were okay."

The most honest thing I've said–well, wrote–today.

I'm currently dangling from the mountain right now.

"Purposefully I hope?"

Nope, but I'm okay. A little cut up, but okay.

Tightness clasps my lungs. Why do I feel like I can't breathe? Is this how he dies? This whole time, have I traveled with him before his death?

Did I startle him and he slipped?

"Oh, no, oh, no, I'm sorry. I hope I didn't cause you to fall."

No, a camper slipped. It's pouring rain.

Quiet shouts float along the breeze outside my window. Was it my imagination? Were kids playing this late at night?

Pounding heartbeats resound in my ears. It takes everything for me not to call the police. Realistically, what could I tell them? That somewhere a man is dangling off a cliff? No. It wouldn't make a difference. I don't know who or where he truly is.

So, then is this it? Is this how Second becomes a ghost? Is there anything I can actually do?

"Oh, no, I'm praying for you."

The only thing I can do right now. A few Hail Marys that will turn into a rosary hopefully will reach Heaven in time.

I appreciate your prayers.

"I won't bother you anymore. Please focus on saving yourself."

> You're never a bother. Don't worry,
> Anderson is going to pull me up soon. I'll
> be fine. It'll take more than this to kill
> me.

Air fills my lungs again. I didn't realize I stopped breathing. His words comfort yet worry me. If falling off a cliff wasn't going to kill him… then what will?

Also, wait. I'm *not* a bother? I literally just interrupted him while he was focusing on not dying. It was a matter of life or death and he *still* talked to me.

"Thank you, Second. It means more than you could know."

The more I converse with him, the more peace with my decision floods my heart. Even if Bryce does nice things once in a while, waiting for those happy moments isn't worth my sanity. Today was a prime example. I offered a solution and he rejected it. Slammed the door in my face and basically said, *Next time, bitch.*

Second is different. If the man my letters are for mirrors anyone else's personality, I want him to be like Second.

Maybe I want him to be Second.

But he's dead, isn't he? He's stuck re-living the time before he died, right?

A chime erupted from my phone. I glanced over to see Aunt Margot answered my text asking where Kayleigh saw her ghost.

My heart caught in my throat as three words lit up my screen:

"Peek-a-Brews."

I slumped back on my bed and ran my fingers through my red hair. The eyes staring back at me from the mirror this morning…

Were they Second's?

No, they can't be. Second said he wears an eyepatch to cover the sight he lost.

Unless…

That's how his body looked when he died. Completely, utterly vulnerable. Did he meet the end as he truly was without the eyepatch covering his regrets?

If so, then the eyes staring back at me are from a man who met an end way too young.

A man who needs to save me in order to move on.

But I don't know how to help him.

Yours haunted.

Violetta

June 20

Hello Love,

I can't wait to take you on adventures. We'll eat popcorn out of aluminum pans and cuddle up by a campfire with warm mugs of cocoa in our hands. When the flames turn to embers, the moon will light our way. We'll wish upon stars and laugh at stupid jokes only we understand.

I've looked forward to my family's annual camping trip since last year's ended. Seven Sparks, two nights, and hundreds of snacks. The woods cried for me and I've ignored them for too long.

Bryce tried camping with us once. It was humiliating. From the moment I stepped outside the RV I knew it would be a miserable trip. In Bryce's eyes, everything I did was wrong. I tried to light a fire and misjudged the amount of wood. He whispered degrading critique to the twins, claiming I wouldn't be able to light a fire if my life depended on it. Rather than defending me, the two joined in his harsh teasing. He ridiculed every path we hiked up, claiming that Park Rangers (knowing my father was one of them) are "lazy fake cops" that can't take better care of the footpaths. He insulted me. He insulted my *dad*. He insulted everything I loved about the woods.

Thankfully, Eleora stepped up to the plate and snapped at Bryce for being a crybaby. My dad, being the gentle giant he was, brushed it off and ignored his grumbles.

But Eleora's defensive tone made Bryce mad even though he didn't reveal it to my family. I was the only one to feel it as he dug his nails into my palm as he held my hand during the last hour of the hike.

After that, I *never* asked if we could bring Bryce along. My parents didn't offer again.

I always wished my boyfriend would be one to camp with me. To explore the woods every other weekend in summer, soaking in the sunshine and breathing in the scent of pine.

But that is not who Bryce is. This trip is the only time the tree-shaped hole in my heart is filled.

I shoved the pains, stress, and confusion of the past few weeks deep down for the weekend. I didn't want to think about how a dead-guy is talking to me through my letters (even though I think about him every minute of the day) nor how the stress of a promotion is consuming my work days nor how breaking up with Bryce is more difficult than building a working spaceship out of a pizza box.

Do you like my analogies? I think I'm pretty funny… or stupid, depending on the day.

Dawn greeted us along the mountains this morning. We always leave bright and early for our trip. We drove in the RV along winding mountains, singing classic rock songs and playing the alphabet game. The sun hung in the middle of the sky when we arrived at the campsite in Longwood Forest.

I hadn't realized how much my heart yearned for the woods until I took that step out of the RV. The familiar scent of earth filled my lungs. We've been camping in Longwood Forest ever since I knew how to walk. My father started his Forest Ranger career between these trees before he moved his family downstate to be at a "less dangerous" National Park. Thousands of acres with hundreds of footpaths stood between me and the painful reality of Bryce.

"All right, Sparkles!" Dad shouted, clapping his hands. "Let's hurry up. I've waited too long to traverse these trails again." Unpacking faster than a pit-crew, our weekend home was ready. A short hike filled the rest of the day before the sun set and we settled in for the night.

Stars sparkled above me as I sat around the campfire with my family. Flames lit our faces like stage lights. Fuzzy blankets bundled our chilly bodies.

Aria and Sage sat on either side of me. White marshmallows steadily browned at the end of our roasting sticks.

Mom and Dad huddled together across from us. Mom tried to feed Dad a s'more, but the graham cracker crumbled and collapsed. They laughed as she shoved its remains in his mouth.

Their childlike relationship gave me hope. A desire for ours to be like that, Love. They're the reason I started writing these letters. My mom began the tradition growing up. As a young girl, she had a long list of "requirements" for her future husband. He needed to be tall, strong, funny, a good provider, understand ASL (or willing to learn), and a billion other things. She encouraged the five of us to pray for our spouses daily. She never *told* us to write letters but it was always implied.

Her eloquence with the written word inspired me to start. The joy on her face when she found Dad's keepsake box after we moved encouraged me to keep writing. I'll never forget the tears in her eyes and the smile upon Dad's lips as they read them together by the fireplace.

That's what I want. It's what I've always wanted.

"Vi, did you steal all the marshmallows?" Eleora called from the camper.

"Yes and I set them free." My own fluffy treat caught fire. I made a wish as I blew it out. A Sparks tradition. A few times, marshmallow wishes have come true. "I wish for them to find their families and be reunited."

"And then, we'll *eat* their entire family," Aria cackled, sinking her teeth into her s'more.

Sage pouted. "Stop, that makes me sad." Wide eyes stared at her treat. "Now, I don't want to eat it."

"If you won't put it out of its misery, I will." Aria snatched the marshmallow out of her twin's hand and shoved it into her mouth.

"Ariaaaaaa!" Sage whined, smacking her sister's leg.

I leaned back on the log as the two flailed their arms at each other like cats.

My mom clapped her hands and the girls froze. Brow furrowed, she signed, "If you fight, your father will eat all the dessert."

A switch flipped and the two sat upright like princesses during teatime. Their quarrel wasn't worth jeopardizing the snacks.

I couldn't help but smile. These chaotic moments are what grounded me. Moments of roasting marshmallows, devouring treats, and counting the stars on a clear night filled my soul. These moments with my family made me Violetta Sparks. During this trip, I prayed for the strength to be happy. I prayed for the confidence to be myself around my family without fear of judgment or worry.

Felicity plopped down to the right of the fire. Popcorn filled her cheeks. Eyebrows raised, her eyes darted to me as she signed, "Are we going to tell another ghost story?"

"Vi won't listen to us, so your story will be wasted," Eleora grumbled.

The smile and peace I had for a moment flew out of my grasp. That was not how the weekend was supposed to go.

Dad wiped his mouth with the sleeve of his red flannel. "What is Violetta ignoring this time?"

"My sisters, who else?" My tone was sarcastic, but my glare shot daggers through Eleora. I didn't want her talking about Bryce. Not this weekend. Not in front of my parents. I didn't want them to worry about me; I'd solve it on my own.

I especially didn't want her to talk about my conversation with Aunt Margot.

"She went to talk to Aunt Margot the other day," Eleora confessed.

And there it was.

"Oh?" Dad popped open a can of beer. It fizzed. "Why did you go see her?"

"To talk about ghoooooossstsss." Aria jumped up, taking the blanket with her. She draped it over her head like a veil and threw her arms up. "I'm surprised she didn't get possessed by Little Ghost."

"Stop, Aria." Mom's eyebrows furrowed and her signs were firm. "That is not a story to be taken lightly. It was a serious incident."

Aria threw her blanket into the dirt and whined. "But Aunt Margot's story is so cool, it's what made me want to study parapsychology." She clasped her hands together. "It's a forbidden romance turned tragedy, plus an otherworldly phenomena the cops can't explain."

"Aria, please be serious." Dad's tone was firm. "Her sister died. The possession is still under investigation by the Church. You can talk about ghosts, but not that one. It's not a laughing matter."

My stomach clenched. How could I have forgotten about that detail? Aunt Margot claimed that Little Ghost possessed Kayleigh's fiance to stop him from killing her. He failed, but those claims went far beyond the police.

Will Second ever possess someone? Will the reflections in the mirror escape their glass prisons, taking over a host to breathe air again?

Should I tell someone about what I saw?

I shook my head hard. I can't lose Second. Not yet. I need to learn more before I give him up.

"I know, Dad, I'm not laughing about Kayleigh's situation." Aria replied defensively. "It was horrible, but I believe Kayleigh is better now." Sympathy replaced her frustration. "God holds her."

"That's right, but we still shouldn't speak ill of the dead." Dad took a swig of his beer before continuing. "It affected Aunt Margot severely. Whether the ghost was real or not, it's not a story to laugh at. If you *must* talk about ghosts, pick Casper or some myth."

"Right, or we could just catch up and talk about happy things?" I asked.

"What happy things? You didn't break up with Bryce yet," Eleora snapped.

Felicity stopped mid-chew and stared at me. The twins silenced their bickering.

Mom couldn't see her lips, so she asked her to repeat it. When she didn't answer, Dad told her.

Head cocked, her lips formed an o. "When did you decide this?"

I bit my lip. Eleora threatened to bring it up this weekend if I didn't cut ties. I had more faith that my sister would respect me and not talk about it during the trip that I've looked forward to for months. The one I counted on for my soul to escape and refresh.

I waved away her question, trying to make light of the situation. "I don't want to talk about it right now. Can we please enjoy this weekend together?"

Dad placed his beer can on the ground. Orange flames flickered in his concerned eyes. "For now, we can table it. But don't think I'll forget this conversation."

Most of the time, he doesn't forget. I have attentive parents who recall even the littlest detail about their daughters. Their understanding is beyond comparison. When I cried myself to sleep at night in highschool, Mom scooped me up as if I was three-years-old. We'd rock back and forth and feel each other's heartbeats. My dad noticed every bad day and asked, "Hey, Braveheart, why don't we grab your bow and go shoot?"

Does Second have a loving relationship with his parents like mine? Or are his parents distant like Bryce's?

"Don't forget to ask her about her Casper," Aria whispered.

I elbowed her and she tumbled off the log. Dramatic sarcastic wails floated to the night sky. Her arms flailed to get Mom's attention. Mom ignored her and pierced five marshmallows with her stick.

I glared at Felicity who looked away. She definitely snitched to the twins. I told her something in confidence, but I should've known that always meant I told *all four* of them.

Dad arched an eyebrow and shook his head. Rising to his feet, he stretched his long arms. "Is Casper a big ghost, little Sparkle?"

"The biggest!" Aria squealed from her new spot in the grass. "He isn't cute like they say. He has long white arms and scary red eyes."

Dad chuckled. He picked up Aria's blanket and pulled it taut in front of him. With long slow steps, he glided around the campfire. He lowered his voice and taunted, "Do you know what happens when little girls get lost in the woods?"

"They get eaten by a bear?" Felicity signed, still not meeting my gaze.

"No, they live happily ever after because they don't have to deal with toxic boyfriends." Eleora shot me a look. "Maybe we should leave Violetta here."

"No, it is worse than happy endings and bears," Dad growled. His head darted to the left. Then the right. In a quick motion, he spun around and stared at Sage.

Eyes widening, she shook her head frantically.

"The ghost finds one girl to claim as their own." One step forward. "To have and to hold." He raised the blanket. "To love FOREVER!" He pounced, trapping Sage in a fuzzy prison.

Sage screamed and punched Dad through the blanket. We all laughed. Each unique to make a cacophony of cackling. Felicity's cheeks turned red and she slid off her log.

Just like that, Bryce was out of the conversation.

Dad pulled down the blanket and let Sage free.

Tears brimmed her eyelids, but a smile formed on her lips. She punched Dad's arms repeatedly.

My family continued to laugh and play as the stars grew brighter. But their chatter faded far away as Dad's words replayed in my mind:

"The ghost finds one girl to claim as their own."

"To have and to hold."

"To love forever."

Is this true with Second?

With heart fluttering.

Violetta

June 27

Hello Love,

Nostalgia is intoxicating. I want to drown myself in it until I'm drunk on happy memories.

The seven of us spent the entire day out in the woods, camping along the hidden trails of Longwood Forest. No matter how many years pass, Dad will never forget the forest he fell in love with at the start of his career. The paths are ingrained in his memory like a song from his childhood. We've ventured down quiet, secret trails only veteran rangers know of.

Every step took me back in time. The days when my sisters and I would play hide-and-seek along the public trails while Dad worked. The summer afternoons we climbed trees and threw pinecones at each other.

Something struck the back of my leg. I yelped and spun around. Aria had an armful of pinecones.

"I guess nothing changes," I snickered. I thought about retaliating, but I picked on my sisters so much growing up that I've chosen to refrain to "atone for my sins." Or that was just Aria guilting me (which is the more accurate reason).

The desire to throw the pinecone at Felicity for spilling my secret strengthened, but since no one mentioned Bryce nor the ghost since last night, I tossed the pinecone aside.

"Except her aim. It's improving," Dad remarked. He tousled Aria's long dark hair.

Eleora scoffed. "Only in cone-chucking. Her archery still sucks."

A pinecone soared through the air and struck her in the shoulder.

Eleora whined, tears brimmed her eyes.

"If you're gonna dish it out, you gotta take it." Dad chuckled. "Right, honey?"

Mom nodded and signed in reply, "But let's not knock out a tooth or lose an eye, please?"

My stomach flipped. Could Second have lost his eye from a pinecone? Did someone get angry and throw it at him with all their might?

"You can't lose an eye from a pinecone, Mom." Aria snorted. "Don't be crazy."

"Are we almost there?" Sage whined. "My feet hurt and I'm getting hungry."

I had to agree with Sage. My stomach growled looking at the big cooler bag strapped to Eleora's back. Inside were cold-cut sandwiches, chilled water bottles, chips, and fudge brownies with colorful sprinkles: Dad's favorite. I'll never forget the first time he brought them home from the store. The twins were little. With a wide smile spread across his thick face, he held five brownies out in his large hands. "Their sweetness reminds me of you five, my little Sparkles," he had said. I plucked one from his grasp and ate it in three bites, begging for another.

Felicity rolled her eyes and signed, "You know we can't eat until we all hit center." Sliding her bow off her shoulder, she plucked the string.

My favorite requirement. It's always been ever since I was little. Archery embedded its arrows into my personality. A dumb reason why teens poked fun at me in highschool, but their teases and remarks didn't matter when the bow was in my grip and my sisters at my sides. Adulthood took us away from shooting together like we used to. But every year, I counted on the camping trip to revive our love for the sport. The anticipation of firing my arrows at the top of the mountain pushed the painful memories away.

"We're just about there, little Sparkles. You can see the top of Mount Maxum from here." Dad smacked a branch off a dead tree. "You know what would make us get there faster?" He yanked a twig off the newly broken stick. Sucking in a deep breath, he jumped up on a boulder, swung down his arm, and shouted, "Charge!"

On instinct, all four of my sisters squealed and ran up the final stretch of the mountain. Sage almost slipped, but her determination pushed her feet forward.

I hung back with my mom, laughing as my dad chased after them. My dad started the Final Charge tradition when we were kids. The command is so deeply ingrained in us that I had to force my feet to stand still and not leave my mom in the dust.

"You know I could beat you in the race if I felt like it," Mom signed with a smirk.

"Oh, I believe it; that's why I didn't run." I winked and put my arm through hers as we ascended the final hundred feet.

Her smile faded as a thought must have crossed her mind. A thin hand squeezed my arm tightly. The air between us grew thick, unanswered questions dangling above us. I knew she wanted to ask me something.

The joy I felt a moment ago flew away like a frightened bird. I sucked in a deep breath and clutched the bow across my chest. "I'm okay, Mom. You don't need to worry about me."

She let out a quiet sigh. "It's my job. Will you at least tell me what's going on?"

I didn't want to. After Felicity betrayed my trust, I wanted to keep my situation close. Keep the secret of Second even closer. I wanted to enjoy the trip. I didn't want to think about the hurt.

"It's just—" I scoffed. "I can't put it into words."

She shot me a side glance and pointed to her own lips.

I chuckled. Her humor in stressful situations always made me smile. "Sorry, bad way to phrase it." I hiked my quiver higher on my shoulder. "I think I'm trying to say that I don't know how to say it."

Mom stopped and tugged me back. We stood in the trail, eye to eye. Bugs buzzed around our heads as if they waited for me to speak, too.

A tug in my heart sent words to my tongue, but they stuck behind my lips. Five heartbeats passed before I opened my mouth.

But Aria's voice shouted down the mountain: "Violetta! Mom! Get your butts up here. I want a brownie!"

The confession crawled back inside and curled up beside my heart. "I'll tell you later. Just know I'm okay, I promise." I gently grabbed her hands before she could sign and led her up the mountain, leaving the truth behind us.

A vast sea of blue and green greeted us at the top. Wispy clouds spread across the sky like paint smears. Fresh pine filled my lungs as I inhaled. My arms prickled as the wind blew through my hair. I needed this. I shoved the words I almost said to the back of my mind. I can't think about the pain. I can't think about the worry. I wanted to be present with my family. I wanted to share a genuine smile. I know my mom is worried, but today is not the time.

"All right little Sparkles," my dad shouted. "Are you ready?"

"Yes!" Aria screeched. She plopped her backpack near a rock and slid her bow off her shoulder. "Let's do this. A sandwich is calling me."

"Make sure you don't miss the target so Dad lets us eat right away." Eleora snorted.

"Be patient, we have to be careful with the wind," Mom signed. She pulled several items out of her thick black backpack. Tucking a roll of targets under her arm, she crossed the cliff about fifty feet where five thick trees stood side by side. She unfurled it and fastened a paper target to each tree with a staple gun. The colored circles with their yellow centers stared at me. Calling me.

Dad licked his first finger and stuck it into the air. "The wind is in our favor." He jogged past the trees and double checked the surrounding areas. He shouted down the path to see if any other hikers were nearby. Ninety-percent of the time no one hiked up that way. The peak was off the trail. A secret only Dad knew from practically living in the woods.

He trotted back over. A wide smile stuck upon his face. "The coast is clear." He stood behind us. "All right, you know the rules so let's get started." He clapped. "Archers to the shooting line."

The five of us lined up in age order. I stood to the far left. The paper flapped against the thin tree before me versus my sisters' thicker targets. My mom loves to give me a challenge.

"First Shooter. Draw," Dad called.

Sage lifted her bow and set an arrow. Her eyes sparkled in the daylight as they focused on her target. She gave a small nod.

"Shoot!" Dad bellowed.

Sage loosed her arrow. It soared forward until it stuck into the tree with a twang. Slightly to the right of the center.

Sage whined and kicked a rock.

"You'll get another try." Dad patted her back. "Second Shooter. Draw."

Aria shot and hit slightly above, but she remained in the yellow. Eleora struck almost center. Felicity had a stroke of bad luck as a surprising gust of wind redirected her arrow to the right, sticking into the blue.

Felicity growled and gritted her teeth, flailing her arms towards the target.

"It's okay, just try again," Mom signed. "Violetta, let your sisters fire their second shot."

I nodded and took a step back so Felicity and Sage could try again. Dad shouted the command, and they fired one after the other: both striking yellow. Not quite dead center, but almost there.

"There you go, that's better." Dad clapped. "All right, one more and then we can eat. Fifth Shooter. Draw."

I tightened my hand around the grip and took a step forward. Sucking in a deep breath, I slid an arrow out of my quiver. I set it and drew back. My eyes stared down the shaft directly at my target. A gust of wind blew across my face so I adjusted my aim. My muscles tensed as I kept my bow drawn. A million thoughts raced through my mind as I waited for Dad to give the command. Anger, frustration, joy, bitterness, everything shot down from my brain, through my arm, and out to my fingertips. I wanted them to be free. I wanted them to get out of the captivity of my head.

I heard Dad inhale. "Shoot!"

Exhaling through my teeth, I let go of my arrow. I sent away every emotion pent up inside me. My work frustration, my despair with Bryce, my strange emotions for Second, all of them soared through the sky. The arrow pierced the tree and my feelings burst from it.

I bit my lip, trying not to think about what was happening outside of the woods. I forced myself to be in the moment.

I needed to enjoy my life.

A strong hand patted my back. "That's it, Braveheart." He pointed downrange.

Dead center.

I took a shaky breath. I don't know why I was so emotional. Tears threatened to burst forth. I wanted to bottle everything inside. I wanted to put a lid on it, hide it from the world, and claim everything was okay.

But I can't do that anymore. The stress is bogging me down, yanking at my ankles until I collapse.

I need to be set free.

Dad clapped three times. "Now, you all can eat."

My sisters erupted shouts of joy and ran to the trees to fetch their arrows. I stood for a moment, watching.

Listening.

Wondering what I'm going to do when I return to the real world.

Wondering what I'll do to set myself free.

With a sense of hope.
Violetta

June 22

Dear Love,

Warmth fades as the sun sets on another beautiful day. A day filled with joy and laughter. As the orange glow dims behind purple mountains, it takes my heart with it. I don't want today to end. Tonight, we return home. Tomorrow, I go back to work. Responsibilities await to shred my peace like paper only to scatter it in the wind.

I wonder if this feeling is why Second ran away. What suffering did he endure during his relationship? What happened that he lost his eye and desire to be loved in one day?

If he is truly a ghost, what killed him?

It's my turn to ask questions now.

He has impeccable timing. Sometimes I wonder if he can read my thoughts imprinted on the pages. If he can, he's good at playing dumb.

"Ask away, Second."

I crave the simple act of communication. I want someone to recall little details like how I like my coffee or what hair cream I use. I desire someone to bring me my favorite candy when I'm having a bad day or say the right thing when I'm feeling down.

Long story short: I need a man who is also my friend.

It hurts that I need to ask for that.

Tell me what your life is like.

"That's not a question, nor did you say please."

Please.

"Fine. Other than waiting for you? I wake up, go to work, take care of my family and friends, go to sleep, repeat."

Why am I holding back? I crave conversation, but I don't give in. Why does my heart want to keep things vague and simple?

Is it because I still think it's crazy I'm talking to a ghost?

Do you enjoy what you do for work?

When I'm not doing someone else's job.

"I do, actually. I am a huge planner and my job requires me to keep things neat and organized."

Sticking to a plan or checking off a list is so satisfying.

My kind of guy. He wouldn't back out of something last minute without an explanation. He wouldn't forget the most important details of an event he promised to help me with.

"Yes! Thank you! Some people don't get it. My sisters for sure."

And Bryce. But he doesn't need to know about him.

How many sisters do you have?

"Four, and they're a handful. We don't always see eye to eye."

And by that, I mean we bicker and argue like sisters do. Lately, I've been the stubborn one—not taking their advice. They've told me to prioritize me first and get rid of Bryce… But they don't understand what he'll do.

You can't take it to heart. I have one

little sister and we fight all the time.
But she still loves me.

Some positive constructive criticism that's not just telling me to get over it? Unheard of for me.

"I know, I know. It's hard sometimes."

I forgot to tell you. Thank you for saving my life earlier today.

"Today?"

Oh, right, time is different. When you told me you didn't want to bother me. You being there actually saved me.

Heat crawls up my neck. I look over at my sisters who are throwing rocks off the cliff side. I hope they can't see me blushing. I saved him? How? He's still talking to me as a ghost—I think. Is he living out his life before his death?

My head hurts just thinking about it.

"I didn't really do anything, but I'm glad to help."

You did, but I have one more thing to ask.

Why is my heart racing faster than an arrow soaring through the sky?

Why did you think you're a bother?

I did ask him that, didn't I? I feel like a chore. Another thing on the checklist to tick off. Bryce doesn't make time for me. I have to be convenient. I am a burden. A scribble in the notes of his selfish-mind's calendar.

"I hate annoying people. I don't want to seem like a burden."

Why would you be a burden?

Ugh, I'm melting. I haven't even seen this man and my heart is a puddle around my feet. Powerful words write the sweetest love stories.

But I can't do this. I can't feel this. He is surely a ghost. A man who died at a young age. I can't pour my heart out to someone who probably doesn't exist anymore.

"Can you ask me other fun questions first? Before we go into the sad stuff?"

Oh, uh, sure. Let's talk fun stuff. How about food? Do you have a favorite?

"These are the kind of questions I love. French fries, hands down. Give me a salty potato and I'll eat ten of them."

My real answer is a little more complicated. I love french fries dipped in maple syrup. The balance of salty and sweet is my guilty pleasure. I haven't had it in a while because Bryce thinks it's the grossest, weirdest thing in the world and made me feel like dirt when I told him.

Junk food? You're speaking my language. Although, I'm a sweet guy myself.

"You seem sweet."

Smooth, Violetta. But why are you flirting with a ghost? Didn't you just say you shouldn't start having feelings?

And why am I writing to myself in the third person?

Second is taking a bit to reply. Maybe my line scared him off.

"Do you like to adventure, Second?"

Absolutely.

My fingers tingle. I am in desperate need of an adventure buddy. Someone who will do crazy, silly things with me. I want to build a pillow fort and watch romance movies, sipping hot cocoa until the sugar hits our heads. I want to picnic by the water after a long walk, watching a sunset even more beautiful than this one. His hand would slip into mine. Calloused palms from hiking. He'd lean forward, his nose pressed against mine, and—

And I'm stopping myself right there.

"Are you adventuring now?"

```
Yep. What do you consider an adventure?
```

Maybe romance movies aren't his thing, so maybe I'll play it safe.

"The wind in my hair, doing something different. Something fun. Feeling like there are no problems in the world. Just me and the person I'm adventuring with."

```
You prefer not to adventure alone?
```

"Adventuring alone is boring, isn't it?"

I'm grateful for my family. If I didn't have them to do silly things with every once in a while, I may be worse off than I feel like I am. My mind always wants to do new things. My feet want to go to new places.

But I want someone to hold my hand and lead the way.

```
You have a point. Who do you adventure
                with?
```

"No one as cool as you, that's for sure."

Damn, I am bold, aren't I?

```
You're pretty cool, too. I'd love to
    adventure with you more sometime.
```

Speechless. My words flutter away from the page like birds. They migrate south and won't come back for a while.

Did he just technically ask me out on a date? Am I reading too much into this?

Yes, yes. That's right. I'm reading into it.

Haha, wait, that was a pun.

"If we're having an adventure right now, can you describe it to me?"

Describe it?

"You said you loved to write, so think of it as a creative prose exercise. And you know I can't see."

Loud heartbeats slam against my ribcage. What does he see? Will he tell me where his soul is trapped?

Okay, I'll do my best. I'm better at
describing on paper than out loud.

"Aww, are you nervous?"

No, I need a moment to gather my bearings.

I bet he's lying.

Darkness blankets the forest. It isn't
frightening nor unnerving. It's heavy and
warm like a sleeping bag by a fire. A cool
earth sleeps beneath our feet. Soft dirt
awaits the morning when critters will
scurry across it. The crickets sing their
lullaby. Harmonious chirps weave between
the trees. Every once in a while, an owl
accents their song like a cymbal crash.

Evergreen trees wave in the breeze. The
air tastes like Christmas. And at the
center of it all glows a beautiful—

Don't stop. Second, keep going. Please. To me, his prose is like a vibrant flower field attracting hundreds of butterflies. It's peaceful, serene. The world fades away as I read his words. Each letter sucks me in and I feel I'm there.

For a moment, I sense him with me.

"A beautiful what?"

I meant at the center of it all grows
a beautiful oak. Its branches reached
towards the glimmering stars. Reaching for
a place where it doesn't have to worry.
Where it's free.

To stand tall in a world that knocks you down. To extend my hands to the sky and grab a fistful of stardust. To sprinkle the gift of Heaven upon me, giving me peace and beauty.

"I envy the tree. Second, that description was beautiful. I feel like I'm really with you. You truly are talented."

Ah, I'm all right. Still learning and
practicing my craft.

While I adore humility, this line sounds too familiar…

"Oh, just take the compliment! I know the feeling of not being able to accept them. It's tough sometimes. Even tougher when you don't receive them much, so that's why I'm giving more than I get."

I didn't mean to get personal. Ink scribbled faster than my brain could comprehend.

Is that why you feel like a burden?

He's quite perceptive. I guess that's another thing we have in common. I see through his words, he sees through mine.

"Maybe. I don't know. I just feel like I am. There is someone in my life that always makes me feel terrible even if he doesn't know it."

Uh, who is he?

I shouldn't have written it. He doesn't need to know about my troubles with Bryce.

And yet, I daydream about Second. His strong face, thick beard, and beautiful blue eye. I wonder what nights would be like together. Would we dance under the stars, sharing our hopes and dreams? Would he scoop me up into his strong arms, kiss my forehead, and tell me how beautiful I am?

Would he make me feel loved?

"My boyfriend."

I wrote it. I did it. He needed to know. I can't lie to him—ghost or no. Lies, deceit, and hurt probably led to the suffering before his death. I never want anyone to hurt because of me. I want all those I care about to be happy.

That's a blessing and a curse.

"Second, are you still there?"

Yeah, yeah, sorry.

I said too much. Stupid, stupid, Violetta. You really are an over-sharer, aren't you?

"Sorry to dump all that on you. I just feel like I don't have anyone to talk to about him."

It's not entirely true. I can talk to my parents, my sisters, and my friends, but this feels different. Second experienced this. He knows the same hurt and pain from someone you've given your heart to. He knows the damage done by a lover who took your heart and crushed it.

> You can talk to me about anything.

Tears blur my vision. Why does this ghost offer his heart? Why does he offer his advice? He knows the bare minimum about me, and yet his desire to be present in my sorrow is the language of a lifelong friend.

"Thank you, Second. I just worry about him finding out from someone other than myself."

Which is true. If someone else told him I was having these thoughts… I don't even want to think about what he'd do.

> I don't even know who you are, so I doubt
> I'll be able to say anything.

I wish he knew. I wish he knew my name was Violetta Sparks. I wish he knew I've been praying for a man like him for ten years. I wish he knew that he would fit in perfectly with my family and their crazy stories and wild outdoor adventures.

But I'm afraid.

I'm getting too attached.

"Maybe it's safer to keep it that way for now."

> When you're ready to tell me your name,
> you let me know. For now, know that I will
> do whatever I can to help.

"Why? I've only spoken to you a few times."

A tear rolled down my cheek. I'm holding back the rest.

> Because you feel like a bother and you
> are far from it. Any time he makes you
> feel like that, you come to me. I will be
> waiting for you.

Dams burst and my eyes burned from crying. I'm glad I'm writing by flashlight on the cliff side. I'm glad my family is back in the camper. I heard a door creak open and slam shut. I don't know who saw me crying, but I hope they don't say anything. Chest heaving, heart racing, I can't control myself.

Never in my life has a man offered me such kindness. Never in my life has love poured through words, wrapping me up like a warm embrace.

"Thank you, Second. I hope to repay you someday. Thank you for our little adventure, today. I hope to have more with you soon."

With my whole heart, I hope.

Yours waiting.
Violetta

June 23

Dear Second,

Your words replay in my mind. You called me to you, giving me permission to pour my heart's contents all over the floor. You've offered to help me pick them up.

I've never felt this way. Giddy and hopeful.

I unpacked the camper with my dad early this morning before work. We left bright and early so I didn't have to take a full day off. My sisters snatched their own packs and scurried to their rooms. Mom dragged a few bags inside to start laundry.

As we tossed supplies around the garage, Dad joked about the roadkill we saw on the way home.

Gruesome, I know. But we're kinda weird like that.

"Listen, I love animals as much as the next dad," he said as he unzipped his backpack. "But it's hard not to laugh when they're belly up with their legs in the air like zombies." Lifting his arms, he groaned and lurched forward toward me.

I ducked under his arms before he could give me an un-deadly hug. "That's because that rabbit was practicing to be a zombie. You should learn from him."

"Grrrrr–" He sluggishly swung himself around. "I think I'm a pretty good zombie who needs curly red-headed brainssss." He pounced and wrapped me up in a tight bear hug, lifting me up off of the ground.

I squealed, kicking and laughing before he dropped me to the floor. "Okay, fine, you'd fit right in during the apocalypse." I knelt and continued unpacking one of our snack boxes.

Tugging his shirt down, he nodded. "That's the better answer. Now, I need some more answers from you." Dad's eyes darkened and his lips formed a straight line beneath his mustache. "Violetta, I'm not going to let you get off easy."

My head snapped up too fast. A crack erupted as I smacked my temple on the side-view mirror. I yelped and rubbed where the warmth bloomed. Tears in my eyes, I winced, "Or painlessly, apparently."

He chuckled. "You brought the pain on yourself. Which honestly is what I need to talk to you about." Baby blue coolers screeched as he slid them over. The larger one still filled with ice and soda creaked beneath his weight.

With a sigh, I plopped down on the smaller cooler beside him. "What wisdom dost thou have to bestow on me today, Father?" Jokes couldn't stop the anxiety bouncing my knee up and down.

My dad's green eyes softened. "Your sisters mentioned over the weekend that you want to break up with Bryce. Your mom is worried about you. Is this true?"

Red crawled up my cheeks. I didn't want to have this conversation. I wanted to jump in my car, drive to work, and pretend this never happened.

And yet, I needed to tell him. Someone. After writing out my thoughts yesterday, I realized I had to say something. Anything. My heart couldn't tell my mom. It probably still can't. I can't bear the thought of tears in her eyes. Cracks split across my soul every time my younger sisters fight with her. No family is perfect. We're flawed and broken. My mom does her best, but I see the strain in her eyes after a fight with my siblings. As the oldest, I need to help her peace. I want to see her happy, which is why I cannot tell her the full truth.

But my dad? Something about his strong presence and soft eyes melted the lock on my heart. A few phrases slid out and waited upon my lips.

I knew he could handle a part of the story better than my mom. The part that confessed why his daughter locks herself in her room, sketched dismal pictures, and wrote tear-stained letters to escape reality.

I took a deep breath, but the words stuck behind my teeth. My lips wouldn't let them out.

"Violetta." Dad's tone lowered. "Tell me. What's with him?"

Five words sucked the memories to the front of my mind. My breathing shook. Bryce's rebukes replayed; his threats echoed between my ears. Every night I didn't want to spend with him. Every harsh touch, bitter word, and painful empty kiss. Every moment he made me feel like a nuisance and then claim I was his future.

Second's words from last night pricked the front of my mind. A man who didn't know my full story made me feel more seen and loved than my own boyfriend.

Why did it take a ghost for me to realize I wished I could take every moment with Bryce back?

"I'm not happy with him," I whispered. Fire burned in my throat. I said it. Five words I feared to say aloud escaped my lips and it hurt just as bad as I thought.

Dad nodded and fiddled with the small flashlight on his keychain. The light strobed as he clicked it on and off. "Have you spoken to him about this?"

"I've tried." The words cracked between my lips. They were true and they hurt. I brought up issues to Bryce only to have them thrown back in my face. The moment I got close to being right, he said he'd end it… But he wasn't talking about our relationship.

"And he wasn't receptive." Dad turned off the flashlight and slid it in his pocket. Bending over, he sifted through his backpack. Paper rustled as he pulled out a wrinkled envelope. Elegant letters spelling *Finn*—my father's name—spread across the front. "You know what this is, right?"

I nodded. I could never forget. "Mom gave that to you when you got engaged." Time aged the edges of the faded white envelope. The story inside has a home on the bookshelf of my mind.

"It's a list of everything she hoped I'd be." Gingerly, he opened it and pulled out the letter. "And it's the first of many." A smile spread across his square face. "I didn't tick half of the hundred boxes in this letter. But, eventually I did." He tapped the paper against my head. "You've written one of these, haven't you?"

My heart quickened. "Of course. Mom had us all write one when we turned 13." The start of my nightly tradition. One gel pen and light blue stationery set in motion years of emotional letters addressed to a man I have never met.

"Have you checked that list recently?"

A knot formed in my stomach. I knew what his next sentence would be.

Dad's dark eyes found the softest part of my soul and he whispered, "Does Bryce tick any of the boxes on the list?"

There it was. The punch to the gut that knocked the wind out of me. One I avoided. One I tucked away in the box at the back of my mind.

Of course I knew what was on my list. I looked over it often. It was the reason I keep writing these letters.

Because Bryce doesn't tick off *anything*.

"I thought so." He stroked his thick fingers along my mom's handwriting. Her poetic words could mark her as a modern Emily Dickinson. Beauty and elegance spoke volumes through her pen ink. "Violetta, you know what I'm going to say next."

I pinched my eyes shut. "Just get it over with."

"Who will tick off those boxes?"

Second.

The letters flow so easily my heart wrote them before my brain caught up.

It's true. Second, you check off those boxes. I hope you don't hear me saying all this. My heart isn't ready to tell you. Every night I dream of a man who will take me dancing under the moonlight. I dream of a man who will bring me roses of red and white, promising everything will be all right. I want to be silly. I want to make jokes and laugh. I want to sing off-key and eat my french fries with maple syrup.

I don't want to walk on eggshells. I don't want to stress about saying the wrong thing. I don't want to stress about seeing another girl in the room, wondering if he will make a move or forget I exist.

"I have to go to work." My broken voice answered my dad better than words ever could. I wished I could've said it. I wished I could've poured out my heart, telling him the whole reason. I wanted him to fight off Bryce alongside you, Second.

But I couldn't put my dad in the middle like that. It wouldn't be fair to him.

He let out a long sigh. He knew it was futile to force the words out of me. "You need to do what's right for you. Please." He put a hand on my back. "You talking to Aunt Margot more about Kayleigh worries me. If she thinks—" He averted his gaze.

"It's okay, Dad." I flung my bag over my shoulder. "Thank you for asking me to open up about what's going on. I will try and become an over-sharer again."

His expression softened. "Just because Eleora called you a 'chronic over-sharer' once doesn't mean you lock your words inside."

I chuckled. It is true that I've been more conscious of what I say because of the rude awakening, but it's not Eleora's perception I'm worried about.

Last time I "over-shared," someone almost died. Expressing my feelings ended in a phone call from the train tracks. My heart can't handle that again.

But sharing or not, I'm falling into the same mistakes.

Will the consequences repeat?

I shook my head. "She called me an over-sharer, but you agreed."

He arched an eyebrow. "I didn't need to hear about your co-worker complaining about an infection in his foot."

A smile cracked my face. "Who just babbled and pretended to be a zombie because of a dead rabbit we passed on the drive home?"

He made puppets with his hands, moving their mouths as he said, "Blah, blah, okay, fine. Truce." Long arms wrapped around me, pulling me in for a tight hug.

Warmth enveloped my soul. Tears threatened to crawl down my face. I couldn't cry. No. I was strong. I was his Braveheart. My small confession showed too much weakness already. "Love you too, Dad." My voice muffled against his chest.

"Violetta." His strong voice sounded frail. "If there's a chance Bryce could hurt you…"

A fiery lump caught in my throat.

He already has. From the harsh words to the tiny bruises on my palm from when he digs his fingers, not wanting to let go, I've been hurt. Broken.

But I can't tell Dad that. I can't bear to see the pain cross his face and erupt in his heart.

"I'll be okay," I lied. "You know whose daughter I am, right? I learn from the best." Gently, I pushed myself away and packed up my things, preparing to go through my day like everything's okay.

I told my dad a portion of the truth, but the picture is incomplete. I don't think I will heal until all the pieces are together.

But I can't glue them together just yet.

Yours broken.
Violetta

June 26

Hi Second,

I didn't write for a few days. I stayed late at work to catch up on a ton of emails I missed. I was only out on Monday for our camping trip and you would've thought I was gone for weeks. Repeated emails from Kirk with a body message of *"Bumping this to the top of your inbox :-)."* If I see another line, I will bump my fist into his face.

Sorry, a little much?

Anyway, Second, if you were looking for me, I'm sorry. Every time I got home from work, I flopped on my bed and passed out. My frustrated sisters griped and complained because I promised I'd help around the house.

To my dismay, Dad told Mom the situation. A portion of it, anyway. She hasn't approached me yet, but I know she told my sisters to go easy.

As I slid my laptop out of my backpack this evening, I heard the creak of the floorboards outside my door. I froze, tilted my head, and listened, assuming one of my sisters crept down the hall to scare me.

The door flung open with a crash as it smacked into the wall. "Boo!" Eleora shouted with a smile that quickly disappeared when she saw my arched eyebrows. "Ugh, no points for me then."

"Nope, what do you want?" Annoyance crept through my voice. It wasn't for her. Hundreds of thoughts swirled through my mind between Bryce, the promotion, you. How I could carry it all with a smile?

Straightening, she grumbled, "Geez, nice to see you too." She crossed her arms. "Don't forget we're meeting up with the Pinkles tonight. Fatima texted me on Wednesday asking to meet at the diner."

I exhaled through my nose. I had totally forgotten. I hadn't seen my best friend, Allura, and her family since our Memorial Day shindig. We Sparks always throw the best summer parties. Food piled higher than our heads, games to occupy any stick-in-the-mud, and plenty of drinks. This past event, Dad allowed Aria a taste of her first "grown-up beverage" as he called it. Although, the disproportionate sweetness-to-alcohol ratio gave her a sugar-high rather than intoxication.

The Kazanskis had been there, too. Bryce had more fun with my sisters than me. Don't get me wrong, I want my boyfriend to get along with my family… But I don't think ignoring my presence should be included.

"Is Allura going to be there?" I asked. I still hadn't heard from her since she's been on vacation. She warned me that she was going to unplug from social media; she took that seriously.

My fingers had hovered over her contact more than once. I wanted to text her, but I couldn't bring myself to annoy her. Layne—her boyfriend—had vacationed with them for the first time. I had a feeling there is something she hasn't told me, but I want to hear it in person.

"Probably, moron." If an eye roll had a tone, it'd match her voice. "Just get changed." She slunk back into the hallway and shut my door.

I let her attitude roll off my shoulders and called, "Whatever, I'll be ready in five." Honestly, I needed more than a few minutes. My sundress stuck to my clammy skin from the summer heat. I needed a shower, but I guessed I didn't have time. Peeling off my clothes, I reapplied deodorant, put a healthy dollop of cream in my red curls, and threw on my favorite light blue skeleton crop top, ripped jean shorts, and black sneakers.

My sisters waited for me in the hallway. Felicity dangled my keys from her finger and raised her eyebrows.

I took them. "Sure, I'll drive."

Aria's hand shot up. "I call shotgun!" She bolted out the door. Sage raced after her, eager to get into the car rather than stand in the sun.

"You guys tend to forget that my car is always locked." The keys clanked as I shook them.

"They'll yank on the handle until you let them in." Felicity signed.

"Also if you ever wanted the front, you could've said you called it first and she just didn't see." Eleora snorted.

Felicity shrugged. "Summer is only so long. I'll be driving back to college before we know it."

June's end crept around the corner. July and August will breeze by. Part of me will miss my sisters being around. Laughter bouncing down the halls, stories of nostalgic games tucked away in the basement, joyful memories misting our eyes.

The other part of me remembered the hurt. Harsh words spat in disputes and bickering across the dinner table.

I clenched my jaw. That was the past. My sisters are basically adults now. They've grown up.

But they're not all there yet.

I looked at Aria and Sage. Terror twins. They'll be leaving for college in a few years. For now, they're tattletales, snitches, and argumentative brats.

"Vi, let's GO!" Aria snapped.

Point made. "Sorry, yeah we're going," I said and unlocked the car. One by one, we slid inside and slammed the doors shut. I jabbed the ignition button and adjusted my rearview mirror.

Two eyes I didn't recognize stared at me.

I gasped and slunk into my seat.

"Geez, Vi, what's the matter with you?" Eleora gasped.

"Was it a bug?" Felicity signed. Wide eyes darted around the car.

I covered my face with my hands. Those eyes. White irises with pale pupils violated my soul. I hadn't seen them since Peek-a-Brews.

Whose were they? Why were they back? Still no eyepatch. What period of your life does this ghost portray? Second, this *is* you, right?

Why won't this ghost speak to me when I see him?

I peered through my fingers. Only my eyes reflected in the rearview. "Y-yeah, it was a bug," I lied, pulling myself together. I peeled out of the driveway, hoping to leave my terrified thoughts behind.

I rolled down the windows, letting my ginger hair whip in the wind. Warm summer breeze kissed my sunburnt cheeks. My sisters sang their hearts out to Aria's pop playlist. The thumping loud bass matched my beating heart. I rarely sang along. Usually, they selected songs outside my preferred genres, so I don't know the words anyway. Every so often, Felicity would throw on a nostalgic song we all knew to include me. I couldn't help but smile.

A phone call interrupted our favorite childhood song. My sisters groaned and complained but then shut their lips tight when they saw the name scrawling across the screen: *Bryce Kazanski.*

Eleora let out a long sigh. "Violetta, are you going to listen to us?"

I tapped the red telephone. The music resumed, and I let out a long breath.

Aria paused the music. "Listen to us about what?"

"Don't worry about it, Ri." I tapped play and increased the volume, hoping to drown out the thoughts swirling in my mind.

Eleora groaned and smacked her head on the car seat. Felicity's eyes glared at me through my rearview.

We listened to the music in silence as we pulled into the restaurant.

Standing in front of the door were the Pinkle kids. Well, hardly kids anymore. We grew up with Allura, Sylvia, and Fatima. They're like sisters to us, making our large family even bigger.

"Violettaaaaaa!" Allura squealed. She ran and crashed into my embrace.

The hug of a dear friend pushed away the anxieties in my mind for a little while. "Allura, I missed you!" I squeezed her tightly. "How are you doing?"

"I'm great!" she exclaimed. Her mint green dress swayed as she bounced on the balls of her feet. "I wanted to text you when I got home yesterday, but I needed to tell you all in person." She held out her hand.

A diamond sparkled on her ring finger.

My jaw dropped and I screamed. "I knew it!" I wrapped my arms around her. "Congratulations!"

My sisters squealed and we took turns hugging and complimenting the sparkly 1.5 karat diamond weighing down her hand. The golden band glittered and accented her dark complexion.

"How did you know?" Allura gasped.

I shrugged. "You never take an unplug from social media seriously. I did not hear a *peep* from you, so I knew something was up."

"You know me so well." She stared at the jewel on her finger. "I'm sorry I've been so distant, but hopefully the news makes sense now."

"How did Layne do it? I need to know!" I exclaimed.

"Let's get a table, and I'll spill *everything*." She put her arm through mine and led our group inside.

The seven of us crowded around the booth of Greasy Skillet Diner. Our waitress Stephanie brought out tall glasses of water with lemons. Sage gagged as Aria and Felicity ate the fruit like candy. Eleora downed three glasses of water within the first five minutes of Allura sharing her engagement story.

"The day was perfectly planned," Allura said, squeezing lemon into her glass. "From the veggie hash breakfast to the afternoon alone by the lake. I couldn't stop smiling."

"Did your family say anything?" I asked.

"I thought Fatima would be the first to snitch," Eleora teased before sucking down another water glass.

Fatima stuck her tongue out. "He needed our help which is *why* it was so perfect."

Allura rolled her eyes. "It was great, no matter what." She held her hand out and watched the gem sparkle in the fluorescent light. "We sat on a quiet beach, watching the sail boats go by. Then he asked me to dance." She pressed her hands to her heart.

Aria gagged and Sage elbowed her in the ribs.

"It's cheesy, isn't it? But I don't care!" She threw her hands up. "He knelt down right there and asked me to marry him. How could I refuse?"

"HOW COULD I REFUSE?" Eleora belted, dramatically pressing her hand against her chest and waving her spoon into the air.

If I had taken a sip of my water, I would've spat it out across the table. For the first time in a while, a genuine laugh erupted from my belly. My body warmed and eyes teared as the entire table cackled at my sister's childhood movie reference.

"Preminger's song goes way too hard." Fatima chuckled.

Sylvia wiped tears from her eyes. "Does that mean Allura is just marrying Layne to become royalty?"

Allura flung her hands into the air. "You girls are the *worst*."

"Oh, shut up, you loved us before Layne." Fatima batted her eyelashes.

Allura rolled her eyes. "Yeah, yeah." She picked up her phone and scrolled through her camera roll. "Anyway, here is a photo right after I said 'yes.'"

I gently took her phone and examined the picture. Allura wore an adorable sage green sundress that complimented her smooth black skin. The dazzling ring sparkled as she showed it off for the selfie. Layne's wide charming smile and bright eyes shone with love for his new fiance.

My heart overflowed with joy for my best friend. She deserved every moment of happiness. Layne is a wonderful man who treats her well. Gentle and sweet to match her boisterous bubbly personality. They fit like puzzle pieces, completing each other into a stunning picture.

Before today, joyful relationship stories sank my bitter heart into my shoes. Bryce and I are pieces from completely different puzzles, mismatched and forced together. The realization of that should've soured the sweetness of their story.

But as Allura told her tale, my body didn't react the way it used to. My heart lightened, butterflies tingled my stomach, and my mind thought of one man:

You, Second.

I hope you aren't around to hear this. For me, little crushes are usually fleeting. A cute guy to open the door for me? I'll think about him for a week. A barista I saw a few times at Peek-a-Brews before he moved? I almost gave him my number.

But this crush on you? It's a little different. It's a force that tugs my lips upward so I can't help but smile when I think of you. Sitting with my best friend, I feel peaceful knowing that she's found someone to cherish her… And maybe I have, too?

I shook my head hard as my mind wandered. I needed to be present, not thinking about a ghost. We chatted and laughed through dinner and dessert. We talked about everything and anything.

Except Bryce. He never came up in conversation around the table. My sisters didn't say anything to the Pinkles about convincing me to break up with him. I was grateful for that. At the diner, he didn't exist. I didn't think about him once. I could eat dinner *and* dessert without asking for a to-go box after two bites because I "shouldn't finish it." I could proudly wear my favorite skull shirt without thinking that "it's weird." I could put my curls up into a ponytail without fear that it'll "look disheveled."

I could be me with my family.

After Stephanie cleared our table and we paid the bill, the eight of us left to talk in the parking lot for an hour.

Then, Allura mentioned him and all the "I coulds" became anxieties.

"Violetta, how is Bryce doing?" Allura asked. "I know tonight was girls only, but he usually asks to come along whenever we go out."

My heart sank into my sneakers. I needed a good ending to the day. "That's because he hates when I go places without him," I mumbled.

I felt Eleora's gaze dig into the back of my head.

Taking Allura's arm, I pulled her off to the side. "Bryce is… um…"

Allura arched an eyebrow. Her dress flapped in the summer breeze. "'Um,' what?"

I shoved my hands deep into my jeans pockets… which weren't very deep because girls' pockets are small. I sucked in a deep breath and said five words I've avoided for a long time: "I want to leave him." Each syllable dropped a link from the chain around my heart.

A smile spread across Allura's cheeks. Dark eyes glowed in the setting sun. Flinging her arms around my neck, she pulled me in close. Being five inches shorter than her, I felt like a little girl drowning in a warm embrace from her older sister.

"I am so proud of you," she whispered into my hair. "I've always said you deserved better."

My arms tightened around her torso. I knew how she felt, but never mentioned anything. I couldn't. Her relationship with Layne sparkled with starlight. I didn't want my clouds to dim it. When she pulled away, a tear rolled down her cheek. "I can't wait to introduce you to some of Layne's friends."

I couldn't help but laugh. "Why didn't you tell me you had other guys in mind?" I punched her arm lightly.

She shrugged. "Some of them are nerds, but I think you should decide for yourself. Besides, I think anyone else is better. You and I both know a rock would be a better boyfriend than Bryce." A moment of silence passed before she wrapped her arms around herself. "What Layne said the other day also hit the point home," she whispered.

The smile disappeared from my face. "What was it?"

Her eyes stuck to the pavement. "Bryce told Layne something that felt a little off." Her dress swayed back and forth as she shifted her weight. "He complained about you the whole time, but then said you were his 'future,' whatever that means."

The panini in my stomach threatened to crawl up my throat. That was the sentence he cried through the phone that night.

Allura fidgeted with her engagement ring. "I only found out before I left, and I didn't know how to tell you, but something tells me you already know this is how he talks about you." She peered over my shoulder. Our sisters preoccupied each other. Gently nudging me, we paced the parking lot.

The wind blew our hair back as we walked away from our siblings' chatter. Time slowed and my heart caught in my throat.

Allura took a deep breath. "Violetta, you should tell someone. What he is doing, what he says to others about his girlfriend…" Her eyes darted to her feet. "It wasn't right. It isn't right. He needs help."

"I've tried to help him." I shoved my hands deeper into my pockets. My fingers threatened to rip through the denim.

"Not from *you*." Allura grabbed my arm. Pain contorted her beautiful face. "This is not something you can fix. If he talks about you to others, I can't imagine what he says to you when you're alone. Something tells me you don't share everything."

"This isn't something anyone else should be burdened with." My eyes couldn't meet hers. I never told her about that phone call. I never told her about the threats when I even hinted about taking a break.

"Most of what happened is in the past. I would like to focus on the future, please."

Allura's grip loosened and her arm fell to her side. "Only because you said 'please.'" Her lips formed a small smile. "But when the memories surface and become hard to push through, please, let me know. Let *someone* know."

"I will," I promised. This time, I meant it. But the first person to know won't be her. I can't bring myself to darken her colorful life. It won't be my dad. It won't be my siblings. It most certainly won't be my mom.

I'll tell you, Second.

I'm going to try and tell you what happened.

Hopefully you can help me.

I want you to save me.

In need of rescuing.

Violetta

June 27

Hi Second,

Today was supposed to be a good day. It started off so great and then took a turn for the worst so fast. My soul is tumbling down a mountainside and there is no way I can stop it.

My phone returned to its regularly scheduled Allura morning texts. I didn't realize how much I missed hearing from her every day.

She texted me around 7:30 am: ***"Want to meet for coffee?"***

I sat up in bed. Red hair frizzed around my face like a lion's mane. I could've teased it and thrown it into a bun if she wanted to meet early. Allura was always an early bird. Me? I was somewhere in the middle. If I could, I'd stay up until 3 am and wake up at 7 am only to crash once a week and sleep for 12 hours.

Do you like to get a reasonable amount of sleep, Second? Or are you crazy like me and stay up late drawing or writing letters?

I replied: ***"Def. What time?"***

Three dots danced in a bubble across my screen.

"9 am?"

Not as early as usual for a Saturday.

"See you then. Usual place?"

"Of course."

I left her on read and slid out of my butterfly patterned sheets. My Saturday morning routine consisted of a quick shower, getting dressed, deodorant, and a minimal amount of eye makeup. I left the freckles peppered on my round face exposed. My skin is not the clearest and I hate putting foundation on it. It makes it worse.

Do you have clear skin, Second? If so, please tell me your secrets?

Although, most guys just wash their face with the same bar of soap as their ass so maybe not. I pray you're the exception though.

Wanting to dress cute (and match Allura's cottage-core energy), I threw on my favorite green sundress and white sneakers. I snatched my purse and bounded down the stairs and towards the door with higher spirits than usual.

"Vi, where are you off to?" a voice called.

Fire burned in my throat, scorching the joy bubbling through me moments before. Heat crawled up from my heels to my cheeks. Every muscle in my body tightened as I peered into the kitchen.

Bryce sat at the kitchen table with my dad. An untouched coffee mug sat between his big hands. Dark eyes watched me curiously.

"Hey, Bryce." My voice cracked. I cleared my throat and tried again with a bit more confidence. "What are you doing here?"

"I came to see you." He waved me over. "I haven't heard from you since your trip. I was worried."

He was worried? How did he define the word?

My dad's stern gaze pulled me into the kitchen. I couldn't leave him with Bryce. I didn't know what they were talking about.

"I know, I've been busy with work," I replied. Not a lie. Exhaustion after an all consuming day in the office shut my mind down. The clock spun faster every night and I could barely keep up.

Bryce sighed. "Sit down, Vi."

I held my breath as I dragged the wooden kitchen chair with a screech across the floor. My dad silently got up and poured me a cup of coffee in the mug patterned with wide-eyed aliens. Bryce got it for me for my birthday even though he thinks it's weird. One of the three things he'd ever gotten me in our two years of dating.

I know gifts aren't important in a relationship. However, something is up when he won't even buy you flowers for Valentine's day, or when you're sick, or even when you ask because you need cheering up.

"Thanks, Dad." I pulled the mug closer and clutched it for moral support. Heat scalded my palms as if the alien's eyes tried to burn through my hands with laser beams.

Bryce let out a deep breath. "I want to make things right."

That wasn't what I thought I'd hear. My eyes darted between Bryce and my dad. "What's up?"

"Your dad was telling me that I haven't quite been there for you lately." He cleared his throat. "I guess it hasn't been easy for you, but I think I can fix things."

My eyebrows raised. "Fix things?"

"Yes. I will make sure everyone sees us as perfect together." He took a long sip of his coffee before placing it back on the round red placemat. "I won't keep you any longer. I know you're off somewhere today, so just text me when you're done. I'll take you somewhere special tomorrow." Raising from his seat, he nodded to my dad and left the house. No kiss goodbye. No gentle touch.

Only a promise that rang like a threat.

I slumped back in my chair. My mouth dropped to the floor and I stared at my father. "What did you say to him?"

Dad shrugged. "Honestly, nothing. He barely spoke to me. I just told him how you needed some time with friends and family."

"And what else?" My grip tightened. I imagined the ceramic cracking beneath my fingers.

"That you needed him to be better," he replied flatly. "Look, I know it's not my place to interfere with your relationship, but you're worrying me, Braveheart."

I ran my fingers through my hair. "It might've become worse, now," I mumbled.

A bear-sized hand gently rubbed my back. "He seems like he wants to make things up to you. Let's see what happens. If he's not the one to tick the boxes?" He jabbed his thumb over his shoulder. "He's outta here."

I chuckled. "You better help me toss him out, then."

"Oh, you won't need me to do it." He laughed. "Your mom is ready to kick him across the country. She'll send him flying."

My smile couldn't reach my eyes. I didn't want her to know. I prayed she'd never find out all the details. Flinging my arms around my dad, I kissed his head. "Thanks for looking out for me."

"Anything for one of my little Sparkles." He patted my arm. "You need to take care of yourself."

I let out a sigh. Take care of myself? How… When I know it will hurt someone else?

I slow-motion punched my dad as a farewell and darted out the door to meet Allura at our favorite coffee shop.

Nerves dragged my feet with every step. An eerie presence floated along the scent of coffee and pastries. Today, haunted house vibes overpowered Peek-a-Brews and its charming vintage decor.

My gaze darted everywhere but the mirrors. The ghastly eyes I've seen twice now stuck to the back of my eyelids.

Seeing visions and talking to dead guys in your letters is not something you easily forget.

After ordering the Stormy Night mocha, I slid into one of the red booths and waited for Allura. As I sat and gawked at the decor, my mind flipped through boxes of memory files. I hoped to pick out a document of daydreams about Second, but the images Aunt Margot kept tucked away scattered along my brain.

Peek-a-Brews was where Kayleigh encountered her ghost the day before she died. Is that what happens when someone is about to reach the end? Aria claims she's obsessed with parapsychology, but she doesn't babble about the phenomena as much as I'd like her to. If I didn't get such an awful attitude every time I spoke to her, maybe I'd ask her.

"Violetta!" Allura screeched, sliding into the seat across from me. Her long cream dress complimented her smooth black skin. Thick ebony hair fell around her long face. She always looked so beautiful and put together—truly an inspiration. "Spill everything about Bryce."

A smile cracked my broken expression. Her blunt desire to know every piece of drama always catches me off guard. In any other circumstance, I would text her and spill the tea immediately. One of my favorites was filling her in on the day Kirk babbled on and on about how his cat kept him up all night, thus decreasing his productivity.

I shrugged. "What do you want to know?"

"Everything and don't leave anything out." Her eyes softened like a mother speaking to a crying child. "And I mean it. I've realized this man has more red flags than I thought, so raise all of them. If you forget any details, I am going to be mad at you forever and ever."

"I can't have that, but this is going to be harder than you think." My throat burned. I never spoke this aloud. Aunt Margot had put the puzzle together without me handing her the pieces. Telling my best friend? Not easy.

A breeze tickled my neck. My spine straightened and I spun around.

"What's wrong?" Allura asked.

My eyes jumped from mirror to mirror. Human reflections filled the glass. I faced forward and shook my head hard. My lips parted but the words caught in my throat when a vanity behind Allura caught my gaze.

A transparent face filled the silver plated mirror. It was the profile of a man with a strong jaw and Roman nose.

A scream crawled up my throat but never left my lips. I pinched my eyes shut.

I heard Allura turn in her chair. "What did you see? Who is there? Is it Bryce?"

My eyelid opened a crack. The only face in the mirror was my own.

My heart beat louder than the bass blasting from the barista's playlist. It hurt as it thumped in my chest.

"Violetta, what happened? You look like you've seen—"

"A ghost," I finished. I said it out loud. There was no going back, I needed to tell Allura something. "Do you remember the ghost story Aria was obsessed with for months when we were teens? The one that actually happened to my family?"

My best friend arched a thin eyebrow. "Go on." She cupped the chai latte in her hands.

"Aunt Margot's sister, Kayleigh, started hearing things before she was murdered. Something she called Little Ghost. Then, she saw his true phantom form shortly before she was killed." My hands slid my coffee mug back and forth across the table. "Now, Aunt Margot thinks something like that may be happening to me."

Allura's thin lips pursed. "What do you mean? Are you hearing things?"

"Not quite, but seeing?" I sounded unsure. I couldn't tell her everything, but I could leave hints. She's good at playing detective. "She is convinced I'm in danger and my own Little Ghost—er, maybe, let's call him…" My warm mug comforted my shaking hands. I looked at my reflection in the mocha and blurted, "Stormy. We'll call him Stormy."

"Ohh-kay." Allura sipped her latte. "So Aunt Margot thinks," she paused, "Stormy is trying to talk to you to tell you… You're going to die?"

The chatter of the coffee shop quieted as my brain processed the words coming from her lips. Hearing them from Aunt Margot is one thing, but seeing the fear in Allura's shaking eyes and those four words tumbling from her lips made it feel different. It made it feel real.

"I don't know," I croaked. "There is something else I need to tell you about Bryce."

Fire burned my eyes and the neurons in my brain fired at light speed. They begged me not to say the words out loud. They begged me not to think about it.

But I had to. No one else knows. If something was to actually happen to me? Who would be able to convince the police what happened? Aunt Margot had to do that for Kayleigh.

I couldn't believe I had to think about that.

"Last year, I wasn't in a good place. I think you remember when I didn't really go out much." Goosebumps raised over my bare legs. "It was because Bryce was making me miserable. I talked with my mom and she suggested I tell him I needed space." The room felt like it was closing in, but I forced myself to continue. "So, I did, but he didn't take it well. At all." My mouth tasted like the desert. I couldn't speak.

Soft fingers touched my arm. "You don't have to tell me if it hurts."

"It will hurt if I say it or not." A shaky breath escaped my lips. "I tried to break up over the phone. I didn't want to do it in person because I was afraid he'd try to convince me otherwise and there would be no escape. Over the phone, I didn't have to see his scowl and I was able to hang up after we came to an agreement. Well, I thought we did. That was until…" I trailed off as the memory resurfaced. A lump caught in my throat, keeping the words down.

Allura's fingers tightened around my arm. Brown eyes magnified as tears brimmed. "Until what?"

Acid burned in my stomach like fire consuming me from the inside out. I sucked in a breath. "He called me back from the train tracks, begging me to take him back or else he'd—" I couldn't say it out loud. I wished he only wanted to run away. I wished he only wanted to travel someplace distant. I couldn't tell her he threatened to step in front of the next train.

Allura's cheeks dampened. She sniffled and dabbed her face with a napkin. I *hated* seeing my best friend cry. I never wanted to cause her pain, but this was because I wasn't strong enough to say no.

She bit her lip. "I noticed the jabs at parties, the awkward moments, and wondered why you were still with him." She shrugged and slunk back into the booth. "Now, it makes sense. Why didn't you tell me?"

Fear clings me to a man I don't like. A man who acts like I'm a burden, yet claims I'm his future.

"I am afraid." Three words broke my heart. Tears streamed down my face and there was nothing I could do to stop it. My shoulders heaved with the sobs. The prying eyes watching us in the mirrors stung the back of my head, but I couldn't stop their curious minds.

Allura jumped up out of the booth and slid next to me. Slender arms draped around my quaking body. I couldn't stop the hysteria. The thought of the past and the fear of the future entwined in a dreadful dance. Emotion poured out with every step until they finished their routine.

We sat in silence after I emptied the napkin holder for tissues. The barista tip-toed to the table and laid a new pack and left without a word. An uncomfortable quiet filled the coffee shop.

I licked my dry lips. "Allura, what do I do?"

She squeezed me tighter. "You need to take care of yourself. This is dangerous and if Aunt Margot sees a pattern?" She shook her head. "History repeats itself in the weirdest of ways. May you please take the mistakes from her story and learn from them? You have to tell your parents first. They'll protect you."

I shook my head. "I'm not ready. My mom already asked me to break up with him once. I *failed* her." Wiping the tears from my cheeks, I whispered, "She doesn't need to know that. She doesn't need the guilt of thinking it's her fault her daughter is still hurting. I want to do this quietly and on my own. I'm an adult, dammit, I think I need to start acting like one."

But is that true?

"Violetta, you don't need to take everything on yourself because you feel like it's a burden to someone else." She rested her chin atop my head, nestling her face in my unruly red curls. "Your family loves you. As much of a pain as your sisters are, they love you, too. And I don't know what this 'Stormy' thing is about, but it seems like it cares about you also." She pulled away for a moment. "Although, if you're actually talking to a spirit, you might need to consult a priest."

I chuckled. "Is it weird that scrupulous me hasn't yet?"

Allura pursed her lips and pulled away from the hug. "A little bit. I still think this overbearing stress might be causing you to hallucinate and that's why you're not scared?"

I drummed my fingers against my lap. I couldn't be hallucinating, could I? Am I spiraling so badly that my mind is making this situation up?

My hand slid to my purse. I thought if I showed her the notebook she could confirm or deny if what was happening to me was real or not. She would be my concrete evidence that I am either crazy or really being haunted.

My fingers recoiled. I couldn't do that. Not yet. More than anything, I wanted you to be real, Second.

I'm not ready to lose you, Second. Not when I haven't decided what to do next.

"Allura, thank you." Resting my head against her chest, I inhaled and exhaled deeply. "Thank you for always listening to me vent."

Slender fingers ran through my hair. "I am always here for you. I hope this helped you decide what the next step should be."

I know what that is, but do I have the strength to do it? I don't want to do it. I'd rather have someone to swoop in and save me.

Ginger curls blocked my vision, but something bright caught my eye. I brushed the hair behind my ear and caught a glimpse of a pale figure of a man watching me through a small mirror in the corner of the room fading away.

Second, if that was you, please come back. I need you to save me.

Yours frightened.
Violetta

June 28

Second. Oh, Second.

Where are you?

Bryce took me out after church today. The day I decided to break it off. He picked me up after Mass and dragged me away from my family. Cold stares from my sisters froze my soul as he nudged me into the front seat of his rusting sedan.

Silence thickened like fog between us. My body remained rigid the entire ride to the restaurant. I rehearsed my lines like an actor preparing for their play. Lights, pressure, action. Dozens of scenarios where I finally end it and set my boundaries flashed through my mind. None of them end well, but we would be in a public place, and Allura was on speed dial.

He blasted his favorite band that we listened to every time we drove. The soundtrack to my sorrowful nightmares. Vulgar songs with degrading lyrics.

Don't get me wrong, Second. I am all for angsty angry rock music. However, these songs have no musical rhythm. They're slurring depressing words with poor guitar and a back beat. Even if I wanted to sing along to appease him, he'd jab the off-button and claim I "ruined it."

Another red flag of the day. I decided to keep tabs after my conversation with Allura. Maybe if I call them out vividly in my letters it will be easier to do what I have to?

Who am I kidding? None of this will be easy.

The moment he turned right on Main Street, I knew where we were going. A new brunch spot in town that charged way too much for scrambled eggs.

We exited the car and climbed the steps. He entered ahead of me, awkwardly holding the door so I could step through. He spoke to the hostess who led us to our tables and took his seat across from me.

Bryce glanced around the wide room. He smirked as he took in the bright atmosphere. "Pretty nice in here, huh?"

I nodded and took the thick leather menu in my hands. I flipped open the pages and tried to find something with a reasonable price tag.

We poured over the menus without a word. Quiet is supposed to be peaceful. When you're with someone you love, it's beautiful. You can hear each other's heart beats, feel each other's thoughts, and drink in each other's presence.

This silence had none of that. It was a knife to the stomach that twisted with each tick of the clock. It dragged, it hurt, and I waited anxiously for him to say something. Anything.

Red flag.

The waitress returned, took our orders, and retrieved the menus. I wished she'd left mine. I wanted to prop it up, creating a wall between Bryce and me.

But there he sat in the same tan polo he always wears on "fancy" occasions. I had bought him other clothes to expand his wardrobe as a courtesy, but they "weren't his style".

"How is work?" he asked after a few moments of staring.

"It's fine," I replied curtly. I forced myself to keep going: "Kirk hasn't been helping again. I wrote a run of show and event details for him—again. Only this time I sent them to all the managers and—"

"Oh, same old. Was hoping for some exciting drama. Let's change the subject." He scoffed, waving his hand.

My cheeks flushed. "Uhh, okay?" When you're in a relationship, shouldn't you be able to ramble freely when asked to share?

Red flag.

"Have you picked up any new hobbies yet?" He straightened the knife beside his plate. "You said your old ones didn't interest you anymore."

My warm face burned red hot. "When did I say that?"

"You mentioned archery and journaling weren't fulfilling

anymore," he claimed. "You wanted to try something new."

I cocked my head to the side. "I never said that. Sure, I want to try new things. I've been into drawing—"

"Yes, that's it!" he interrupted—again.

Red flag.

"How is your drawing?" He continued, "I'm sure you can become a digital artist with the right equipment. Seems more beneficial than archery. You can probably do commissions to rake in more income."

My fingernails dug into my thighs. "Why would I need to get more income?"

"Well, you want to move out, don't you? And places like this," he gestured toward the restaurant's high ceiling and glittering chandeliers, "don't come cheap. I pulled an extra shift at my second job to take you here. Not easy."

I didn't ask to go somewhere fancy. I didn't ask to be taken out at all. I thought he was doing something nice to make up for being such a jerk. I thought he would apologize and tell me it was his fault.

But that won't happen.

Red flag.

I bit my tongue and nodded.

He smiled. "I'm glad. Look, the commission idea is just a backup plan in case you don't get that promotion at work."

Before I could defend myself, the waitress placed plates of steaming hot food in front of us.

Bryce drowned his blueberry pancakes in maple syrup. He jerked his chin toward my plate. "Glad you got the protein, but that's enough for two people. Save some for tomorrow."

Fire bubbled in my stomach. My muscles ached and my head throbbed. Again, he mentioned my weight. Sure, I am big boned. Sure, I am "fluffy."

I am fine with it.

The fact that he isn't?

Red. Flag.

My hands trembled as I lifted my fork. I stabbed a steaming potato. Today, it repulsed me and I was devastated. I loved potatoes. They're my favorite food. Every shape and form is beautiful. Thin, chunky, curly, all of them.

Why can't he love me for my form?

I just compared myself to a potato… I really am upset.

The final red flag. I couldn't handle raising another one. My arms hurt from carrying them all. I needed to put them down, cross the river, and burn the bridge.

I placed my fork down and cleared my throat. "Bryce, I need to tell you something."

Pancake stuffed his cheeks. "What is it?"

Words stuck to the roof of my dry mouth. I took a deep breath and said, "I think something needs to change." But a loud clatter of dishes crashed behind me.

Bryce looked over my shoulder. "That sucks. They should've paid attention." He didn't hear me and continued slicing his pancakes.

I tried again. "Bryce, we need to—" Clapping erupted as the wait staff sang 'Happy Birthday' to another patron.

Bryce rolled his eyes. "Never do that for me, m'kay? No matter how long we've been married for."

My eyebrows shot up and my racing heart stopped dead in my chest. Married? When does he think we'll get married?

"Bryce, I don't think so," I croaked.

"You don't think what?" His eyes darted from my face to my plate. "You should eat, it's getting cold."

And that was that. He rambled on about the perfect ratio of pancake batter to water and other random things that fascinated him, not caring what I have to say. Even if I wanted to get a word in edgewise, he wouldn't let me.

I packed a box of leftovers enough for 2 people.

Breakfast ended and we drove back to my parents house. My legs bounced the whole ride home. I couldn't break up with him in the car. It wasn't safe. If he decided he didn't like it, he may have done something irrational.

The sedan screeched to a halt in the driveway. "Glad we finally got to go out. Sucks it was for breakfast, but we'll do a late night date soon." He winked and my stomach dropped.

I nodded and slid out of the car. He didn't try to kiss me goodbye.

He didn't even offer to get out of the car.

Red flag.

I jabbed my key into the door and slipped inside. The brass handle felt like a weapon as I locked it behind me. My only defense against the man outside.

The man Allura and Margot think might *kill* me. The man who might hurt himself if I leave. The man who drops me on a doorstep, feeling broken.

A haunted quiet floated through the hallway. Cold tiles greeted my feet as I removed my sandals. My family hadn't returned from their Sunday errands. My date with Bryce wasn't for him to work on our relationship. It was a checklist tick. A front for my family to see that he's trying to do better.

I was *so close* to telling him things weren't working. The words started to come out, but he wouldn't accept the hint. I wanted to at least plant the seed and let my tears water it. Perhaps it would grow into a giant tree that I could climb. It would take me to the stars where I could build a home among them.

I dragged my feet up the stairs and sat on my plush white rug. Bryce's voice garbled in my head. Negative memories scraped and clawed at the door I shut them in.

My eyes shook and my body quaked. Trembling fingers grabbed my sketchbook. I needed to draw. I haven't done it in a while because writing letters to you, Second, preoccupied my hands.

Writing the memories isn't enough. They need to take shape. I need to see their monstrous form to know they are leaving my mind.

Charcoal stained my pale skin like ash as I scribbled the thoughts onto paper. Harsh lines imitating angry words filled the pages. I tore it off and created another. Then another. Then another.

Tears stained my art. Black puddles morphed and spread. I lay my back against my bed and stare at the stars on my ceiling. I muttered the same prayer over and over between gasping breaths, trying to calm my racing heart.

A gentle breeze tickled my legs. I left my window open a crack. My legs quaked as I rose from the floor to shut it. Clenching and unclenching my fists, I tried to steady my emotions.

I closed my eyes and prayed. I prayed for peace. I prayed for the thoughts to leave.

I prayed for you, Second.

Opening my eyes, I looked in the mirror. A fragile girl with puffy green eyes stared back at me. Red hair curled like an uncontrollable fire. I burned and I needed someone to put me out.

A gust of wind rushed through my room, scattering my nightmarish drawings everywhere. I stumbled over my notebooks to slam it closed.

But the room didn't stay quiet. A whisper floated between my ears. I couldn't make it out, but the peculiarity of it snapped me out of my hysterics.

It sounded like a crackling, broken radio of a man saying these words: imagination, chili, too spicy, things.

My shoulders dropped as the sound tickled my ears. A laugh escaped my lips. I laughed and laughed, rubbing my palms across my face. "I'm going insane." I plopped on my bed and picked up my white leather notebook. I opened to the front where Kayleigh wrote only three sentences before her ex crashed into Margot's car.

Three wrong words break a heart.
Five wrong words consume a soul.
Ten wrong words last eternity.

Margot claimed Kayleigh started seeing and hearing the ghost before she died.

Maybe Allura is right. Will I become a ghost like you, Second?

I've finished transcribing my day as evidence Bryce will not listen to me. He won't let me go. I want someone to do this for me.

I want to scream for you. My lips want to cry out, "Second, he's not listening!" with the hopes that you are.

```
I'm so, so sorry. I have to talk to you
                 later.
```

Tears dampen my cheeks. Not later. Now. Please. I've been waiting for you. Countless nights I've waited for you.

Second, I need you now.

Yours forever patient.
Violetta

June 29

Hello Second,

"When will you be able to talk to me?"

I write my cries, desperately in need of advice from someone I can't see. I need to hear—or read—words that are reassuring. Perhaps it will push me in the right direction.

My sisters filled my evening with a night at the bowling alley. My head fogged from the previous day's breakdown, so I welcomed the distraction.

Neon lights illuminated the alleys. It was Moonlit Mondays at King Pin-guin. My sisters insisted we wear light colors to glow blue in the dark. White shirts make me feel like a marshmallow, but I obliged to make them happy.

I sat quietly on the edge of the plastic loveseat, watching Sage throw yet another gutterball. Aria's obnoxious cackles overpowered the rock music. Felicity and Eleora returned from the snackbar with hot dogs balancing on four plastic cups of soda.

"A glizzy for you." Eleora handed me my combo. "And the rest of your cash."

"Thank you." I took the cup and shoved the change into my pocket, careful not to drop the hotdog.

"Felicity, Felicity!" Aria waved her hands until our sister noticed. "You're up!"

Felicity rolled her eyes and hopped up the step to take her turn.

Aria padded over and snatched her dinner. "Thanks, Mooom," Aria drawled before taking a large bite.

"Sometimes I feel like you only bring me along for my wallet," I teased.

With full cheeks, she replied, "You are correct." She plopped beside me. "I am a broke future-college student."

"Get a job then, you freeloader." Eleora snorted. Mustard dripped onto her lap. She jumped up with a squeal and ran to the bathroom to hopefully save her white pants.

My phone vibrated against my leg. I bit down on the rim of the cup to hold it between my teeth, careful not to make the same condiment calamity as Eleora. I yanked my phone out of my obnoxiously tiny pocket and opened it without seeing who it was from.

It was from Allura: *"Hey girlie! Checking in and seeing how you are doing and if you've heard from Stormy."*

I heard a quiet scoff and pressed my phone against my chest. Aria glanced at the device and mocked. "What are you hiding?"

"Don't worry about it," I retorted, turning my body away from her. My heartbeat quickened as I texted back: *"I have and I'm nervous that you're right about Bryce. Will tell you more later. Wanna do it in person."*

An unread message bubble taunted me before I could lock my screen. I steeled myself to open Bryce's and get it over with: *"Have fun with ur sisters. Glad it's not me. Hate bowling. Try not to break anything lol <3"*

A heart emoticon and "lol" is like putting a happy-face mask on a murderer in a horror film. It doesn't make the message any less messed up.

"Violetta, your face looks scrunchy, you'll get wrinkles," Eleora said, returning from the bathroom. The stain on her pants was gone, but a few wet marks from where she scrubbed remained. "Your turn, by the way."

I shoved my phone back into the pocket. "Sorry. Aria, can you hold my stuff?" I handed over my hotdog and soda. "Don't eat it!" I called over my shoulder.

I grabbed a blue sparkly ball. The weight felt good in my palms. Throwing heavy objects to knock things over with a satisfying crash was the pastime I definitely needed. Bryce's message stained my mind. I prayed to get it out of my head. I couldn't break anything in a bowling alley unless I chucked the ball into the ceiling. I wasn't that strong.

Second, are you that strong? I imagine you must have a thick frame and strong arms from pulling yourself up mountainsides all day. I imagined you bowling beside me, cheering me on. We'd have some friendly competition, but you'd be proud whether I hit one pin or ten.

I don't think you would throw it into the ceiling like I've seen on the internet. If you did, I bet you'd feel so guilty. You have too many green flags to break-and-run.

I also hope you didn't catch me writing all that. (If you did, I meant every word.)

As I bowled and knocked down six pins, my mind wandered thinking about you. A smile cracked my hardened face.

My eyes caught Aria's for a moment. Her head cocked, watching me carefully. Intently. I stuck my tongue out and bowled again, knocking down the rest of the penguin pins.

"Ugh, now you're beating me," Eleora whined.

"Felicity is way further ahead though." I pointed to her twenty point lead.

Felicity shrugged and signed, "I'm the penguin's deadliest predator."

"That was dumb," Aria teased. "Vi, hurry up and take your hot dog before I eat it."

I took it from her and sat back down.

Felicity leaned forward. Ketchup stained the corners of her lips, but I didn't tell her. "So, my birthday is in five days," she signed, her curious eyes darting from face to face. "What are you planning for me?"

Sage quietly sipped her soda while Aria looked at her oversized clown shoes.

Eleora and I exchanged glances. She shook her head.

"We can't tell you anything," I said. "You know planning parties is part of my job, so rest assured it will be the best twenty-first birthday you've ever had."

"It will be her only twenty-first birthday, idiot." Aria punched my leg. "But no one tells me anything, so I couldn't tell you if I tried."

"No one tells you anything because you are a snitch." Eleora swigged the rest of her soda and wiped her lips with the back of her hand. "No one can trust you."

"That's not true! I haven't told you guys about—" Our eyes met and her lips shut. "Nevermind. Sage, it's your turn to bowl."

She stood silently, exchanged a glance with her twin, and went to the lane.

My heart clenched. I didn't like that exchange. They know something, and I'm afraid to find out what it is.

"No, what is it?" Felicity signed, leaning in. UV lights turned her white smile purple. Gossip was her favorite pastime. It didn't matter if it was between sisters or some stranger we saw across the street, Felicity hung on every word.

"Forget whatever it was, because I think we need to talk about the elephant we left behind at the campsite?" Eleora's eyebrows shot up. "Violetta, why did Bryce pick you up and take you out yesterday? I thought it was over?"

Felicity shook her head, red hair bouncing back and forth. "No, I heard Dad talked to him telling him to be better. Mom is furious." Her sign for "furious" reminded me of an explosion and did not help my nerves.

"Why haven't you talked to her?" Eleora asked.

"There are too many questions, take turns." I melted into the chair, wishing I could turn into a puddle and evaporate. This was supposed to be an escape, not a therapy session. I already went through it with Allura. My sisters weren't trust-worthy–especially not the twins. They were close to the Kazanski girls.

"Violetta, what happened yesterday?" Felicity signed. "You didn't come down for dinner the other night, and you've barely touched your hotdog."

The half-eaten sandwich grew heavier in my grip. The smell of the mustard burned my nose and I wanted to gag. I couldn't think about yesterday. I couldn't bring it up. I didn't want to bring it up.

But I had to say something.

Needles pricked the back of my eyelids as I pinched them shut and took a deep breath. "I tried to break up with him yesterday," I whispered.

Felicity was the only one to understand me and she gasped. "You tried to break up with him?"

Aria wasn't paying attention, but Eleora read her sign. "Wait, what! What happened? Is it over?" She whispered.

Prickles turned to tears as the corner of my eyes brimmed. "I don't think so. He didn't really hear me."

The two groaned and threw out their arms. Sage returned and quietly asked Aria to go up and take her turn. She didn't acknowledge anything we said. She sat and bent her neck forward to keep her eyes on the phone laying on her lap.

"Okay, but I have to say this is progress." Eleora clapped. "You took our advice for once. So, when are you going to try again? You clearly don't have any dates coming up."

"They're coming over for my birthday, aren't they?" Felicity signed slowly. A shadow covered her eyes. "Are you going to break up then?"

I shook my head. "I don't want to ruin your birthday. I can wait."

Her face softened. "Thank you, but I don't want you to wait any longer. I'd rather you have peace on my birthday than be frustrated."

"Why not do it before then so he doesn't even come?" Eleora suggested.

I shrugged. "I don't think I'll see him before then. Besides, I want to do it in a public place in case he…" I trailed off. Soda dampened my palm from a crack in the side of the plastic cup. I didn't realize how hard I squeezed it.

Felicity and Eleora glanced at each other but said nothing as I handed off my hotdog and jumped up to get a replacement cup.

The mirror-plated bar reflected the disco lights illuminating the dark bowling alley. Sparkling stars danced beneath the drinks the bartender slid across the counter.

I plucked a few napkins from the holder. "Excuse me?"

The bartender turned. A burly man with thick brown arms and kind eyes tossed a towel over his shoulder. "Yes, miss, what can I do for you?"

"May I have a new cup? This one broke." I lifted the dripping plastic.

"I'll give you new soda, too. Place it there." He retreated to the back of the bar to grab a sturdier cup.

Colorful alcohol bottles lined the mirrored wall. A rainbow of escape or deadly intoxication depending on who you are. I drank recreationally, but never to the point of unconsciousness. Lately, I haven't drank at all. My moral compass fears that if I start and fall in love with the release from the stress of Bryce, work, family, and now Second. It may tether me and never let me go.

I forced my mind to read the labels to calm my erratic thoughts. As I counted the amount of gin brands he had, a breeze rushed through, rattling the bottles.

My heart shuddered. I think I was the only one to see it. My eyes darted to every mirror behind the bar.

When I looked down at the counter, I saw him.

A strong white hand lay next to mine pressed to the mirrored bar top as if it tried to escape. The faded image of a ghastly man with a strong jaw and anti-gravity hair flickered. No beard, but the shape of his face was familiar. No eyepatch, but white filled both eyes.

I couldn't tear myself away. I stared at the figure trapped below me. My hand slowly slid across the counter, desperate to press my fingers to his. Begging to feel him. Praying it would electrify me. Closer and closer until our pinkies almost touched.

"Miss, are you okay?"

My head snapped up, startling the bartender. Water dripped onto the counter. I didn't realize I was crying.

"I-I-I am sorry." I yanked another napkin out of its holder and dabbed my eyes. "I've been having a hard time."

"You're about twenty-five, right?" He took a step back towards the bar. Thick fingers grasped the neck of a rum bottle.

A splash of rum to swirl my thoughts flirted with my heart. It might be easier to confront my sisters. If I get that out of the way, maybe another shot would make it easier to tell my mom. Another shot and then maybe I could call Bryce and end it.

I shook my head. I wasn't in a good-place to flirt back. "Twenty-three, but I don't have my wallet on me. Just the soda is fine, thank you."

He put the bottle down and handed me the soda. "If you change your mind, liquid courage might help."

"Thank you, I appreciate it." With a nod, I took my soft drink and walked back to my sisters. The conversation shifted to the "unfair" lead Felicity has in the game and how it was my turn to bowl.

The night proceeded as nothing happened. The loud sounds of the alley couldn't drown out three paths fogging my mind: Second, the bartender's advice, and Bryce.

I don't know what I'll choose first.

I need your help.

Ever desperate,
Violetta

June 30

Second,

I am a little match trying my hardest to keep a dark world bright.
But I'm burning out.

I sat across from Kirk in the conference room. He reclined in his
leather office chair, drumming his fingers against the mahogany table.
"Why is he always late to these things?"

"This is the first time you're early," I retorted. My fingers flew
across my keyboard. Three bridal clients needed vendor updates
"immediately" (even after I sent them an email yesterday). So, I had to
work during our review meeting. I hate dealing with bridezillas. First
off, they're so rude. Second of all, they always think they know what
they want, but they wait until the last minute to tell you. When you
hire an event planner, shouldn't you let *them* plan the event?

Well, unless you hire Kirk. Then, you need to do it all yourself.

"Why don't you work on your next run-of-show," I muttered.
I was in no mood this morning to be nice to him, but I couldn't be
mean either. Mid-year review approached. If I wanted the promotion,
I needed to be firm, but not an ass.

Besides, I haven't decided the path I would traverse down. I didn't
know where my life and relationship with Bryce would end up over
the next few days.

"You're probably right." He sighed. He swung his legs up onto the
table, slid his laptop onto his lap, and flipped open the lid. He exhaled
and opened a new document.

He surprised me. I didn't think he'd actually try to do work.

Perhaps he sensed our boss was about to walk in thirty seconds after he typed the client's name.

"Good morning, Violetta. Kirk," Lucio greeted. A stack of papers and a laptop tucked under his thick arm. "I can't believe summer is a third of the way over. Our biggest events are approaching quickly."

"Yes, July is my busiest month with summer weddings," I said as he sat down with a grunt. "I have many cranky brides who are looking at the heatwave and regretting their dates."

Lucio scoffed and adjusted his rumpled shirt over his round belly. "They do every year, don't they?"

"Most of them just get divorced anyway, so I don't know why they even bother." Kirk snorted. He picked at something stuck under his fingernails. "Wasting fifty grand on a wedding only to cheat on the guy the following year."

I bit my lip. He was right, and it sucked. It wasn't just about the money. I hated the thought of heartbreak. The lies. The cheating.

Despite the gritty music I listen to and the skull t-shirts I tuck into ripped jeans, I am a hopeless romantic. My heart yearns for happy endings. For myself, for my sisters, for my friends, for every bride I work with.

My heart shatters and blood boils when it ends in pieces.

"That's their decision, Kirk. Our job is to make their best day ever memorable." Lucio opened his laptop. An ascending tone brought it life. "Now, I hate kicking off meetings with bad news." He rubbed his mustache. "Jessica is no longer with the company."

My heart beat loudly in my chest. I knew it was coming. My mind prepared for it, but it was finally here. The reminder I wouldn't have anyone in the workplace that understood hit me in the gut. She had left because her family moved downstate and she couldn't afford to move out yet. The positive side? She would live close to my uncle, Rowan, so I'd have someone to stay with when I visited her.

"Oh my goodness," I replied. I didn't want to tell him I knew, it wasn't my business.

"Yep." Lucio leaned back and crossed his tattooed arms. "She said her family is moving and she wanted to go with them. She also said it would be a good change for now because the pressure was getting to her." He laughed. "She called herself a little puppy who couldn't deal with the dogs."

I smiled. That's a Jessica thing. Her goth style and monotone voice juxtaposed with her dry random humor and sweet nature brought me joy.

I'm going to miss her. I need to text her when I'm in a better headspace.

"The 'dogs' meaning?" Kirk arched an eyebrow.

"Not you. You're a poodle." Lucio laughed. "The brides. The mother-in-laws. I guess you can only take so much." He glanced over at me, warmth in his eyes. "Proud of you for sticking with it, Violetta."

My ears reddened. My boss was proud of me? I had never heard him say that in my three years of working here. Hearing those works from a businessman I respect? I couldn't be more thankful.

Lucio has always inspired me. He started Grandview Entertainments as a small hole in the wall downtown with five team members. Now, we have about a hundred employees working in the fourth floor of a new commercial building with a view of the city rushing by. Brides, corporate conferences, rich parents everywhere booked years in advance to work with our team. We've grown as a business and made a name for ourselves in the industry.

Clearing my throat, I replied, "Thank you, Lucio. It means a lot."

"Can we get on with the meeting?" Kirk groaned. "I've got docs to write."

Lucio waved a hand and picked up his pile of papers. "Fine, fine, we'll go over our plans for the next month. We have busy weekends ahead."

As Lucio talked through the list, I felt a fire ignite in my heart. So many things to do. Weddings, graduations, corporate team events, bat mitzvahs, sweet sixteens, showers, and more. Summer was for parties and our job at Grandview Entertainments was to make sure everyone had a grand ol' time. I loved the process and couldn't wait to dive in.

The only problem? With Jessica gone, no one was there to clean up Kirk's act… except me. Knowing my people-pleasing ass, I would end up following through with his clients.

But August was coming. The end of tri-2 when the promotion for Senior Event Manager would open. The one constant in my life. The one thing I've continued to pursue and not deviate from.

With this promotion, I could move out. It would be enough to start my own life. I could get away.

Am I a little young? Yeah. Am I qualified? Absolutely. Do I deserve it? Definitely.

I am doing whatever I can to get this promotion. I've had my resume and proposal collecting dust in my desk drawer. I'm waiting for the day it opens and I can present my case to Lucio. He only had two Event Coordinators now: Kirk and me. Unless he goes external, I've got a good chance.

After an hour and a half, Lucio rose from his chair. Cracking his back, he groaned and said, "It's tough getting old. Don't grow up too fast, Violetta. You'll turn into ugly old bags like Kirk and me."

"Speak for yourself." Kirk shot up from his chair. "My skin is better than ever, thank you very much." He snatched his laptop off the table, spun, and stalked out of the meeting room.

"Boy, he's uptight, ain't he?" Lucio shook his head. "Oh, before I forget, did we call the sponsors for the charity gala?"

I nodded and gathered my blue patterned notebooks. "I did that last week. Most of the same from last year. No one new just yet."

He grunted and scratched the side of his temple. "We need more to make this year's gala bigger and better. Any suggestions?"

Lucio sought my insight more often than I asked for help. Whether it was because he trusted me or I was in the field more, I couldn't be certain. I appreciated being involved in decision making and hatching new ideas. "We could lower our sponsorship minimum. You would have more independent businesses supporting us than major corporations. Grand Little Lives is a beautiful charity helping children with cancer. I know more businesses want to support, but if we make a special tier for start-up and independent businesses, we may get more sponsors."

The corner of Lucio's mouth turned upward. "I like your thinking, Violetta. If you have any in mind, let me know." With a nod, he left the conference room.

His kind words made me smile, but internally, the reasonable side of me panicked. My workload increased with Jessica's absence which

I anticipated. I was ready for it. This additional task of locating over a dozen small business sponsors was not one in my mental checklist.

It's not that I don't want to do it. I was sure I could handle it, but how can I focus on putting on a smile for sponsors when my personal life tugs at the back of my mind?

Second, what should I do? How can I survive this *and* Bryce at the same time?

My job is to plan everyone's happiest memories.

When can I start making my own?

Yours exhausted.
Violetta

June 30 / July 1

Second,

I can't sleep. It's almost midnight. Something woke me up. Was it work stress thinking about my future projects? Relationship stress wondering what will happen when I finally break it off? I poked my head out every window and glanced at every mirror. Only darkness greeted me.

I don't know. All I'm certain is there is a sinking feeling in the pit of my stomach. Bryce's refusal to listen to me, my family's advice, and Allura's anxieties swirled in my mind. Something is going to happen, but I'm not sure what.

Oh, Second, what do I do? How do I handle this situation with Bryce? Allura's words from the coffee shop the other day are the monster in my closet, preventing me from sleeping: *"So Aunt Margot thinks Stormy is trying to talk to you to tell you… you're going to die?"*

Nothing about my situation is a simple breakup. In theory, yes, the breakup is step one to making everything okay.

If Allura and Margot are right, one of us doesn't make it out of this story alive. Something bad will happen despite my choice.

But I don't know what to choose. My heart is torn. Claws of anxiety, stress, guilt, and distress tear at it until it's shredded. I want to curl up and hide in the RV. When I wake up, I want the warm sun to be on my cheeks. I want birds to sing sweet songs. I want God's creation to be green, fresh, and rejuvenating.

Mostly, I want to wake up in a world that Bryce isn't a part of. I want to wake up next to you: a handsome, bearded, wannabe pirate. I want to feel your warmth. Your hand brushed up against mine. Your lips inches away from my forehead.

Tears are brimming my eyes now. How can I fantasize about a man who is most likely dead? Or worse, a figment of my imagination?

And yet, my heart longs for no one else.

Oh, Second. Please. Help me.

Hey, are you okay?

I choke back a sob. I have never been so happy to see four words in my life. He's back. He's listening.

But what will he say?

"I-I don't know, Second. I feel very off lately. I don't know what's wrong. I need to talk to you." Most of this was true. 98% of the time I can pinpoint my pain. I know exactly what's on my mind and heart.

And yet, today, that 2% uncertainty aches more than the 98% I am aware of.

Is there anything I can help with?

Warmth flushes my cheeks. Now that he's here, I don't know how to put it. I've gotten advice from almost everyone I'm close to. They all say the same thing. Aunt Margot, Dad, Felicity, Eleora, Allura. All of them are begging me to do the same thing: get away from Bryce.

How can I run away from someone guilt tethered me to? I need more advice. I need something more, but I don't know what.

What does Second want me to do? If my life follows Aunt Margot's sister, then this ghost is meant to save me. Or try, at least, before I'm murdered.

Okay, I need to calm down. My heart is racing and my breathing is shaky. Bryce won't kill me. He says I'm his future. Sure, he gripped my wrist a little too tightly a few times and blue bruises bloomed. Yeah, those tiny scars on my palms are from when he dug his nails into my palm, reminding me never to leave. That means he wants me alive. Right?

Tell me everything.

I will be honest, I am dumbfounded by his persistence. Never has a guy—other than my dad—offered to sit and listen to a few moments of my struggles. Bryce is my first serious relationship. I went on a few dates in high school and had a group of guy friends before we all went separate ways for college. Even in the most vulnerable moments, most of them wanted to hear the basics and move on. No drama, no depth.

But Second? He wants every detail. Every instance that makes me hurt. At least, that's what I hope this means.

So, I'm going to start with work. A public job the world sees on your professional social media is easier to vent about than the memories we hide from the internet. "My workload has gotten pretty heavy over the past week. We have a major event next month, and if I don't perform well, I won't get the promotion I've been begging for for two years."

What are they expecting you to do?

"What are they expecting me *not to do*?" These next sentences won't be as eloquent or coherent as I usually write, so hopefully Second bears with me. I need to vent. "I may be just an Event Coordinator, but I do so much more. I am an event planner, project manager, community outreach team, and communications facilitator. Oh, and my boss wants me to spearhead new sponsorship opportunities for our gala. Which is fine and I love my job, but I do so much work for not a lot since I came into a higher-ish position when I was young. If I don't get a promotion soon, I won't be able to move out and start my life. But so many factors are in play—not to mention my co-worker Kirk is basically useless. I've taken on a lot of his projects and it's taking its toll."

My hand cramped. I just scrawled a bunch of pathetic, poorly written, info dumpy backstory. I hate doing that to him. To anyone. Makes me feel weak, whiny, and amateur.

Why don't you speak up for yourself?

"Because I can do his job better." It's easier to answer that question from a work perspective about my situation with Kirk. Standing up for myself in front of my sisters? That's a harder path to take. One I don't want to go down right now. "He is unreliable. He barely completes his projects. And I can do his job anyway, so I just end up taking over and making it ten times better."

Sounds like you're a perfectionist.

He's right. Yes, I am the kind of person that critiques every little thing I do. Just like I did with my writing before. I'm writing to a ghost. Does it have to be perfect? No. It doesn't. The way I wrote that sentence is how I speak. Will I criticize myself for it? Absolutely.

"I guess you're right." But it isn't entirely my own fault. I don't want to be a perfectionist. But when you're constantly under scrutiny… "And that's another thing: he always makes me feel like I have to be."

"He" as in your Kirk?

He's playing dumb. This is the worst. Well, I wanted his opinion, so I have to shake my head and tell him the truth.

Then, your boyfriend?

I swear he can read my other words, too, sometimes. "Yes, and he is driving me up a wall."

Okay, wait, so are you a perfectionist because it's who you are or it's who this boyfriend wants you to be?

A question I can't answer. I think it's perhaps a bit of both. "I think who he wants me to be. He is pushing me to get the promotion. At first I thought he was just being supportive, but—" The memories of Bryce and my date on June 28th flood to the forefront of my mind. When he called me fat, didn't listen to a word I said, told me I needed to earn more money, and other things I wish I could forget. An army of red flags to strike me down.

But?

"Now that I'm thinking about it, he kinda digs into me if I mess up." Now, I'm the one to play dumb. Of course I know this, but I want to play innocent and see what honest advice he'll give me.

What things would he say?

"A few weeks ago, I missed our date for a multitude of reasons and he was rude about it. When we finally went out, he was being all passive aggressive at the table. He was saying things like, 'I know you care more about your job than me' and then like, 'You should work harder if you want to eat at fancy places.' And then he'd tell me not to eat so much."

That's stupid and contradictory.

Finally, a guy who sees it. "Right?! He's constantly making me feel guilty. He tends to make me sound stupid in front of my family— which frankly, should be impossible." I recall a time a few months ago when I fumbled in the kitchen and broke a glass. The entire night he made a mountain out of a molehill. It started with rude comments, funny faces, and exchanged jokes with my sisters. Then, the running gag remained all night long. No one handed me anything in fear I'd break it. Everyone carried things for me like I was a child.

"I can be a bit klutzy sometimes and he loves to tell everyone the embarrassing mistakes I make. Serious mistakes and not." And it's only a one way street because God-forbid I tell anyone what mistakes he's made…

"Also, he—" I almost wrote it. My pen was *so close* to finally telling someone the truth of what he did. The first time I realized the mess I was in. The first time my heart tore in two, unsure of what to do. "I'm sorry, I should stop."

No, no, what else?

He really wants to know? Is this the part where the ghost says something profound to save my life? To fix my broken heart?

As much as I want to, I can't tell him about Bryce's phone call. But I can tell him about the consequences of my boyfriend's actions. "After we're together, I end up—" How do I tell him about this? The nightly venting sessions in my journals. The boxes of tissues piled up in the corner because I go through one a night. The terrifying sketches scattered across my desk. The overthinking brain that won't let me sleep at night because I thought I said something stupid in front of Bryce that he won't let me live down.

I suck in a deep breath and finish my sentence: "He makes me cry more than he makes me smile."

That says enough.

A few moments have passed. Did I say too much? Have I opened up more than I should've?

"Are you there, Second?" Please, be there. I need your advice. Please. "I never told another guy about this before. I was told guys didn't care about this kind of stuff."

Everyone says that. Whoever told you must forget that if guys didn't actually care, they wouldn't be in relationships.

My hand freezes, the ballpoint hovering above the page. If that's true, why is Bryce in a relationship? What does Bryce *actually* care about? "I-I guess that makes sense."

It takes two to tango, sister. Also, this guy sounds like a total brass.

A brass? Does he mean ass? I laugh through the tears, and I thank him for that. Maybe he doesn't like to swear. I could probably learn a thing or two from him. After working with Kirk, I have the mouth of a sailor sometimes. It's not my favorite trait.

"Second, you never cease to surprise me. Thank you for understanding." I meant every word. I wish I could show him how grateful I am. But I don't even know what he is...

I didn't do anything but listen.

"You'd be surprised how many people fail such an easy task." I think of my recent conversations with Bryce. Drama morphed from all of them because he refused to listen to what I had to say. All he heard was himself. "So what would be your advice?"

Dump him.

I sit for a moment, processing the two words. After pouring my heart out, these are the only words he can offer me? Him, too? Aunt Margot, Dad, Felicity, Eleora, and Allura all have said the same thing.

Is the answer really two words?

If the ghost sent to save me is also saying it, then it's about time I do something about it. And I mean really do something about it.

But it's not that simple. It really isn't.

"I can't." It's true. I'm living at home. He lives right around the corner. My sisters hang out with the Kazanskis a lot. In fact, Aria and Sage are going there tomorrow. He and his family are coming over for Felicity's birthday. Our paths will always cross.

If I dump him but don't escape him... What will happen?

Why not? If you dump him, you won't feel the need to be a perfectionist. Then, you

can focus on enjoying your job rather than
stressing.

Oh, Second. Truly oversimplifying the problem. But you know what? I appreciate it. It's consistent. Simple. Maybe hearing it from the ghost that is supposed to save me hardens its meaning. Life doesn't need to be overcomplicated. I don't have to burn myself jumping through flaming hoops in order to find happiness.

And yet, it's not going to be easy.

"You're right. Just because I understand him doesn't mean he understands me."

Will Bryce ever understand me? Not at this time in his life. After some help, maybe.

But Second understands me. He's shown me something I've always desired isn't as unrealistic as I always thought.

"Thank you, Second. You're definitely a writer because your words are wise."

Damn, that was corny as hell. Oh well, I said it. And you know what? I'm not going to regret it.

It's just unfortunate experience.

A lump catches in my throat. The summer wind blowing in from my open window raises the hairs on my neck. Did he gain this knowledge on his deathbed? As a ghost, does he wander the earth holding this wisdom in the palm of his hand like a bouquet of roses, patiently waiting for a woman to hand them off to?

As much as I want to learn more about him, my heart cannot handle it. It's one in the morning on July 1st. The still night calls me to rest. "Well, if you've experienced what I have, then my heart breaks for you. Next time, it's your turn to talk."

I meant every word. I want to know about him. Every ache, pain, and sorrow that sits in his core. I want to know the darkest secret that chains him to this earthly plane.

But first, I need to let him save me so he can save himself.

And that starts with getting rid of Bryce.

Yours resolved.

Violetta

July 7

Hi Second,

Something happened today. Something that shouldn't have.

I sat around the dinner table with my parents and Eleora. Felicity was at work while Aria and Sage hung out at the Kazanski's. Bryce texted me, wondering where I was. I told him I had to plan Felicity's 21st birthday party with my parents. Surprisingly, he seemed fine with me staying home tonight. There was no, "You're always busy. Come over later." or "Whatever, talk whenever." It was just "Sounds good. Talk later." followed by a heart.

Completely unlike him.

"Should we rent a pavilion at the park?" Mom signed. "We can invite more people that way."

"No, the police might catch us," I replied. "Gotta keep our party on the DL."

Dad laughed. "I don't want them taking our fireworks. I bought the big ones this year. Brought them over from Pennsylvania."

"Did you get that $500 one?" Eleora asked with wide eyes. "The one with the grim reaper on the front?" She slurped her cherry soda.

Mom shot Dad a look who shrugged. "I'm not spilling any beans on my fireworks stash." He waved his fork at Eleora. "It's going to be a surprise for your sister."

Felicity shared her birthday with America. July 4th was always a big deal for the Sparks. Dad's brothers and all our cousins come over for a long night of food, drinks, games, and fireworks.

Felicity loves fireworks. On her first birthday, we went to a fireworks display at our local park. Dad thought it was a bad idea, but

Mom insisted their Deaf little girl would be fine. Felicity was more than fine with the bursts of color filling the skies. She was enchanted. Her eyes lit in the red and golden glow. She bounced happily as the boom echoed off the valley. A wide smile spread across her chubby cheeks. Every year, the explosions still make her heart skip a beat. The vibrations shooting through her chest make her feel alive.

"So, Violetta." Dad took the final bite of his steak. With a mouthful, he asked, "How should we begin the planning process?"

I dragged my roasted potatoes through hot sauce. "As always, I need a 50% deposit today. No taxes if you pay cash."

My dad laughed. "I'll slip you the envelope in the alleyway so the IRS won't see us."

"Deal." I popped a potato in my mouth. My tongue tingled. I liked certain spicy things. I was pretty white, though, so buffalo sauce was probably the hottest for me. "What's our budget?"

Dad chuckled. "That's up to the boss." He nudged Mom as she brought a forkful of veggies up to her lips.

A carrot abandoned ship and rolled down her skirt. She clicked her tongue. Arching an eyebrow, she shook her head and signed, "That comes out of the budget."

Eleora plopped three carrots onto Mom's plate. "Does this triple our budget?"

She eyed the carrots, then my sister. She pursed her lips and nodded.

Eleora pumped her fist. "Okay, Dad, go buy the big Grim Reaper fireworks to add to our stash. Violetta, let's get food from her favorite taco place."

I smiled. "You read my mind."

By the time our plates were cleared, we decided the caterer, times, the guest list, activities, and what cake to get. Birthday parties were the easiest event to plan.

And, I had to say, I was pretty good.

We were cleaning the kitchen when Eleora's phone buzzed. A sinking feeling stuck in the pit of my stomach as she read the text.

Something wasn't right.

Eleora's eyes widened, but her lips stayed tight.

I stopped loading the dishwasher. "What happened?" I whispered.

Eleora glanced around the kitchen. A greasy pot distracted Dad at the sink and Mom disappeared into the laundry room.

Red crawled up her cheeks. Her eyes met mine as she mouthed, "He knows."

The utensils in my hand clanked as my grip tightened. "He knows? He knows what?" I whispered.

Eleora's lips formed a straight line as she looked back at her phone. The ascending tones of repeated incoming messages filled the awkward silence. Nervous eyes darted between the screen and me. Sweat beaded on her forehead. "Before I show you, I want you to know I had nothing to do with this."

I tossed the forks back into the dishwasher and held out my trembling hand. "Please, let me see."

Distress painted her cheeks like rouge. She placed the phone into my palm.

Air caught in my lungs as I read through the chaotic single lines of text Sage sent to Eleora in a matter of seconds.

"Rly nervous rn at the Kazanskis"

"Want to go home, something feels weird."

"We were only trying to help Vi and tell him for her"

"Why is Bryce so weird?

"He's like yellin and stuff about Vi being a liar"

"Freaking me out."

"Can you come get us? I don't wanna be here."

"His sisters weren't supposed to tell him now."

"We told them so they could tell him later."

"Aria is whispering something to his sisters to calm them down hopefully."

"Oh no."

"One of them ran to tell Bryce."

"I heard him yell again."

"It's worse."

"So much worse."

"I don't know what she said."

"Don't tell Vi."

"Please."

"Don't tell her."

"We just wanted her to—"

The phone slipped out of my trembling hand before I could read the final text. Eleora's quick reflexes caught it before it could clatter onto the dishwasher racks. My heart thumped loud in my ears. I couldn't take any more.

I know I'm supposed to dump him. I promised I would. Everyone told me to. You told me to, Second. But *I* was supposed to do it. I even formulated a plan this morning to soften the blow.

Now, every hope of this being a peaceful parting shattered like glass.

Now, my sisters are involved.

I thought they trusted me to finish this on my own. I told them I would. I promised them.

They ripped that chance right from under my feet.

They betrayed me.

I pulled my phone out of my pocket. My shaking finger typed in my passcode and checked my messages.

Nothing from Bryce.

That was not a good sign.

Yours horrified,

Violetta

Second,

Where are you? Please. I need advice. I still haven't heard from Bryce. This secret stayed between Eleora and me. I haven't confronted Sage and Aria about it. They don't know I saw the texts and frankly, I don't have the courage to call them out, yet.

Anxiety claws at my lungs. Air seeps through the scratches, making it hard to breathe. Of all the weeks for this to happen, why this week? Why did it happen when my boss scheduled a progress review that could make or break my future plans?

I sat at my desk at work, staring out the window. Cars beeped as they rushed by. People shuffled across the sidewalk. Secret thoughts, hopes, dreams hiding behind their eyes. I wished I could swap places with one of them for a day. See what their lives were like. See if things would be better. See if things could change.

A cold cup of coffee rested between my shaking hands. Fog invaded my brain, clouding any positive thoughts or confident sentences. Lucio would call me in shortly for my mid-year review. I was not in a good headspace to plant the seed for the promotion in August. I said a prayer for guidance but feared that doubt would take over.

Why? Of all the personal problems my sisters could scatter across the lawn for all to see, why this one? Why did they take my biggest struggle of breaking up with Bryce and carelessly place it into their own hands?

I know I claimed I wanted someone else to do it for me a few weeks ago but that was before my resolve. That was before I realized the danger I was in. Before I realized how frightening Bryce might become. Before I realized someone might die.

I tapped my phone screen every ten seconds. No notifications.

I slid my journal out of my purse. The white leather cooled my sweating hands. I flipped open the pages. Hoping, praying your words would appear.

The pages remained blank.

My stomach twisted. I was so stupid.

I am relying on someone I've never met. Some phenomena I don't know what to make of. I've always been strong in my Faith. Maybe I'm just putting too much trust in something else.

I pinched my eyes shut and took a deep breath. I said a quick Hail Mary to try and calm my nerves. My prayer life has been lacking lately. The stress, the confusion, the letters to you, Second, all of it ate up my quiet time. Allura claimed I should see a priest and ask for spiritual direction since I'm conversing with a phantom. I knew I should, but a piece of me is holding onto this secret. A miracle I believe is between me and God, not the devil. I hoped.

Despite my torn heart, my whole life seemed like a prayer. I wanted to thrust every move, action, word, and thought up to the heavens. I wanted God to take a look at what I've done, pat me on the head, and say "Violetta, it'll be all right."

But right now I can't feel His touch. All I feel is the aching, stinging, twisting pains in my gut as a blank phone screen stares back at me.

Maybe that's why I hold onto the hope of you saving me, Second.

I prayed Bryce was okay. Just because I didn't want to be with him didn't mean I wanted anything bad to happen to him. My heart can't bear any life lost, no matter how cruel.

"Violetta," Lucio called from the next room. "I'm ready when you are."

I sucked in a deep breath, letting the air expand my aching lungs. I breathed in until my chest hurt. I exhaled slowly and headed into the office. Snapping the journal shut, I placed it and my phone on the desk. I didn't want to be distracted when I presented my proposal at the end of my review.

But as I slowly closed the door, I thought I saw a sparkling light illuminate the journal at my desk.

Yours prayerful.
Violetta

July 3

Second,

Another day without you. Another day without hearing from Bryce.

I couldn't write about the rest of the evening yesterday. My mental exhaustion sent the pen flying from my fingertips last night. My mom asked if I was okay, and I had to lie. Again. The only truth I shared was that my mid-year review went well, but I was still nervous. I prayed that was enough to satisfy her curiosity.

Knowing my mom, it won't be enough, but I'm not ready to tell her anything else.

I didn't speak to Aria nor Sage when I dragged my feet down the stairs and into the kitchen this morning. My entire body felt heavy as if chains linked around my ankles, yanking me downward.

"Morning to you too, sunshine." Aria scoffed when she stepped out of my way. "Why are you so cranky?"

Did she really not know? She and Sage had gotten home late from the Kazanski's last night, so I couldn't confront her about it then. Part of me wanted to talk to her about it this morning, but Felicity's birthday is tomorrow. I couldn't risk having her and Sage be in a hissy fit and refuse to help. Girls can be caddy.

Do I want this over right away? Yes. But Felicity doesn't deserve to worry on her 21st birthday. I could force myself to play nice one more day. I had to. The twins tore apart my trust. The tension and anger would fill the air like a deadly fog. Felicity's day needed to be bursting with light. I'd suck in a deep breath and keep the clouds away.

Stomach clenched as I lied. "I'll tell you later." The words burned.

"You two have time to help me today? It's for Felicity."

Sage nodded tightly. "Dad gave us a few things to do before leaving for work today." Her voice was quiet like a mouse fearing the claws of a cat.

"Yeah, what *else* do you want us to do?" Aria sneered. A harsh secret hid beneath her bitter tone.

What did they tell the Kazanskis? What happened while Bryce was there? What do they know?

I sucked in a deep breath. Her words stung. Cut. I couldn't bring it up. Not now. How could she not realize what she'd done, betraying me? Why was she giving me an attitude for planning our sister's birthday party? I felt like the meme of Dwayne Johnson repeating "Don't cry, don't cry, don't cry" over and over again. Bottled emotions ready to burst.

"Don't worry about it then," I snapped. "I guess you already have your marching orders from Dad."

Aria arched an eyebrow. "If you leave us a list, we'll do it."

My lips formed a straight line. My pride wanted me to storm away and do everything myself after work. I didn't want to face my sisters. I didn't want to deal with them. However, the practical side of me forced myself to pull a pen and pad out of the drawer. I scribbled my instructions.

Aria tore the sheet and shoved it in her pocket. "We'll handle it."

Without another word, I poured lukewarm coffee into my travel mug and headed out the door.

Every moment at work drew out like slowly dripping water from a faucet. I had much to do, but I didn't want to do any of it. I collapsed into a working slump and couldn't stand back up. The weight of Sage's texts tugged on my mind.

What did Aria whisper to the Kazanskis? What made things worse? What made Sage afraid?

Why did they betray my trust?

To my relief, Kirk worked a tad more diligently than usual so my lack of productivity didn't set us behind too much. I wondered what Lucio said during his manager review. Probably nothing terribly mean. Lucio wasn't that kind of boss. However, he never shied away from constructive criticism.

My review had very minor criticism. All positive "good jobs" or "excellent progress." He was exceptionally proud of how efficiently I saved Kirk's ass with that last client. I guess CCing the boss on that email worked in my favor.

"I appreciate your proposition for your growth here," Lucio had said. "I will highly consider it."

I couldn't even relish in the hope of a positive review. My personal situation plucked the hope I had. The ambition and drive to do my best for this promotion were slowly being dragged away from me.

My mind wandered from lunch time until 4 pm. The moment the numbers changed on my phone, I shoved my laptop into my backpack and ran out the door.

As I walked to my car, my phone vibrated against my thigh. I slid it out of my pocket with trembling hands. Was it Bryce? Did he finally have the strength to call me?

It wasn't. It was Allura.

Relief flooded half of me. The other half remained anxious. I slid my finger across the screen and tapped "speaker." "Hey, Allura."

"Oh my gosh, Violetta! Fatima just told me Eleora got some crazy text from Sage. What did the twins say to Bryce? Was it about the breakup? Are you okay? Why didn't you call me?"

Why hadn't I? Ugh, who was I kidding. I knew why. I only had the mental capacity to tell one person my innermost feelings and emotions. Only one person per day could hear my problems.

Lately, that person is you, Second, but I don't know where you are.

"I'm sorry, girlie. I think I've been in shock. I couldn't think straight. I think they told him I want to break up."

She paused. "Are you serious? Has he said anything?"

I fumbled my keys out of my purse. "Not yet. That's what's worrying me."

"Ah, crap. Are you okay? Do you want Layne to reach out?"

I paused. A little *mano a mano* chit chat between the two guys might be good. But then again, Bryce believes guys who talk about their feelings are wussies. Well, he used a worse word.

"That settles it. I'm having Layne reach out," Allura decided.

"Wait, maybe that's a bad idea." Was it though? Layne could be subtle… sometimes.

"Okay, but if you change your mind please let me know. Don't forget, we know what he's capable of. We're trying to protect you and your sanity. And him, too, I guess. But mostly you."

I smiled slightly. "Thank you, Allura. Maybe it will be good if Layne just sees where he is. Maybe having someone to keep tabs on him is a good thing. Please have him be discreet."

"I'll tell him. Now, do you need anything for tomorrow?"

I slid into my car and shut the door. "No, thank you, though. I'm going to meet Eleora at the store. My sisters are finishing up the decorations. Thankfully, Felicity is pulling an overnight shift. She won't notice the decorations up around the house until tomorrow."

"She notices everything, so don't fool yourself," she replied with a forced laugh. Anxiety hung on the call. "Are you okay? Really?"

I took a shaky breath. I wasn't okay. How could I be? I think my sisters tried to break up on my behalf. The man who claims I'm his future is ignoring me. The last time I tried to break up with him, I got an unforgettable phone call.

"I'm going to have to be for Felicity," I replied.

She exhaled. "Okay, fine. But If you need me, I'm here. Love you."

I said likewise and hung up the phone. I scrolled through my messages. Bryce's face sat neatly in a bubble down a ways. He hadn't messaged me since he told me to have fun with my parents on July 1st.

What has he been up to? Where has he been?

The twins never mentioned anything was out of place with the Kazanski family. I also didn't ask. Eleora never mentioned she heard anything since then either.

I guess tomorrow will tell. The entire Kazanski family received an invitation to Felicity's Fireworks Frenzy (Yes, that was my idea. Yes, I'm a sucker for alliterations). Bryce has never missed a Sparks party.

If he doesn't show up, then I have a reason to panic.

And if he does show up? I'll probably panic then, too.

Because he's a ticking time bomb and who knows when he'll blow up.

Yours taking cover.
Violetta

July 4

Second,

Today was supposed to be fun. July 4th with the Sparks is supposed to be the most chaotic, memorable, explosive event of the year.

Unfortunately, more than fireworks blew up today.

This entry is going to be long; I already know it.

Felicity slept in until about 11 am. It was perfect. My sisters and I put the finishing touches up around the house. Balloons colored red, white, and blue dangled from the ceiling where we fastened them with office tape. Teal streamers trailed doing the walls like hanging vines. They swayed as we walked between them. Homemade signs covered in crude doodles of Felicity hung crooked along the hallway walls. My pride and joy was the stick figure of Felicity riding what is supposed to be a firework. The first drawing of mine in months that wasn't tainted by bad memories.

I had finished hanging the last art piece from Sage when I heard Felicity's footsteps. I spun around to see a bright smile on her face as she stood between the streamers.

"Happy birthday," I said, extending my arms to show off the decor.

She beamed and signed, "Thank you, Violetta."

Mom and Dad gave her a big hug, pecking her forehead with kisses like they used to do when we were little. She stuck her tongue out and tried to shimmy away.

Aria tried to scare her from behind, waving her arms and laughing.

Unfazed, Felicity rolled her eyes. "The only time you scare me is when you drive."

"I'll take it as long as it counts for points." Aria chuckled. She held out a tall box. "Can I give this to you now or should I wait?"

"You need to give it to her now!" Eleora exclaimed with her arms behind her back. "Because I have the other one."

Felicity looked to Mom, who nodded. Eleora and Aria presented their gifts at the same time. The birthday girl sat at the table and tore apart the pink balloon wrapping paper. She pulled a wine glass out of a cardboard box. *FELICITY* painted across the front in rose. Then, she opened Eleora's gift: a bottle of champagne. Well, technically, it was from both of us, because she is too young to buy alcohol.

"Your first drink as a 21-year-old law abiding citizen!" Eleora exclaimed. "Sage bought you orange juice. We're gonna have mimosas."

Felicity laughed and popped open the bottle. Sage dropped to the ground as the cork soared above her head.

"Careful now," Dad warned. "Can't have anyone lose an eye."

"Like you almost did to me on our anniversary?" Mom smirked and elbowed him.

He pressed his lips to her forehead. "I apologized so many times."

Felicity poured the champagne into her new glass. A little too much. The ratio of juice to alcohol was definitely off.

As Dad placed six glasses on the table, a knock echoed down the hall. Eleora spun around and ran to the door.

"That might be my brother," Dad said. He poured small amounts of champagne in the empty glasses. "Sage, please get a few more. Uncle Rowan, Aunt Caitlin, and the kids might want some."

"Hi Uncle Kettil! Aunt Margot!" I heard Eleora greet.

"Oh, nevermind. Just two, Sage," Dad corrected. "It's your brother," Dad signed to my mom.

"Ugh, why is she here so early," Sage murmured. "She's crazy."

"Sage, be nice," Mom signed, brows furrowed.

Uncle Kettil appeared in the doorframe. Blue paper streamers dangling from the ceiling draped around his face like curly hair. "Seems like I finally fit in with all the beautiful ladies." He pushed a streamer behind his ear.

"Hey, Kettil." Dad gave him a firm handshake. "Glad you were able to escape for a bit to party with us."

"Are you crazy? I would never miss a Sparks event." He patted his rotund belly. "You guys always have plenty of food for a big whale like me."

"I hope you remembered it's Felicity's birthday and not just a buffet for you," Eleora quipped.

"No matter the occasion, it's always a buffet for Kettil," Aunt Margot interjected. She appeared in the doorway with a small package wrapped neatly in brown paper. A thin string of twine tied into a bow atop. "However, I certainly would never forget precious Felicity's birthday."

"Thank you," Felicity signed with a smile and gave Aunt Margot a hug. She gingerly took the present and placed it on the table. "Should I open this now?"

Margot waved her hand. "Save it for later. It's a bit personal."

The two made their rounds, hugging us individually. Uncle Kettil was jolly and goofy—his usual personality. Aunt Margot however seemed extra bubbly today. Her eyes brighter somehow.

She wrapped her thin arms around me and kissed the top of my head. "How are you doing, Violetta?"

"Fine," I replied, forcing a small smile. The best I could give.

She arched an eyebrow. "I haven't heard from you in a while, hoping that's a good thing. Let's catch up in a bit, yeah?"

I nodded. I supposed she thought my lack of communication was because of an improvement. I wished she was right.

We made our way to the backyard and began the party as always: drinks, food, and music. Felicity's playlist blared out of two floor speakers on our deck. The bass raised all the way so you could feel the beat in the middle of your chest.

We were blessed with an acre of land; plenty of room to spread out and run around. We had corn hole, volleyball, and disc toss. Our parties wouldn't be complete without yard games.

The other guests trickled in within the next hour. Uncle Rowan, Aunt Caitlin, and our cousins showed up next.

"Rowan! You're missing one," Dad said, embracing his brother.

"Riley won't be home for a few more weeks," Uncle Rowan said, taking a dark beer from the cooler. He popped off the cap with his teeth. "Even with one missing, the house seems quieter."

"I don't know how that's possible since you're raising an army." Uncle Kettil scoffed.

"You'd be surprised how only six in the house makes a difference," Aunt Caitlin spat. She always butted heads with Uncle Kettil. The barrel of a man means well, but he comes off as harsh and bitter.

Kettil opened his mouth to speak, but Aunt Margot jumped in: "Where is Riley?"

"He's away at a boy's summer camp," Aunt Caitlin explained. "He's done it for a few years but doesn't like to talk about it much for some reason."

My grip loosened around my plastic cup. The drink slipped from my palm and splashed onto the deck.

A summer camp? Second, do you know a Riley? *Did* you know a Riley? Before you died? I mean, if you are a ghost?

Uncle Kettil blew a raspberry. "Party foul."

Aunt Margot jumped to her feet and grabbed a roll of paper towels. She held it out and our eyes locked.

I knew what she wanted to ask.

I took the roll from her. "I'm fine, I promise."

Her lips formed a straight line, but she kept quiet and returned to her deck chair.

My heart wanted to ask more about the camp, but my tongue tied. I couldn't say anything before they were onto a new conversation.

"Hey, Violetta!" Two hands clasped my shoulder. "What's happenin'?"

"Hi, Brigid." I smiled and patted her forearm. "Are you living it up with Riley gone?"

"Eh, I barely notice he's not around. He's usually so busy with work, the summers feel normal." She crossed the deck and flipped open the cooler lid. She wore an adorable light blue sundress and a sunhat. Forever classy, my cousin.

"Love the outfit," I complimented. "Where'd you get it?"

"The same thrift store where I get everything." She winked and popped open a soda. It fizzed as she gulped it down. "Now, where is your boyfriend? You seem sad and lonely. He's usually early."

Heat bloomed in my cheeks. I felt Aunt Margot's eyes pierce the side of my head from her spot beneath the canopy. "His family is coming later. Oh, and the Pinkles won't be here until dessert."

"Brigid! Violetta!" Eleora called, waving her arms. "Come join us!"

Felicity violently chucked a volleyball over the net. It soared through the air until it smacked my cousin Niall in the head. He swore and returned the favor. Only his aim sucked and it hit his twin sister Riona.

Brigid ran down the steps. I waved saying I'd join them later. To be honest, my trembling hands wouldn't be able to hit a volleyball even if it froze in time before me. My thumping heart told me it was time to talk to Aunt Margot.

"Violetta, come help me mix some drinks in the kitchen."

I turned around to see Aunt Margot holding two empty glasses in her hands. She jerked her head toward the door.

Opening the sliding glass door, I followed her inside.

"Violetta." She placed the cups onto the counter. "Why is he coming over today? I thought we talked about this."

I opened the fridge. Its chill sent goosebumps over my skin. "I tried to tell him."

She opened a new bottle of vodka. "And?"

I shrugged my shoulders. "He completely ignored me. Dismissed me." I snatched a bottle of cranberry juice and slammed the door shut. The glasses on the counter rattled.

Aunt Margot took a deep breath. "Have you heard voices? Seen things?" she whispered. "Anything since I gave you the notebook."

My breath caught in my chest as I gave a small nod. She was someone I could trust with the full story. Someone who understood. Someone who wouldn't betray me. Someone who would more easily accept the fact that a dead boy gave me the last bit of courage I needed to do something about my toxic relationship.

Aunt Margot's eyes darkened. She poured two shots of the liquor into the glasses. Then she brought the bottle up to her lips. "I'll be damned." She took a swig. Her face twisted. "I was right."

"You were," I replied softly. "I couldn't believe it when his words first appeared."

She arched an eyebrow. "How does he speak to you?"

I took the bottle from her. The bartender at the bowling alley said liquid courage might help. My nerves were at war with my heart and mind. I needed to drown one of them out.

It would only be for today, I told myself. I planned to enjoy a drink, but I wouldn't indulge. I couldn't.

I knocked back the shot. The vodka felt like flames trailing down my throat. Burning and raw. I welcomed the physical pain to take me away from the sorrow in my mind.

My head lightened and I finally said, "I've heard some whispers and reflections, but he speaks the clearest through the notebook you gave me." Saying it aloud brought a small sense of freedom I didn't know I craved.

She humphed. She refilled my vodka and sloshed cranberry juice into both glasses. "I knew it. I knew there was something special about that book. Kayleigh *told* me. Somehow." She shrugged and held her head. "So, what does it want you to do?"

I thought about our last conversation. Despite the gravity of the situation, I couldn't help but laugh. "He told me to dump Bryce."

"Smart ghost." Leaning against the beige counter, she crossed her arms. "Tell me what happened."

I had another sip of courage and caught Aunt Margot up on everything. Second, the camp, the nice things he'd say to me, the way he makes my heart flutter.

And then I told her about Bryce. The red flags, the comments, and my sisters betraying me by spilling something to the Kazanskis and making Bryce mad. I briefly told her about the phone call I received last year when I tried to end it the first time.

The color in Aunt Margot's face drained as fast as her glass. By the time we finished, we each downed two vodka cranberries.

"My dear, he cannot come over here." She refilled my glass. "Why is he coming? Do you know what exactly your sisters said to make him that mad? Did they tell him to break up with you?"

"All I know is Sage said they were trying to help but he got really mad. I've assumed they tried to break us up so I didn't have to do it." I shrugged. I tried to sip from my glass but—like an idiot—missed my mouth. Juice sloshed onto my hand staining it red. "Aria said something else to him and he was furious. I haven't heard from him, I'm worried and stressed, and my sisters betrayed my trust again." Tears brimmed and I wiped them away quickly.

The door quickly slid open. "Violetta, where have you been?" Aria complained. "The Kazanskis got here forever ago and we've been playing frisbee. Get your booty out here."

I looked at Aunt Margot. She shrugged. "Do you know what you're going to do?"

Of course, I did. I always did. But the truth and confrontation are never easy.

Ice clinked in my glass. Red liquid swirled like a small whirlpool. Scrunching my nose, I lifted my glass and chugged it. The cold cocktail ran down my throat. Juice dribbled down my chin. I felt like a vampire downing its final pint of blood before stepping out into the sun.

I was ready to get burned.

I teetered my way outside and into the lawn to see him playing games with my family as if he always belonged. I guess he did, kind of. But he only belonged with them. He didn't belong with me.

If he really cared about me wouldn't he have found me right away to say hello? Wouldn't he have invited me to hang out? He didn't even *look* at me when I walked over.

If he was mad at me, wouldn't he have called me out? Wouldn't he have pulled me aside to have an argument?

He didn't do either. He acted as if I didn't exist. As if nothing was wrong.

"Ready to play?" Eleora held the disc tight in her grip. "Let's go."

And that was it. We played Ultimate Frisbee without another word (well, I just ran back and forth unable to catch a thing). The evening went on and Bryce didn't speak to me.

Unease knotted and twisted my stomach. My heart throbbed and my eyes burned.

I was *livid*. He didn't even have the decency of talking to me. To want to hear the truth of whatever my sisters told him.

The rest of the night proceeded as planned: games, barbecue dinner, dessert, and then fireworks.

Pink and orange painted the horizon as the sun set. Fireflies danced along the grass, making constellations in our backyard. The summer breeze cooled my heated skin. Everything about this night was romantic. Sweet. A cute couple probably cuddled up on a picnic blanket to watch the county's fireworks.

But Bryce? He was on the other side of the deck, talking with Brigid. A charming smile spread across his face. She giggled at everything he said.

He was flirting. With *my cousin*. In my family's backyard.

"Violetta!"

I didn't turn to greet Allura. I felt her arms wrap around me in a bear hug. "Where is the bastard?" she whispered in my ear.

"Flirting with Brigid," I sneered through gritted teeth.

Allura's eyes darted around until she saw it. Disgust stuck upon her face. "Oh my gosh. Violetta, he's gross."

Dad clapped his hands and told everyone to take a seat. Felicity's Firework Frenzy was about to begin.

Everyone settled into their chosen spots to watch the show. My dad, Rowan, and Niall brought boxes of fireworks into the middle of the yard. Niall fumbled and dropped an armful across the lawn. Scoffing, Eleora ran to their aid.

I went up onto the deck and stood beside my mom. Alcohol muddled my mind as I rested my head on her shoulder. Slender fingers massaged my scalp as if she tried to smooth out the jagged thoughts occupying my mind. It had been way too long since I'd been present with my mother, feeling her warmth. Feeling her strength against my body.

The unanswered questions from our time in the forest still hung between us. I avoided every glance, indirect comment, and sad smile. I wanted to tell her. I thought the cocktails coursing through my blood would make me brave. At the bowling alley, I was certain two shots would've been the courage I needed to say that she was right.

The bravery I needed to say I tried to leave him like she said, but he wouldn't let me. The fortitude to admit I needed her help despite the hurt I know she'll feel.

But we didn't communicate. We stood quietly, waiting for the fireworks to begin. Despite that, her comforting body beside me encouraged me more than words—or signs—ever could.

"Time for the show to begin!" Eleora shouted.

A spark ignited and the fireworks display commenced. Whistles soared through the air until they ended with bursts of bright colors. Glimmering yellow, blue, red, and green fireworks painted the sky. The booming echoed off the mountains. Each explosion rattled in my chest.

I looked over to see Felicity's gaze fixated on the sky. Her eyes sparkled; her smile widened.

Today was for *her*. It wasn't for Bryce and me.

But I couldn't help it. Bryce stood at the bottom of the deck, arms crossed. Gaze fixated on the sky. Not once did he glance over at me. It's as if I didn't exist.

A feeling I get from him too often.

Mom's hand squeezed my arm. A gentle touch strengthened my broken spirit. Even if I couldn't face telling her the truth, the first thing I could do is make it up to her. I wanted to make up for the heartbreak I caused her for the past year.

I blew out an exhale. Fists balled, I marched down the stairs and across the lawn to stand next to him. I clasped my hands so he couldn't see me trembling. "Hey, Bryce."

"Vi." He nodded.

Four fireworks went off. He didn't say another word.

My turn: "Why haven't you talked to me today?"

"You don't want me to," he replied curtly.

"And who told you that?"

He tilted his head to where his younger sisters sat. The Kazanski girls giggled and chatted with Fatima and Aria while Sage carried a plate overflowing with snacks.

"And what did they tell you?" I asked, heart hammering against my ribcage.

"Nothing much." He scraped his nail between his teeth. "Just that you've been talking to someone else and don't want to see me anymore."

Ice crawled across my skin. My brain shut down.

My sisters told Bryce I was *cheating* on him?

"They said *what?*" I couldn't believe it. There had to be a mistake. My sisters betrayed my trust by getting involved in our breakup. In time, I could probably accept that they were trying to help. But to tell him I was a cheat? To lie and not defend me? To fuel flames that would burst into a roaring fire?

How could they? I would *never* cheat. I would never treat anyone, not even him, the way I'm treated.

"I suspected it." He spat out a piece of food caught between his front teeth. "It's whatever, Vi. You know I chose you over Melissa, right? Guess I'm not good enough for you to choose me. I don't know how anyone else could ever meet your 'standards,' though."

Tremors shot through my body. My heart thumped so loud I couldn't tell my pulse from a firework.

How *dare* he believe I was a cheat? The audacity to accuse the person he claimed to be a "people pleaser" and "too nice."

"You know I would never do that," I snapped. Explosions drowned out the rage in my voice.

He shrugged. "I thought you wouldn't at first. After thinking about it, it all makes sense. I guess I don't really know you, do I?"

That last part was technically true. He doesn't know me at all, but I thought he at least would know I'd be faithful.

"Look." He turned to face me. He looked me in the eyes. I thought they'd be sad because I didn't want to be with him anymore. I thought they'd be angry because he thinks I'm cheating.

What's worse? They were completely normal. No emotion in his face. His eyes met mine like I was a stranger on the street. But his lips wove his lies: "You know how I feel about you. How you're my future. But whatever, forget about me if he can take better care of you."

I didn't know what to reply. His contradictions made my head hurt. I wanted to scream.

"Get it over with. Whatever you need to say, just say it." He turned away from me.

That should've been the moment. I should've broken it up and let him think what he wanted.

But I was afraid.

My watch buzzed. A message crawled across the screen.

"I bet that's him now." He scoffed. "Just give me time to think about what we should do."

That was it. I couldn't take it. He couldn't even give *me* the decency of letting me choose. "It's Allura, you jackass," I sneered.

Tears brimmed my eyes. I stalked back into the house as slowly as possible. Only a few side glances, but no one stopped me.

Once inside, I ran up to my room and slammed the door. I sank to my feet.

The fireworks finale masked my screams.

Yours exploding,
Violetta

July 5

Second,

How many times do I have to say, "Second, I don't know if I can do this." How many times must I cry out, begging for help.

It's after midnight. Everyone is still here, slowly packing up to leave Felicity's party. I tried going back down, but I couldn't stomach it. I told everyone I felt sick and ran back upstairs.

I need to talk to you.

"Second, he is with my family right now. I can't do this."

I will write a million sentences until you reply.

"Second, please."

Please.

I need you.

Kayleigh's ghost couldn't save her.

Please, save me.

I'm here.

My heart flutters while my head swims. Muffled voices call for my name. Finally, guests are leaving.

"Second, they're calling me downstairs. What do I do?"

Is it about dumping your boyfriend?

It is so much more than that, but I don't know what to say. "Yes, I'm trying, I promise, but he isn't letting me." A fiery lump catches in my throat.

Why won't he? Just lay down the law. He's
toxic.

Heat crawls across my face. Second loves to oversimplify the problem, but that's not his fault. He's not here. He's not here to swoop in and stand up to Bryce for me. No. I'm left to do that and fix the shattered pieces my sisters destroyed.

I won't say that to him, though. He's here to help me. He's trying to help from the bits and pieces I share with him. "I know, I know that's what my friend says, but he is trying to manipulate my family now."

Won't they listen to you?

"It's not that easy!" My pen digs into the page, harsh and angry. I want to tear the pages out. This entire situation is ridiculous. A drawn out drama that should've been over ages ago. I loosen my grip and let out a deep breath. "They have connections with him, and they'd probably hate me if I broke them."

As I write the words, I realize: is this a valid reason why I can't pull on my big girl pants and break off my relationship? These past few days, I didn't say anything to Sage and Aria because I wanted to protect Felicity. She didn't deserve this drama on her 21st birthday. Eleora kept quiet because I asked her to keep this a secret.

But are my sleepless nights and sorrowful days what my sisters really want for me? Sparks blood courses through our veins. We'd take up our bows and fight for each other.

Then again, why did Sage and Aria spread those horrible lies? If they were fighting for me, would they have really come up with such a damaging rumor?

What makes you happy?

My heart jumps in my chest as four words shock my soul. "What makes me happy?" A question my dad asked me—in his own words. One that I didn't want to answer. One I feel like I've needed to answer for a long time. "I love my family. I love the way the wind feels in my hair or the sound my arrows make when they hit their mark. I do love my job and my work—except Kirk, of course. Coffee is something I look forward to. I look forward to your words."

My hand glided so fast along the paper I thought it would catch fire. My eyes burn with each word. My long paragraph was true… but I know what Second is getting at. He wants me to say–well write– the truth. To spell out the reality my father tried to convince me to confess. To recognize what's going on in my life.

```
                I appreciate that.
```

"Of course. I wish you could be here to do this for me."

```
It would be easier if someone else could
   solve it, but you have to stand up for
yourself. Out of all the things that make
   you happy: your boyfriend wasn't among
                  that list.
```

There it was. The point. The whole point of our conversations as of late. The whole point of why this drama erupted in the first place.

I am not happy in my relationship.

```
     So, what are you going to do now?
```

"I am going to tell my family the truth." At some point. I need to process. I need to get away. My sisters were wrong to get tangled up in my personal business. Did they just want to help? Maybe. But this is making everything worse—not to mention damaging my reputation and self-esteem. How many people will Bryce run off to and convince I'm a cheat?

I took a deep breath. This too shall pass. Everything does, doesn't it? Time will tell, but the road is tough. It cannot be traveled overnight. I need to make a promise to myself. "I will do what it takes to make me happy."

Make you happy and peaceful. Some happiness is fleeting. Most of it robs peace. But I'm confident getting rid of this guy is what you need to move on.

"Yes. Move on." Two words have the heaviest weights. I take two steps forward, but the baggage of worry, anxiety, and fear pull me back. I want to move on. I really do. "My heart needs to move on to give myself peace."

Will you come back to tell me what happened?

Magical sparkles crackle and ignite as this sentence appears on the page. A burning question for him. Will I come back? I've never gone anywhere. Then again, Second's existence is different. I need to stop trying to understand it.

"Of course. But please, be here. I know time is weird, but I have a feeling I'll need you more than ever."

I promise I will be here for you. Keep calling for me, I'll answer.

I pray to God he will keep his promise.

Yours waiting,

Violetta

July 7

Second,

I am unwell. I barely eat. I barely sleep. Moving on is not that easy. Telling the truth is not easy. Obtaining happiness is not easy.

I let it brew for a few days. I played the scenarios over and over in my head.

I am *not* crazy. He was a total asshole. He toyed with my heart like a cat plays with string. Whether he realized it or not, his claws were out, ripping me to shreds. He claimed he needed time to process. He believed the lies my sisters spread.

My mom asked what happened, but I brushed her aside again. It hurt, but I needed to finish this before I spoke to her. I couldn't let her down anymore. I promised her I would do this. I promised my *sisters* I would do this.

After he called me a cheat, I only told Allura and Aunt Margot. They both gave me the same advice:

Dump him. Confront your sisters.

I did the latter today.

I got home from a busy day at work. My feet ached from running to-and-fro at an event venue with a client. One of our customers had an all-day conference and I handled the logistics because one of our event planners called out sick.

Long story short: I was cranky, frustrated, and nervous.

I sat around the dinner table with all my siblings for the first time since July 4th. I excused myself each night and hid in my room, claiming to be sick from the party.

Today, I had to say something.

A colorful display of salsa, sour cream, cheese, jalapenos, and other fixings covered our long table in small white bowls. Warm spices tickled my nose. I normally loved taco night, but the sight made me sick.

I watched Aria shove a burrito into her mouth. The content spilled out of the back. Just like how she spilled the beans with the Kazanskis.

Haha. Bad pun. I may be depressed, but that doesn't mean I won't try some stupid joke.

I pushed away my full plate. A million thoughts swirled through my head. Was it actually Aria? Should I tell her in private? Should I really expose her betrayal to everyone?

I shook my head. I had made up my mind. I needed witnesses. Aria had a habit of twisting words and changing stories which is probably what happened with the Kazanski sisters.

I cleared my throat. "Aria, Sage, I need to ask you both something."

They stopped midchew. Four wide eyes stared at me.

My nails dug into my thighs. "What exactly did you tell the Kazanskis?" I needed the truth. No more speculation. No more guessing. I deserved to know what actually happened.

Aria froze. Sage choked on her lemon-lime soda. Eleora roughly patted her back—it was less than helpful.

"Tell them what?" Sage asked slowly.

"You know exactly what." I tried to sound confident. Strong. But my voice cracked with each syllable. Tears welled in the corners of my eyes. I hated crying in front of my siblings. I thought they always saw me as weak. Pathetic. I was supposed to be the strong older sister. The one who took life head on and taught them the ropes.

Lately, I feel like my sisters have had to drag me along with them.

Sage placed her cup down. She rubbed her hands anxiously on her jeans. She tilted her head down so no one could read her lips. "I just told them that you might need a break from Bryce."

Eleora choked on her water, droplets dribbling down her chin. "Excuse me, you what?"

Mom's eyes darted up. Dad repeated Sage's statement to her.

"Mom, Dad, it's not that big of a deal," Aria defended.

"Yeah, Violetta is miserable so Aria said we were doing her a favor," Sage argued. "She didn't want to tell Bryce herself, so we told the girls to tell him on her behalf." Brown eyes softened. "He was angry, though. They told him while we were there. It wasn't fun, so no wonder she didn't want to do it alone."

No. They weren't doing me a favor. They were digging my grave. His grave. "You told him I was cheating on him," I spat through gritted teeth.

"What?" Sage exclaimed. "No, I didn't!"

"Then, who did?" I shot up from my chair. Silverware clattered and liquid sloshed out of cups. "I saw the texts. You and Aria were talking about me to them, then Bryce got mad, and now he is calling me a lying cheat now because of you."

"I never said you were a cheat," Sage yelled defensively. "I said you need to have better standards and Bryce isn't it. I never mentioned another guy. I didn't even know anything about another guy."

"Okay, then who spread that lie?" Dad butted in. Angry eyes met all of ours. "This is a private matter between your sister and him. She needs to deal with this on her own."

Mom threw her napkin onto the table. Her hands flew as she signed, "It's not private anymore. I'm about to call Lena and demand she make her son apologize."

Fear clawed my heart. Not his parents. Bryce can't have his parents involved. That makes everything worse. "Mom, please. Don't do that."

Mom's jaw clenched and fire roared in her eyes. "If someone doesn't confess what really happened in five seconds, I will lock you all in your rooms for the rest of the summer."

Eleora held her hands up. "I was with you when it all went down. Wasn't me."

"I had no idea this happened," Felicity signed. She swallowed her taco. "I knew Violetta wanted to break up, but I didn't know Bryce knew. I never would've shared anything."

"Aria and Sage were over at the Kazanskis when he found out," Eleora snitched.

"But it wasn't us!" Sage squealed. "I only told the sisters it needed to end because something wasn't right. That's true, right?"

"Then why does he think my daughter is a cheat?" Mom signed, browed furrowed and teeth bared. "Why is he slandering her?"

Aria remained quiet.

Mom's eyes narrowed. "Aria Rosemary Sparks."

Aria placed her broken burrito onto her plate. "Violetta has been talking to someone else."

My face paled. "What are you talking about?"

"Don't lie!" Red flushed her cheeks. "You write about him in your stupid diary. You did it all during the camping trip. You cried and were a baby about it. I saw you sitting at the cliff that night. Allura texted you about him, too. You call him 'Stormy.' I saw the text when we went bowling."

Six pairs of eyes shot through me like arrows. I never felt so humiliated.

"There is no real guy," I growled.

"Then who do you write about, huh?" Aria mocked. "Do you have some secret ghost like Aunt Margot's sister? Is that why you were suddenly seeing Aunt Margot more often?"

"Aria," Dad scolded. "Don't you *dare* bring that into this."

"But what if Aria is right? What if it isn't a coincidence?" Sage defended her twin. "She wants to break up with Bryce and is writing about some guy we don't know about? She seems spooked and stressed lately, so what if that's it?"

"I'm sitting right here," I snarled.

"It all happened when she started talking to Aunt Margot," Aria continued, ignoring me. "Just saying, it's all suspicious." Her eyes widened and she pointed a fork at me. "Unless you're not seeing Aunt Margot at all! Your location shows you've visited her a few times, but you could also be leaving your phone at her house."

My cheeks burned and red flickered before my eyes. "How dare you."

Mom's gaze darted across the table. "Aria, put your imagination in a box and lock it away. These accusations are out of hand." With shaking hands, Mom refilled her water glass, took a slow sip, and set down the pitcher. "The damage is done," she signed firmly. "No more talking about your sisters to others. You girls are supposed to defend each other. Not destroy each other."

"That's why we told the Kazanskis," Aria claimed. "Violetta is so annoying, complaining and oversharing about Bryce. I hear her crying all the time. If he's so bad, why didn't she leave last year when you told her to? She promised us she would leave him, but she hasn't done it yet. We tried to do it for her just so she'd finally just shut up and stop whining." Eyes widening, she jolted and clasped a hand over her mouth.

An arrow struck through my heart. Blood seeped out the wound, dripping to my feet. I wanted to drown in it and never surface.

I would've hoped my sisters would want to help because they loved me. I wished they would have trusted me. I didn't break up last year because I didn't want him to hurt himself. I suffered to keep him alive. I suffered to keep the peace between the Kazanskis and the twins. I suffered to protect my family's peace.

Everything I put myself through was for nothing. It never mattered to my family.

"Think of me however you want," I croaked. The dishes clattered as I shoved myself away from the table. "I'm sorry I brought my misery on all of you. Just stay out of this from now on." Without another word, I shot up out of my chair and stalked out of the kitchen.

Scrambling up the stairs, I packed a bag and grabbed my keys. My dad's voice cut short when I slammed the front door behind me.

Your runaway,
Violetta

July 10

Second,

I don't know where you are, but I've been at Allura's for the past few days. I couldn't be at home after my fight with the twins. Nothing they did was out of love. They betrayed my trust and spilled my secrets because I was an annoying nuisance they wanted to turn off like a radio.

Thanks to them, the rumor is spreading like a weed. Layne spoke to Bryce who is alive and keeping busy with texts and phone calls.

Everyone we know now thinks I'm a cheat.

I lied when I said I will do what it takes to make me happy. I am not ready for confrontation. Do you have any better advice? Any kind words to wrap me up in like a warm blanket? I need comfort. I need love. Honestly? I need a time machine to go back and stop any of this from happening.

I texted my boss, Lucio, the night I left my parents asking him if I could work from home. I said I had "lady problems" and couldn't even sit in an office chair. He let it slide. He was always so understanding.

"This entire situation is mortifying." Allura clutched her stuffed golden doodle tightly. "It's a miscommunication trope gone rogue."

"Everyone hates those tropes, so no wonder they hate me," I murmured. Sliding a pink bowl across the bed, I tossed a piece of popcorn into my mouth. I haven't eaten a real meal in days. Only chips, popcorn, chicken nuggets, salted caramel candies, and french fries. Well, french fries are real food. At least I could dip them in syrup and enjoy myself without being criticized.

"No one hates you, Violetta." Allura scooted across the cream floral comforter. "The ones who accept this lie are stupid losers anyway. The ones you really care about you would never believe it."

I dumped a bag of chocolate candies into the popcorn bowl. "Guess my sisters don't care about me because *they* seem to believe it."

Allura's gaze narrowed. "I'm sure that's not true."

"Then why did Aria and Sage say all those things?" Tears threatened to flow again. I thought I had run dry. "Why did Aria jump to conclusions from one text she saw over my shoulder? I promised them I would make a change and solve this problem on my own. Why did they get involved?"

"They were worried about their big sister. Sure, it was messed up how they went about it. Aria had no right to say all those horrible things, and what they did was totally wrong." Her lips formed a straight line. "I've been meaning to ask..."

My heart raced as she took a breath to ask the question I waited for:

Gentle eyes met my soul as Allura asked, "What is really going on with this 'Stormy' thing?"

My pulse hammered in my head. It beat against my skull, trying to let my mind escape. Perhaps with half a brain, I could've played dumb.

But I didn't. I slid my backpack across the floor and pulled out the white leather journal.

It was time to show someone. Allura knew *something* about a ghost. Whether she believed it yet or not didn't matter. She needed to know. I needed her to believe me. If something was going to happen to me, she needed to know every detail. I needed someone else to believe in you, Second.

"Recap the story about Aunt Margot's sister, Kayleigh, so I know how much you remember." I untied the string and flipped through the pages.

She cocked her head. "We talked about it recently. She was the one whose murderer was convicted because of written documents."

I arched an eyebrow. "And?"

Allura clutched the stuffie closer to her chest. "She saw a ghost before she died." Wide eyes watched me carefully. "I thought you said it was only Aunt Margot who thinks you also have a ghost which you called Stormy. When I texted you, I was hoping you'd get the code for 'what's going on with Bryce.'" She swallowed. "Is there really a ghost talking to you like with Kayleigh? When you mentioned it at the coffee shop, I thought you were stress hallucinating or something."

Fingers trembling, I opened up to one of my longer letters with you, Second. As I turned to *June 22nd*, my breath caught in my throat. Everything ached as I turned the notebook around to present it to her. It was as if I tore out a piece of my heart for public display. This was personal. Rare. Supernatural.

It was a gift I didn't want to share.

"Do you see these words?" My shaking finger rubbed against your sentences. A spark tickled my fingertips. Static, maybe? Or something magical?

Gingerly, my best friend took the book and read over the first two pages. "These words don't look like your handwriting?" It came out as a question.

I swallowed hard. "That's because it's not."

Allura's breath shook. "W-what are you trying to say?"

"See how I wrote in pencil for this entry?" Supplies clattered in my bag as I rummaged for an eraser. I grabbed a new pencil and erased my first few words. "That's my handwriting, but watch what happens next." I rubbed back and forth across your first sentence. Pink particles spread across the paper. Your words remained.

She shook her head slightly.

"Now rub your fingers over it. It's not indented like a pen." I grabbed her hand and pressed her fingertips against the page. A knot formed in my stomach. Your words are the closest thing I have to you. Bringing Allura to them felt like an invasion, but I needed her to know. "It's as if the text was always there."

A small gasp escaped her lips. She traced your sentences and then mine. Your words were permanent. Imprinted on the pages as if from a press.

"Are you saying these words just appeared?" Disbelief shook her voice.

I bit my lip and nodded.

Hands to her head, she said, "No, no, no, Violetta. This isn't real. It can't be."

"I know it sounds crazy and it may be hard to believe." I placed a hand on her shoulder. "But Kayleigh saw a ghost before she died. A ghost that was supposed to save her and move on from this life." I pointed to her vanity. "Remember when I got startled at Peek-a-Brews? That was because I saw male reflections in the mirrors. I've heard whispers. Everything that's happened to me happened to her."

Allura snapped her head up. Life drained from her cheeks. "Violetta. Don't tell me Bryce is *really* going to try and…" Her words trailed. "When I asked if he would—I didn't think…"

I nodded. "Something really bad is going to happen and I don't know who is going to get hurt worse."

With gentle hands, she flipped through the entry, scanning the pages and trying to comprehend what I shared.

I didn't stop her. I chose the entry where I told you about Bryce. Was it personal? Yeah. But she is my best friend, and I needed someone else to know that I wasn't crazy.

She scoffed in disbelief. "Violetta, first off, this Second guy seems incredible."

My heart flipped. Hearing your nickname out loud from another person solidified your existence even though I haven't heard from you in a while. Allura calling you "Second" means you're not a made up character in my head.

I nodded. "He is. He is the kindest, sweetest, most genuine guy I've ever spoken to." My heart fluttered. I wished it would stop. "He's understanding and doesn't think I'm annoying or stupid."

"So, he's nothing like Bryce." Allura attempted to sound lighthearted but a serious tone hid between the words.

"Exactly," I whispered. Heartbeats thumped hard in my chest as I said the words I dreamed to scream out loud: "I want the man I'm with to be just like Second."

It's true, Second. You really are everything I've ever wanted in a man. A piece of my heart hopes you're listening. You need to know the impact you've had on my life from a few kind words.

Allura gently closed the book and wrapped the thin leather cord around it. "Violetta, you know I only want what's best for you. Is this a ghost? Maybe. If he was malicious, he probably would want you to stay with Bryce or tell you to do something horrible. So, I don't think he's a *bad* ghost." She shrugged. "I'm not sure. You gotta be careful, though."

"Are you going to say what I think you're going to say?" I cradled the popcorn bowl like a child, shoving handfuls into my mouth like a squirrel.

"Have you talked to someone other than Aunt Margot about this?" Her eyes hid her true words.

"I just told you," I quipped.

Her head dropped to the side. "No, Violetta. If this is a spirit, this is serious. Why don't you tell Father McFadden?"

I swallowed the salty sweetness of my snack. Have I thought about it? Yeah. Have I been afraid to? Absolutely. Maybe because I think I'd rather be crazy than conversing with some demonic entity.

In reality? I don't want to lose you, Second.

"You're right, you're right." She was. I had avoided it. I don't want to risk never speaking to you again. When we converse, there is a peace I haven't felt in a long time. A sense of determination that I can find someone better. "I'll ask Father after Mass if he has a few minutes to talk." Tears welled at the corners of my eyes. I didn't realize how afraid I was of sharing this. I didn't want someone to take you away from me, but I also didn't want to be doing something I shouldn't.

Allura took my hand and squeezed it. "Violetta, you're not doing anything wrong." Brown eyes softened as she continued, "I don't want you to fall so far for Second that you lose track of yourself. If this is something supernatural and serious, I don't want you to break your own heart." She let out a quiet sigh. "At the end of the day, you have to decide. You have to step up to the front lines, defend yourself, and forge your path."

I clutched her hand. I always knew that, didn't I? But maybe I didn't want to know it. I wanted to be saved like a princess in a tower. Saved by someone stronger. Braver.

I'm a tough girl, I know. I can take care of myself. I can lead and protect others.

But I want someone to protect me.

Your fragile princess.
Violetta

July 12

Second,

I chickened out. I couldn't give you up. I'm hoping, praying, clinging onto the slim chance you'll reply to me again.

I went to Church with Allura this morning. I still haven't returned home. I texted my parents telling them I was okay and needed space. Felicity and Eleora texted me a few times, checking in on me, and updating me on what's happening at home. Mom ripped the twins a new one. They've been grounded for a month and are banned from ever going back to the Kazanskis. Dad also called Bryce's father. Bitter words spewed between them, ending in curses and broken friendships.

It's not what I wanted. I didn't want this discourse to break apart my family. I wanted to end things with Bryce quietly.

Now, the world knows, and I can't hide it anymore.

I've never felt so betrayed by Sage and Aria. My sisters. The girls I love more than anything. The ones I would do anything for.

They shattered my soul and trampled across the pieces.

Tremors shook my fingers as I made the sign of the cross at the beginning of Mass. Sweat dampened my forehead. One hour in church became a hundred years. Hollow prayers tumbled from my lips. My heart should be peaceful before Our Lord. Church is my safe haven. It is the place outside of my room where my broken soul finds comfort.

Not today, because Bryce's sisters sat three rows ahead of us. His youngest sister's perfectly braided hair with thin pastel blue streaks stuck out in any crowd.

Scenarios flickered through my mind. I imagined the two girls whispering to each other with dark eyes glancing back at me, infuriated expressions when they mouthed "cheat." Enraged that I destroyed their friendship with Sage and Aria. Bryce's blank glare from Felicity's birthday stuck to the back of my eyelids. Second: your silence screamed louder than the sorrowful voice in my heart.

A hand shook me back to the real world. The Mass had ended and it was time to go in peace.

But discord wrangled my soul.

The Kazanski sisters rushed outside without a word. I know they saw me. Their backs stiffened as they shuffled past us and disappeared into the sea of parishioners.

Allura threw her purse over her shoulder. "Let's go talk to Father McFadden," she whispered. "He's a good friend of your parents. He'll understand."

My nails dug into the wooden pew. "I can't. They're here."

"Let's go try, please? I'm not leaving you." She picked up my bag. "Even if you don't tell him about Stormy—er Second—you can at least ask if he has a moment for spiritual direction."

My feet were glued to the floor. My limbs quaked. I couldn't do it. I wanted to do it, but I couldn't.

Allura took my arm and gently nudged me out of the pew. We genuflected toward the altar and headed out to talk to our pastor.

Warm summer sun greeted my face as we stepped outside, but my blood ran cold.

The Kazanski sisters were talking to Father McFadden. He listened intently as they chatted with furrowed brows and shaking hands.

The hum of the congregation mingling drowned out their words, but I read Father's lips. One sentence was all I needed: "Wasn't his relationship with Violetta Sparks?"

The outside world closed in. A weight sat on my chest and I couldn't breathe. "Allura, we have to go."

"What are they saying? What happened?" she panicked.

I shook my head furiously. "I can't do this. We have to go. Now. I don't know what they said, but I can't talk to him right now. "

Allura obliged, took my hand, and dragged me away from the lies the sisters scattered like seeds. Whether they fell on rocky ground, the path, or good soil, I'm terrified of what they'll grow into.

Yours petrified.
Violetta

July 15

Second,

I went home after hiding at Allura's for about a week. Felicity and Eleora texted me saying the fire started to dwindle, but warned me to tread carefully. If they and Allura didn't keep me grounded, I would've spiraled further down than I already have.

I snuck inside the front door when only Felicity was home. Dad and Eleora were at work while Mom took the twins out to volunteer for the soup kitchen all day.

A curly head of red hair poked down the staircase when I closed the front door. Soft eyes met mine as Felicity slowly walked down the stairs. "How are you doing?" she signed.

Slipping off my shoes, I shrugged. "I'd be better if the twins would've just let me handle this on my own."

Lips pursed, she replied, "I know they were only trying to help, but I agree this was not the best way to go about it."

I shoved my palms into my eyes. "I was so close. I finally was going to do it myself. I promised you guys. I promised–" My words trailed off as your name was left unsaid, Second.

Gentle fingers pulled my hands away and Felicity's image blurred before my eyes. I was tired of crying, but I couldn't help it. It's all I knew how to do.

With slow intentional movements, Felicity signed, "It's okay. This is not an easy situation. I don't know the full story, but we don't like to see you hurt." Water welled in her eyes, magnifying them like a pleading child. "Please, tell me what's really going on. I can't help you when I don't know."

Fractures spread across my heart. Felicity's tears. I couldn't see her cry. My first sister. The baby who made me recognize I needed to protect the ones I love. The little girl I watched cry at night, worrying the kids in preschool would think she was different because she was Deaf. The teenager I held heartbroken after a stupid boy dumped her. Now, the young woman who wept for the sister who was supposed to be strong for her.

Keeping secrets was not protecting them. It was lying to them. Breaking them.

The pain I caused them was worse than revealing my weaknesses.

"I'm sorry, Felicity." My voice broke. Three words shattered my resolve to keep them safe from myself. "It's so much worse than you know."

Tears streamed down her cheeks. "It is?"

"Yes." I placed my hands on her shoulder. "But I am not going to make you cry. Not you, not Mom, not Dad, not the other girls, no one." I gently shook her. "I will fix this."

She sniffled and shook her head. "*We* will fix this. You aren't doing this alone anymore. I'm sorry we didn't support you more than just yelling at you to break up with him."

A quiet laugh escaped my lips. "You were right though. It's something I should've done a long time ago." I ran my fingers through my curls. "It's much harder than you think. Much more dangerous than you think." The words spewed out easier now that I unlocked my box of secrets for Allura. While I didn't want to tell Felicity everything, getting closer to the truth brought an unexpected peace.

Brows furrowed, she signed, "All the more reason to end this for good. I don't care if the twins never see the Kazanskis again. Let's get him out of here forever."

A smile cracked across my hardened face. "Forever."

Yours resolved.

Violetta

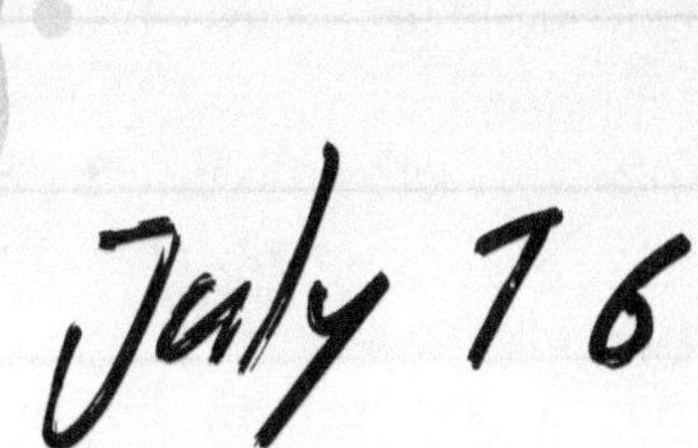

July 16

Hi Second,

"Sharing pain with someone who understands is the first step to mending a heart."

That's what I said to you, isn't it?

Why didn't I take my own advice sooner? A year of heartbreak, secrets, and hurt could have dissipated with one conversation.

This morning, a pain weighed down on my soul despite my vulnerable, hopeful moment with Felicity. I survived the workday by going through the motions, my mind completely numb.

Returning home, I climbed the stairs to my room, plopped onto my bed, and threw my purse to the floor. Aria and Sage once again were out volunteering with our mom. Part of their punishment was community service supporting our church every day for two weeks. Mom's summer break now filled with sergeant duties, ensuring the twins learned from their mistakes.

My mom shouldn't have had to do that. She didn't need to take her time off to punish her daughters because I couldn't speak up. Last year, Mom warned me. She *told* me to get away. She hated the way he looked at me. She hated the way he acted around me. She hated his prideful demeanor.

But she played nice. I told her everything was okay and that we weren't going to take a break.

I lied to her.

I needed to stop.

I needed to fix it.

The phone in my hand grew heavy as I debated calling Bryce to get it over with. To tell him I didn't care about his lies nor the rumors. To tell him we're done and nothing he could say would change that.

But I wasn't brave enough.

Felicity's tears filled the cup in my heart, threatening to overflow with sorrow. Was I ready to stand up for myself and make it up to my mom? Yes. At that moment was I strong enough mentally to counter his manipulative lies? No. Fury, sorrow, disgust swirled in my soul, clouding my thoughts. I needed to exert the negativity and clear my head to steel myself against his attacks.

Black coated my hands as I sketched my thoughts onto a page of my notebook. The lines were fluid, simple, but sad. Anger dissipated and sorrow remained. Dismal images of my emotions. Horrifying, but satisfying. Bryce's lies, painful grip, and harsh expressions slowly faded in my mind as they solidified onto paper.

Mom gently pushed her way into my room without knocking. I didn't hear her and the twins come home. I looked up from my page to see her soft, kind expression.

"Honey, please share your heart with me," she signed. Sadness hung on her eyelashes. "I've been thinking about this since it happened. Your dad is beside himself, saying he should've done more. He wanted to talk to you sooner—as did I—but I said to give you time." She tilted her head to her shoulder. "We also needed to have a serious conversation with your sisters." Her shoulders lifted with a small shrug. "I put out their fiery emotions. It's only a matter of time before their kindness rekindles."

A smile softened my hard expression. My mom's dramatis and eloquence ignited my heart. I forget how alike she and I are. Emotions woven into every phrase. She's a woman I'll forever look up to.

But I've let her down.

Chocolate eyes sweet with love met my broken gaze. "Please, Violetta. Tell me what's going on."

I let out a long breath and glanced at the floor. I should be able to trust my mother with everything, but this was a burden she didn't need to carry. As the oldest, I am meant to lift the stones crushing my family, not drag them down harder.

Mom's fingers gently lifted my chin upward. Long black hair

fell around her cheeks. Thick lips formed a straight line as my mom signed, "Stop protecting me."

My stomach clenched and fire pricked my eyes. She was right. She was strong and courageous. She was dad's first Braveheart. Ferocious and ready to go to war for her family, no matter what.

But Mom couldn't fight for me if I didn't recruit her for the battle.

Fingers clutched my charcoal pencil until I heard it crack. "I want to get away," I replied but my voice was too small for her to read my lips. I enunciated: "He is not good for me. He does not care about me."

Mom sat on the bed beside me. Carefully, she took the pages and pencil from my blackened hands and placed them on the ground. "What does he do to hurt you?" Water brimmed her eyes. "You never tell me."

She was right. I didn't. I put my trust in her sister-in-law, my best friend, and a ghost. I knew I could tell my mom anything and everything, but she has four other girls to help. She guides a classroom of students that look to her as their second mother, asking for advice and courage before they go out into a big bad world.

But I'm exhausted trying to solve this on my own.

A gentle hand rubbed my shoulder. Kind eyes met mine. A small smile broke the dam I built within my heart. Struggles, sorrow, and confusion pent up in my soul burst with the kind touch of a woman I love and respect more than anything.

A woman I've been ignoring when I needed her most.

My lip quivered and my eyes watered. The floodgates opened.

I sobbed.

Tears streamed down my cheeks like waterfalls, dragging down the anguish I've kept inside for far too long.

I couldn't enunciate clearly through my hysterics, so I slowly signed, "I am so tired, Mom."

Pain cracked her beautiful face as I told her about Bryce's red flags I tallied over the past few months. I showed her the texts, recounted the jabs during dates, the bruises in my palms from his harsh hands. An array of arrows pierced my soul as I recounted the phone call when I first tried to break up with Bryce. As I revealed I stayed with him so he wouldn't hurt himself. As I relived the fear when Allura's concern that he might kill me seemed slowly closer to reality.

Every vulnerable moment I tucked into the broken corner of my heart bled from my fingertips as I signed between my sobs.

Trembling hands clasped mine as I failed to sign effectively. Mom's lip quivered and she shook her head. Rage filled her eyes as tears streamed down her face. Pressing a fist to her chest, she signed, "I am so sorry."

Shaking my head, I tried to speak, but words evaporated between my sorrow.

Soft palms clasped my cheeks. Two rapid heartbeats passed before she pressed her forehead against mine.

Warmth bloomed in my mind. Gentle pressure from someone I love with my entire being thrust the anguish back into its dark depths.

Why did I push her away for so long?

Why did I hide my pain from her?

Why didn't I trust her?

It's because I was afraid of hurting her.

It's because I was afraid of failing.

It's because I wasn't the Braveheart my parents claim me to be.

Flinging my arms around her, I pulled myself close to her, breathing in her scent of vanilla and honey. "I'm sorry, too. I'm sorry. I'm sorry. I'm sorry," I repeated until it became mumbles against her shoulder now damp from my tears.

She scooped me up like a child and pressed me against her chest. Her cheek nestled into my hair as she pressed her lips to the side of my head. Strong heartbeats comforted my shaken soul.

I would never hide my life from her again.

Gently, I pulled away. "Thank you, Mom."

She pecked my cheek with a gentle kiss. "Thank you for finally telling me. I'm sorry you've been hurting for so long. The moment Bryce entered the picture, I knew something was wrong."

A gut punch. "Why didn't you tell me?"

She plucked at a string on my bed before signing, "I mentioned it to your sisters. Aria and Sage claimed I was overreacting." She clenched her fists tightly for a moment, then continued. "Since they're friends, I brushed it off, thinking I didn't know them very well."

The twins mask ugly situations like it was as simple as putting on makeup. They think it will fix things, but if you don't care for your skin first nothing will get better.

With a sigh, she continued, "I asked Felicity and Eleora, and they said to give you time. I'm sure that was before they knew. I should've gone with my gut, and I didn't." Despair slid across her face. "That was *my* mistake." She rubbed her hands across her cheeks before continuing, "As time went on, I noticed things I didn't like. My biggest hurt?" She nudged herself closer to me. "Seeing your sad face. I've wanted you to get yourself out of this for a long time, but instead of getting in the middle of things, I stayed on the sidelines holding the medicine bag for when you needed me."

I knotted my fingers and sniffled. "But I didn't ask for the first-aid."

A smile reached her tearful eyes. "I'm glad at least one of my girls can complete my outlandish metaphors."

"Have you seen some of the things I write?" I laughed. "I learned from the best. My sisters did, too, but theirs are more humorous than dramatic."

She shook her head. "That's their dad, for sure."

My smile faded as I swallowed the lump in my throat. "Speaking of writing, I need to show you something." I wiped my nose with my sleeve. "The reason why I've been talking to Aunt Margot is because she thinks my situation is like her sister, Kayleigh's." Hands trembling, I pulled the white leather notebook out from under my pillow. "Remember how Kayleigh saw and heard things before she died?" Static sparked my fingertips as I flipped through the pages. "Aria mentioned someone named 'Stormy.' I am not cheating on Bryce," I added firmly.

Mom gave a small smile. "Violetta, you know I never believed that lie for a second. But a story like Kayleigh's? That's the part that makes me nervous. Why did Allura think he might seriously hurt you? Who is Stormy?"

"That's my nickname for…" I couldn't choke out the word so I signed, "ghost." I held out the open journal, ready to let my mom into another vulnerable place of my heart.

Eyes widened as my mom took the journal in her hands. Fingers ran over the supernatural impressions on the pages.

"I was going to talk to Father McFadden and see his thoughts, but Bryce's sisters were talking to him after Mass, so I couldn't."

"Is this real?" Curiosity painted over the sorrow on Mom's face. "You wrote these letters every day?"

"Yeah, but Second doesn't always respond."

"But you wrote these every day?

My ear dropped to my shoulder. "I've written them every day since my thirteenth birthday, just like you did for Dad."

A soft laugh escaped her lips. She flipped through the pages. Her eyes fell upon one of your quotes, Second. My cheeks flushed as she read my innermost thoughts and a phantom's response.

She smirked and eyed me. "This ghost sounds pretty cute," she quickly signed.

Red crawled up my neck. "Mom!"

She laughed, lightening the heavy tension present moments ago. "He seems so sweet and nice."

"You don't think this is weird?"

She shut the journal and handed it back. "Of course, it's weird, but that's because it's different. You know what I really think it is?" Her index finger booped my nose. "A miracle. A prayer answered."

"What do you mean?"

"I've prayed for you girls every day of your lives. When you turned thirteen, my recurring prayer was that you would find your happiness. These past two years," she shrugged, "I realized you needed extra prayers. I wished I was stronger last year when you first tried to break up with him."

"No, Mom, don't do that," I shook my head. "You saw it before I did. I tried to follow your advice, but I wasn't strong enough."

She pursed her lips and exhaled through her nose. "Violetta, you are an incredible, beautiful, young woman. Bryce is a menace. A devil in disguise to tear apart God's beauty." Balled fists shook before she continued, "We are never letting him in this house again. *You* are never seeing him again. If he ever shows his face? I don't think I could restrain my fury." Biting her lip, she gave her head a hard shake. "Anyway, back to this hot ghost we like."

The moment she signed "hot" I couldn't withhold a laugh. "Don't call Second hot, that's so weird."

Gently, she poked my ribs, tickling me. A few laughs satisfied her before she signed, "Your smile is one reason why I think this conversation with this spirit is a miracle. Another reason," she tapped the notebook, "is because Second reminds you of who you are."

Second, your words weighed the journal in my hands. I felt them between the pages. Each letter ingrained into my memory. Each kind word and thoughtful remark painted every corner of my brain until the walls were bright, colorful, and joyful.

A reflection of who I wanted to be.

"I miss Violetta." Three words broke my heart. A truth I never said aloud. Three words that hid between the pages, unpublished and forgotten.

"You can bring her back." Mom's five words consumed my soul. Five words sparked a flicker of hope. Hope that I craved like a drug. One that would get me high on a future where I could be free. Where I could be saved.

That future starts with me.

But Second, you're a part of this journey whether you like it or not.

Thank you for waking up the real Violetta.

Let's set her free.

Yours still waiting.
Violetta

July 17

Second,

I have bad news. Bryce called today.

It did not go well.

My phone buzzed as I walked out of a meeting at work. I glanced at the name scrolling across my watch screen. I held my breath, nodded to Lucio, and ducked down the bright hallway. I needed to answer it. I couldn't keep waiting for the best time to call him. The opportunity presented itself and I had to take it. I owed it to Aunt Margot, to Allura, to Felicity, to my mom…

I owed it to myself.

I slid my finger across the screen and pressed the screen to my ear. "Bryce," I answered coldly. I wouldn't be pushed around. Not today. Not ever again.

I was Violetta Sparks. Braveheart. No one would manipulate me again.

"Violetta, I've made a decision. Let's meet to talk." His voice was sharp around the edges.

I snuck inside the staff bathroom and locked myself in a stall with a click. "You've made a decision?"

"Yes. I know you'd probably prefer it if we did it in person. So, let's meet up after work today and talk about what to do since you cheated on me."

Knuckles turned white as I gripped my phone. "I didn't."

"Liar," he hissed.

A knife through the heart. "What exactly did your sisters tell you?" I asked as firmly as my unsteady voice would allow. "You make this accusation during Felicity's birthday, then claim 'you need time' to think before 'you' decide what you want to do."

"My sisters said you've been seeing someone else and that's why you haven't wanted to hang out."

Red flushed my neck. "I haven't seen anyone. You made that assumption without speaking to me. You haven't made time for me. We've only gone out when it's convenient for you."

"Oh, sure sure. Blame me," he whined. "You've ignored my calls and denied any time I wanted to hang out."

I was done making excuses. I was done biting my tongue. I thought of all the advice I've received. I thought of the sleepless nights, the distressed days. I thought of each time my hand quaked picking up my pencil to write in my journal or my shaking grip when I shot my arrows. The tears that streamed down my face whenever I thought of love. The pangs in my stomach whenever I thought of my future.

I should never be this anxious.

I should never be this worried.

I should never be this sad.

I needed to do it for myself.

Time for me to decide my own fate.

"Bryce, I tried telling you before but you never listened." My fingers trembled and my throat dried. Straightening my back, I spat into the phone, "I want this to be over. I'm tired of you lying to me and making me look like the problem. I never cheated on you, but you can believe what you want. I never want to see you again. We are done."

The line was quiet. Its silence cut through my racing heart. Was this it? Is this all there was? Was it over?

Two beeps. The call ended.

He hung up on me.

I am not sure what to expect next.

~~Anxiously waiting.~~

Violetta

July 18

Second,

I haven't heard from Bryce since the phone call. An uneasiness sat like a rock in the pit of my stomach. Something wasn't right.

After work, I shut my bedroom door, pulled my journal out of my laptop case, plopped in my swivel chair, and rolled to my desk. I reached across the white wood to grab a purple pen when I noticed a small bag of salted caramels on my desk. My favorite candies. A sticky note stuck to the side. Doodled small hearts and initials "A+S" covered the pink paper.

I haven't spoken to the twins since July 7th. They hadn't made an effort to reach out or apologize. Mom kept them busy with volunteer work to help them think about their mistakes. My favorite candies offered in peace was a start. I tore open the bag and popped one into my mouth. The chocolate melted on my tongue as the sugar hit my soul. A sweet gesture that I wouldn't turn down no matter how badly my pride was hit.

A knock rapped at my door. Sage poked her head in before I answered. "Violetta, are you coming down for dinner tonight?" Wide eyes watched me cautiously like a cat carefully observing a vicious dog from behind the couch.

I sucked in a deep breath. I didn't want to be the annoying pup that growled and bit everyone that walked by. I wanted to be the one to protect and defend. I can't do that for my sisters if I'm holding a grudge.

I can forgive, but I won't forget. I need to start forgiving.

"Depends," I said.

Her lip pursed. "Depends on what?"

I stood up and put my journal down. "Depends on if you'll give me a hug." I opened my arms wide.

Sage's eyes watered and she crashed into my embrace. Her body shook as I squeezed her tightly. A lump caught in my throat. I didn't realize how badly I needed that.

"I-I am sorry." Sage sobbed. "I didn't know how s-serious it was. A-Aria said we were h-helping." She buried her nose into my shoulder. Tears dampened my shirt.

"I know. You've seen me sad and you both heard Eleora and Felicity talking about me breaking up with Bryce." I ran my fingers through her hair. "You didn't know the whole story of why I didn't break up right away."

"We still don't know the details," a voice snapped.

I looked up to see Aria standing in the doorway with her arms crossed. Her lips pursed as words stuck in her mouth. She fidgeted from foot to foot before she spat. "Why didn't you say how serious it was? Is it all true?"

Rocks formed in my stomach. "Is what true?"

Dark eyes widened with tears. "Was he really hurting you? It wasn't just because he was a weirdo and not romantic?"

Bitterness melted around my heart. Aria truly thought I was only being picky and stubborn. In her practical mind, breaking up was simple. A few words, departing glances, and it was over. Similarly to how you think, Second.

"Who told you that?" I whispered.

"Felicity, but don't get mad." She put a hand up. "All she said was he is more dangerous than we think."

"I believe that," Sage whispered. "He scared me when we were at their house last time."

Arms crossed, Aria dug her toes into the carpet. "I really thought I was helping you by telling the sisters you needed a break. Messed up of them to tell him while we were there."

"What *really* happened?" I pressed.

Aria let out a long exhale. "Sage and I were trying to tell them that you and Bryce weren't working anymore. I suggested maybe we all work together to encourage you two to take a break. Agatha was stupid and ran to tell her brother right away."

Sage pressed her hands to her ears. "Bryce started yelling. I hated it."

"He was being a total crybaby," Aria mocked. "Whining and yelling saying 'Violetta's my future' and 'she wouldn't dare try to leave me again.'" Long fingers tugged at a dark curl draped around her cheek. "Then I said the thing I shouldn't have said."

I arched an eyebrow. "Which was?"

Red flushed her cheeks. "I didn't like his tone. He was rude and mean. It made me realize maybe something more toxic was really going on between you two. So?" She shrugged. "I stretched the truth a bit by snapping back saying, 'Violetta doesn't need you anyway. I think she's found someone else already who is ten times better than you.'"

Emptiness filled my mind as her confession hung in the air. I had no thoughts, no words, no response to her confession. My arms wrapped tighter around Sage as I continued to hug her.

"It was wrong, I'm sorry," Aria mumbled. "I didn't know how messed up he actually was. If I could take it back, I would, but I can't. And now?" Curls bounced back and forth as she shook her head. "I destroyed our friendship with Christine and Agatha. Dad is ready to pick a fight with any guy who looks at us. Mom is furious. And…" Her voice trailed off. "We hurt you. The lies they're spreading are ridiculous. I only said that you found someone better because I saw a text about someone named Stormy from Allura and you wrote about a guy in your journal. Not real evidence or anything." Fists at her sides, she closed her eyes and spat, "I was wrong, I'm sorry."

Another burden lifted from my heart. Aria and Sage cared about me as I do them. With a tearful grin, I replied sarcastically, "Wait, what was that last part?"

Aria growled and stomped over. Flinging her arms around Sage and me, she grumbled, "I am *sorry*. I am sorry I called you annoying. I'm sorry I got in the middle of your relationship. I'm sorry I messed up." Resting her forehead on my shoulder, she mumbled, "I just don't like when my sister is upset and possibly hurt."

I rubbed my hand through her silky hair. "I forgive you. I promise, things will get better."

She sniffled. "Good. Just stop faking it, too," Aria demanded, wriggling out of the hug. Affection wasn't exactly her forte. "Break up with Bryce and start healing. I don't know what really happened between you guys—you won't tell us and neither will Mom. But if he's really dangerous? You need to do something about it if we can't help."

Bryce's phone call lingered in the back of my mind, but I shoved it away. I finally did it. I broke up with him. It's not perfect or the true ending, but it was the start. I promised that whatever came next I would handle bravely, but not alone.

My family cared about me. Deeply, truly, wholly. I would return the favor by being truthful.

"I am slowly healing now." I released Sage from our long hug. "There was good to come out of all this." Cold air filled my lungs. I hadn't told my family yet. It was time. "Bryce called me."

Four eyes widened. Air stilled between us, waiting for me to speak.

"I told him we're done," I stated. Five words erupted like fire in my soul. I burned brightly rather than turning to ash. The start of something new. The start of me upholding the name of Braveheart.

Aria's jaw dropped. "Wait, excuse me? You broke up with him?"

I bit my lip and nodded. "He didn't take it well, so I'll need your help with the rest."

Light ignited Aria's dark eyes. "Deal." Dancing in place, she sang, "I think we need to celeebraaaate."

"Guys, dinner!" Eleora shouted from downstairs. "C'mon, I'm starving."

Flicking off my desk light, I laughed and said, "Let's go eat before Eleora eats her own foot."

"With her big feet she'd have enough to eat for a month." Aria gently punched my arm and ran back out of my room. "But I'm going to see if we have champagne."

"Please don't make a big deal out of it!" I shouted, but it was too late. I heard Aria announcing my accomplishment to my family downstairs.

A squeal echoed through the hall. "No way!" Eleora screamed. The pad of feet running from the kitchen filled the house. "Violetta!

Get down here and let's have a drink!"

My smile softened. I appreciated them relishing my bravery. It uplifted a heavy situation. I tried to force my distanced mind to return to the present. Despite the vocal joys, Bryce's silence before ending our phone call haunted my memory.

After a year of waiting, I finally broke up with my toxic boyfriend.

But something still wasn't right.

Sage and I stood in silence for a minute. She sniffled and wiped her nose with the back of her hand. "Violetta, I know you don't want to talk about it because it hurts. But is there something you can tell me?"

I snapped myself back into reality. "What is it?"

She let out a shaky breath. "Who were you writing about? Really? Aria still thinks there is something else going on especially because you keep talking to Aunt Margot. Will you please tell me?"

I bit my lip. Conviction to keep my promise forced the truth out of my mouth. "Remember when Mom told us to write letters to our future spouses?" I began.

Sage nodded. "I still have mine."

"That's important, I'm glad you do." I picked up my notebook. Dust and dirt slowly darkened the white leather. "Well, I write to him every day."

Her eyes widened. "You do?"

I nodded. "Yeah. I sit down with my thoughts and tell him all about my day as if he was really here. As If I was telling him a story over dinner. I wanted to make this a gift to him. I told Allura about it and she calls him Stormy."

Sage smiled. "I think that's really cool, Vi. I'm sure he will appreciate it someday. I know Dad did when Mom gave him her letters."

I nodded. "Yes."

"But, is that all of it?" Her voice sounded unsure. "If you're not cheating on Bryce with someone, then have you really seen…" Her voice faltered.

"A ghost?" I finished.

Her lips formed a straight line as she nodded.

"Well, I haven't *seen* one," I sucked in a deep breath, "but one has spoken to me," I said on the exhale.

Sage's eyes widened. "Like Aunt Margot's sister?"

"Like Aunt Margot's sister." This small confession made the secret of Second lighter to carry around my siblings.

Sage's face paled. "Is he friendly?"

I nodded. "Very. He is sweet, too. Whether he is real or not, all I know is he's helped me realize that everything I want in a man was never in Bryce."

Color returned to her cheeks and she smiled. "Then, I'm happy he found you. But please be careful, okay?" She bounced on her toes, then came in for another hug. "I don't want anything to happen to you."

My heart stopped in my chest. I hugged her tightly. "Nothing will, I promise."

But I wasn't so sure.

Is everything over? Will I never hear from you again, Second? How do I know if you fulfilled your duty?

Kayleigh's ghost failed to save her.

I prayed mine would help save me.

Your human,

Violetta

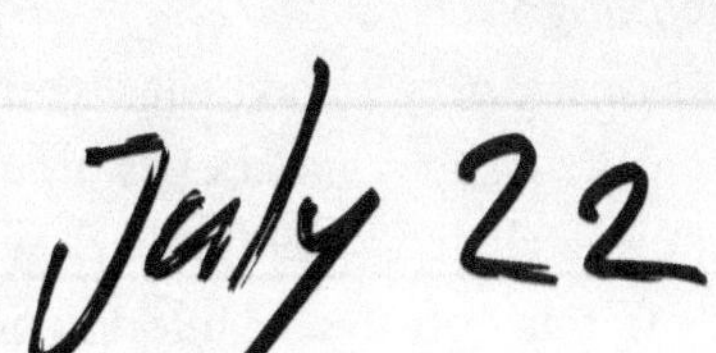

Second,

It's been about five days since I broke up with Bryce over the phone. I haven't heard a word from him. My sisters haven't heard from the Kazanskis either. I thought this breakup would bring relief. I thought I would feel a weight lifted off my shoulders. I thought my heart would be happy. I thought I'd be even braver.

I'm not.

I'm afraid.

My conversation with Sage and Aria lifted the pain only temporarily. Sipping bubbly champagne around a cheerful dinner table and chatting about silly stories granted escape for only that night. Anxiety fills my soul with holes so any peace trying to fill it slips right through.

Something bad is going to happen. I fear the worst isn't over yet. I'm trying to become the Braveheart I promised I'd live up to, but it's not instant. I'm trudging through mud, dirty and broken. It might take me forever to get there, but I fear I'm running out of time.

Peaceful melodies filled my ears as my dad's radio sang from the kitchen counter. I sat at the table with an uneaten plate of cherry pie in front of me. Dad bought the homemade confectionary from a farmer's market as a treat. Its sugary sweet scent should have made my mouth water, but the sticky red filling reminded me of a deep blood that made my stomach turn.

Dad hummed the tune of the folk band and cheerfully cleaned the dishes while mom tucked herself into the office to lesson plan for her future classes. A pink apron that said "World's Greatest Housemaid" pulled taut against his broad chest. The giant of a man with a warrior's build wore it proudly after Aria purchased it for him as a joke on Father's Day last year.

Glancing over his shoulder, his lips parted to speak, but quickly closed them when his eyes fell upon the wasted pie slice in front of me. "Violetta, is the pie not good?"

I shook my head. "I'm so sorry. I can't eat it tonight."

Thick lips frowned as he flung a towel over his shoulder. Tapping the radio off, he pulled out a chair and plopped down, shaking the table. "I think I've put off this conversation long enough."

Fire flamed in my cheeks. We needed to talk, but I didn't want to. I held the truth from my dad. I hurt him. I failed him, too. I wasn't the Braveheart he needed me to be.

Thick arms rested on the table as his light eyes watched me closely. "You didn't tell me everything after the camping trip."

My head hung low, curls covering my face. "I told you what I could."

Fingers drumming against the table, he replied, "You told me the bare minimum. This is serious, Violetta. Your mom told me more."

I snapped up. "She did? What do you know?"

"Everything." He held out his hand.

Stomach clenched, I hesitated before placing mine in his. Small and fragile compared to his large calloused palm.

Gently, he turned my hand over. He inhaled sharply and traced the tiny scars scattered across my palms. The marks Bryce's nails left whenever he squeezed me tightly, demanding I never leave.

"They're small," I whispered.

"But they exist." A heartbeat passed before a tear rolled down his wide nose.

My dad cried.

I made my dad cry.

A hand gripped my heart, squeezing until I thought it would stop beating. "Dad, please don't cry. I'm sorry." I placed my other hand on top of his. "I wasn't brave enough. I let this go on for too long because I wasn't strong enough to stop it. I'm so sorry."

In a small voice, he asked, "Violetta, do you know why I call you

Braveheart?"

The question stunned me. Memory files fluttered in my mind as I sought out when my nickname began. The origin blurred and melded with other recollections from my childhood.

"I thought it was because I look like the Scottish princess and the 90s movie I never saw," I confessed.

A small smile hid under his mustache. "You not seeing the movie is one way I've failed as a father." Squeezing my palm, he continued, "The other way I failed is not empowering you to live up to the true reason I gave you that name." He leaned back in the chair, tilting his head upward. Warm light cast shadows under his eyes. "Do you remember your first camping trip?"

I nodded. "You took Felicity and me to Longwood Forest when I was seven." Stars sparkled in my memories as I recalled my sister and me sitting beside our dad, looking up at the stories God wrote in the sky. "I was so scared of being in the woods without mom." I bit my lip. "Felicity was braver than me and she was only five. I remember her saying she'd fight any spider or bug that tried to crawl on me while I slept. She wanted to become super strong to take down a bear someday, too."

Dad chuckled. "She promised to protect you. Do you remember what you said after that?"

I paused, thinking back to that night. Evening and morning blurred together as I recalled the moments that impacted me most. This one wasn't among them. "I don't know."

"Never had a little girl said something so profound." A proud smile spread across his cheeks. "You looked at your sister, small tears in your eyes, and said, 'I'm supposed to protect you, but if it'll make you strong enough to fight a bear, then you can protect me.'" He leaned forward, comforting warmth radiating from him like a campfire. "You recognized your weakness and surrendered yourself to make someone else stronger. You sacrificed becoming the hero so someone else could be." He shook my palms. "*That* is why you're Braveheart. You let Felicity help you even if it hurt your pride as the big sister. You let her grow in herself if that meant you'd take a step back. It's your humility in asking for help despite needing to be strong that makes *you* my Braveheart."

Clock ticks shouted in the quiet that followed his story. Heartbeats thumped in my chest. Never had I thought of bravery like that. "I thought asking for help was a weakness."

He shook his head. "It's a strength. You hiding your pain, suffering, and something as serious as this toxic relationship was your weakness." His strong palm pressed against my cheek. "You're Braveheart because you weren't afraid to let others be strong for you. Bryce took that from you, manipulating you into hiding what he's done and what he *threatens* to do." Flames ignited in his eyes, rage ready to consume him. "He ripped you away from who you're supposed to be." Rage turned to determination as he promised, "Together, we'll bring Braveheart back."

Five words consumed my soul. Memories from the past two years blurred as tears streamed down my face, dampening my father's hand pressed against my cheek. He was right, I never asked for help. I thought I had to do it alone. Fear tethered me to Bryce's darkness, but I didn't ask anyone to turn on the lights. Years of pain, hurt, and distance from my family could have been solved by opening up. If I hurt them with the truth sooner, the pain of putting me back together could've been avoided.

I needed to let someone else be the hero of my story.

Ugly sobs stuck in my throat as I nestled my cheek in dad's hands. "I'm sorry, Dad. I'm so sorry."

Scooting closer, he wrapped me in his arms. "Don't apologize, Violetta. Thank you for finally letting us in." Chapped lips kissed the top of my head. "Thank you for being my Braveheart."

My world expanded as I made myself smaller in his embrace. "I'll promise to live up to that name."

"You already have," he whispered against my head.

No matter what happened with Bryce next, I vowed to myself that I wouldn't solve the problem on my own. I wouldn't run into it without telling others for fear of letting them down.

I'd let someone help save me.

Ever brave,
Violetta

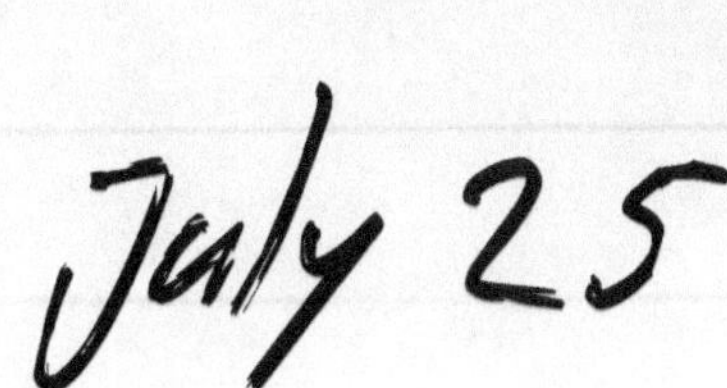

Second,

I haven't heard from you in a while. I hope you're doing okay. Not sure what you're doing on this plane of existence, but I pray you're safe.

I hope you'll hear me soon. I promised Dad I'll be Braveheart and let someone else be the hero of my story.

Is that hero going to be you? Will you come and become real like Little Ghost was for Kayleigh?

I haven't seen the phantom reflections in a while. My parents know about those interactions as well. It's comical to watch them eye a mirror, searching for something. Once in a while, Mom will ask if I've seen anything, but lately the answers have always been no. A piece of my heart is relieved but sorrowful.

For a few days, I thought the absence resulted in a "mission success."

But then Bryce texted me: ***"It will be your fault."***

Five wrong words consume a soul, Kayleigh wrote at the beginning of this journal.

The worst is ready to consume mine.

Yours anxious,
Violetta

July 26

Second,

It's happening again. The reason I didn't break up with him forever ago. The reason I had locked in a box and buried deep into the recesses of my mind.

All bets are off. The cards are all on the table. Bryce is playing his hand.

Aria ran into the living room with her smartphone tight in her grip.

Mom paused the movie and asked, "What's wrong?"

"The Kazanskis can't find Bryce," Aria answered flatly.

Color drained from my cheeks. My heart thumped hard against my ribcage. It happened again. Memories swarmed to the front of my mind: the phone call from Bryce last year as the wind rushed into the receiver and the blare of the train horn as it rattled down the tracks.

I shook my head. No.

It wouldn't happen again. It couldn't happen again.

Mom jumped up from the couch and crossed the room to stand beside me. "This is not your fault," she signed. "There is something deeper with Bryce that we cannot control."

She was right. His reaction to this situation goes deeper than I can imagine, but I don't know how to fix it. I will not dive back into a relationship to try and hold it together by a thread because of this threat.

I will do this right. I will stand up for myself, but I won't do it alone.

"Maybe he just played hooky and is sleeping around or

something," Eleora mumbled through a mouthful of popcorn.

Aria shook her head. "He left a note for Violetta. It's not a good one."

My heart sank into my shoes.

Mom's eyes widened and she glanced over at me. "This isn't your fault," she signed again, breathing quickening.

"He is still alive," Aria clarified quickly.

My heart beat a little slower. "What did the note say?"

She scrolled to the top of her text messages. "It said that you are his future, no matter what happens. He was upset you couldn't take responsibility for your actions when you cheated on him. He wants you to say sorry and get back with him."

"Bullcrap," Felicity signed, her brow furrowed. "Didn't you see the way he flirted with Brigid at my birthday party?"

"He what?" Eleora cried. "No, he didn't."

Felicity nodded. "I notice everything. I knew Violetta didn't feel well that night and he was the reason why."

"Why is he doing this?" Sage whimpered. She curled herself into a ball. "Why is this happening?"

All eyes were on me. I bit my lip. I parted my lips to tell them what happened last year. To tell them the truth why I stuck with him.

Mom shot me a glance, keeping me quiet. "Bryce is not okay, but it's not Violetta's fault," she signed. "We need to pray for him, but we can't solve the problem. You girls stay out of it, okay?"

Sage and Aria nodded, but Felicity and Eleora exchanged glances.

My phone vibrated before I could say anything. I fumbled it out of my pocket to see "*Allura*" with two hearts scrolling across the screen. "Hello?"

"Violetta, did you hear what Bryce did?" Her voice rang.

"Only he is missing and left a note. Did something else happen?"

"No nothing yet. Just that. But he's blaming you for his absence." She paused. "Is it happening again?"

Tears brimmed. "Yes, Allura, it is."

"What are you going to do, Violetta?" Aria asked.

I took a shaky breath. My mind throbbed with the thought of going through that again. Of walking on eggshells, fearing the worst.

But this time, it will be different.

Everyone knows the truth about Bryce, to some degree. My parents know his condition and are doing whatever they can to help. This time, I won't do it alone.

"Become the Braveheart I needed to be," I responded.

The valiant.
Violetta

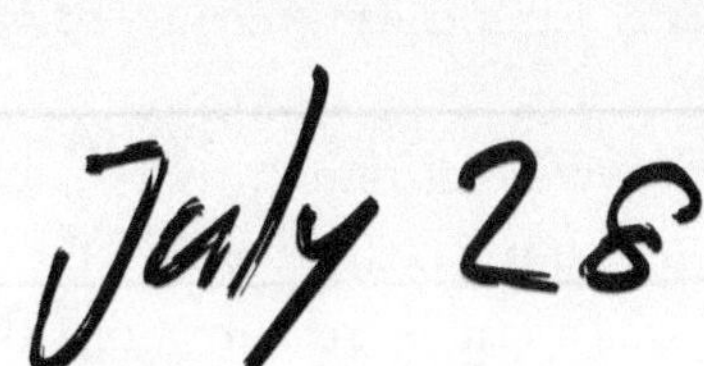

July 28

Second,

You promised.

You told me if I needed you, I could call upon you and you'd be there.

Second, where are you?

You couldn't have left. Not now. Not when I needed saving the most. Bryce is still missing. My parents called Mr. and Mrs. Kazanski, explaining what happened between us last year. His parents were beside themselves, but didn't blame their son. They blamed me for his condition. They called me a liar and a gaslighter, claiming Bryce to be the victim of our relationship.

The Kazanskis filed a missing persons report. The first time he disappeared was for less than 24 hours, and he contacted me within that time.

This time is different. It's been two days and now the police are involved. The Kazanski sisters spun the story and I was called into the station to be interviewed... twice.

Exhaustion tugged at my limbs from hours spent sitting in a cold interrogation room. They only let me go because I had a solid alibi, my parents' testimonies, my sister's text, and a few journal entries from the first time he disappeared.

As I sat with the blue notebook from last year, my heart clenched. Shock numbed my entire body.

Kayleigh wrote journal entries as evidence.

I never thought the love letters to my future husband would be used to convict someone.

My story is becoming like hers.

I prayed they wouldn't end the same.

I don't want to recount the questions the mustached officer drew on as I responded with watery eyes. His careless fingers as they flipped roughly through the pages stained with tears. My heart can't handle it.

I sit in the back of my parents car, praying, begging, to see your words.

Second, I thought you were different.

I thought I could entrust my heart to you. I thought you would carry it gingerly as if it was a fragile treasure. Something you never wanted to break. Something you wanted to hold onto and never let go.

Let's face it: the reason I am so upset?

I thought you were the one.

I thought you would come to my side and rescue me. I thought you would have all the answers. I thought I would at least get to see you before you moved on like Kayleigh saw Little Ghost.

You told me to get on with my life. You told me everything would be "okay" if I did.

Well, Bryce is still missing. There are more notes. The police might think I did it. And my heart is shattering into a million pieces.

If your job as a ghost was to save me, you're failing.

I hope you make it to the afterlife somehow.

Despaired.

Violetta

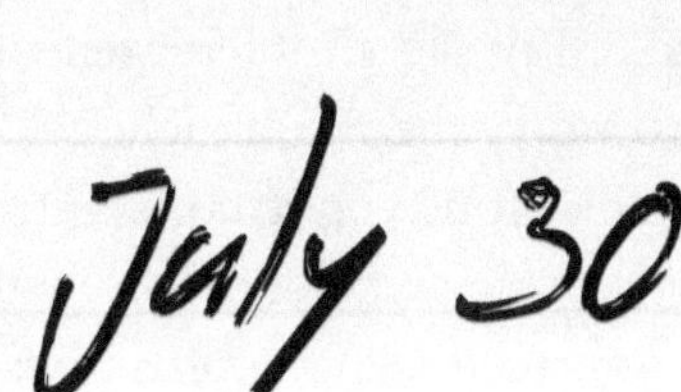

July 30

Second,

Bryce called me today. The first time anyone had heard from him in days. It came from an unknown number and I almost didn't answer it, but something told me to slide my thumb across the screen. "Hello?"

"Vi, it's Bryce."

My heart jumped. "Bryce, where are you?" I looked at the screen. The number wasn't his, but it belonged to our local area code. I screenshotted it and sent it to my parents who had contacts with the police.

"You should know where I am," he snarled. "You're late."

My words caught in my throat. "What are you talking about?"

"I'm going to finish what I started if you don't show up soon."

My body shook. Tears streamed down my face. It's happening again. The reason why I stayed with him is coming back to haunt me. Memories of the train horn rattled my soul.

"Bryce, you need help. Tell me where you are and I'll let the police know so we can come get you."

"No police. Just you," he snapped. "I won't do anything until you arrive."

I swallowed the lump in my throat. "Bryce, why don't we stop this now? I can call Melissa to have her take care of you. She seemed to be worried."

"Again with Melissa," his voice grew louder. Angry. "She was never going to be my future. She only eased the pain. You take it."

There it was. Three wrong words broke a heart and it shattered mine. The reason why I stayed with him. The reason his manipulation and gaslighting kept me wrapped around his finger.

I feared if I didn't help him, no one would.

But I can't anymore.

I just *can't.*

"Fine, I'll come to you. But please at least tell your family you are okay. There is no need to worry them so much."

"Only if you won't tell anyone you're coming to me."

"Okay," I lied. "If you want me to come alone, I can't get there until Sunday." I needed time to think of a plan. I wasn't going to do this blindly. It wasn't safe and he needed more help than I could provide.

Silent pause screamed through the receiver. "Fine, I will be okay until then."

"Will you tell your parents you're okay? You do know the police are looking for you, right?" Harsh tones wove into my reply. I tried to remain level, but fury quelled inside.

"Yes, I know. They almost found me," he snapped. "They think I'm not well, but I'm fine. I don't know what you told them but it was really messed up that you said I 'need help.' You're the one who needs help, Vi."

"I only told them—" I held my breath and tapped the corner of the phone against my forehead. I exhaled sharply, pressed the phone back to my ear, and continued, "Listen, I will be there Sunday. Alone. Do you need food or anything? Are you all right?"

He laughed quietly. "This is why you're my future. Always looking out for me. I have plenty to eat. I'm safe. I will call you Saturday night with the location. I have something special for you when you get here. I'll make all this go away."

The line went dead.

I thrust my phone into my pocket. I sat at the edge of my bed, staring at the stars on my ceiling. Praying, wishing, hoping that my ghost will come to save me.

But you're not here, Second. My mind claims you failed, but my heart keeps trying to give you another chance.

That's my problem, isn't it?

I need to tell you: "I've done something I regret. Now, I'm paying for it."

Yours distressed.
Violetta

August 7

Second,

Bryce contacted his family yesterday, letting them know he was okay. He even *apologized* for worrying them and for wasting the police's time.

I only know this because the detective called this morning.

Dad sat at the piano early this morning, playing a melody from our childhood. I wanted to sing along, but I wasn't ready just yet. I wouldn't sing until Bryce was safe.

Instead, I sat on the floor, playing cards with Eleora and Felicity, grateful for a distraction. Mom dragged the twins grocery shopping, ensuring they continued to do extra chores to "build their character."

Felicity danced triumphantly after winning another round of poker when my dad's phone rang. The song stopped abruptly as he pulled the cracked smartphone out of his pocket. His chipper voice turned solemn as he conversed with the man on the other end.

"Violetta," Dad whispered, looking over his shoulder. Eyes darkened, he signed so as not to interrupt the call, "The police are calling off the search, but they want to talk to us."

Cards bent in my tense grip. I didn't want to do that again. I had already told them everything. I had shown them my private journal entries. My dad had shared the phone call details with them. I didn't want to talk to them anymore.

"What's going on?" Felicity signed.

Dad signed back, "One minute," as he continued to speak to the officer.

Eleora shook her head and dealt another hand. "I hope this will be over soon. If your life was a book or movie, Violetta, I would've fast-forwarded to the end by now."

Picking up the forest green cards, I laughed. "I would've skipped these scenes, too."

Felicity frowned. "I think a writer would call that 'character development' and everyone has to go through it."

"I'm fully developed, don't worry about me." Eleora stuck her tongue out and fanned the cards in front of her face. "Vi, no matter what happens don't run off on your own again, okay?"

I clutched my three-of-a-kind against my chest. I hadn't told my sisters about Bryce demanding me to see him. My parents and the police were the only ones who knew.

"Thank you, Officer Budman. We'll be there soon." Dad hung up the phone and spun around on the piano bench. "Violetta, we need to talk to them about tomorrow."

"Excuse me, what?" Eleora's eyebrow arched. "What's tomorrow?"

I sucked in a deep breath and answered, "Bryce wanted to see me. He didn't tell me where he is, but I think he'll call sometime today to let me know."

"Can't we just leave him to rot?" Eleora murmured.

"Eleora Mae." Dad shot a glance. "You know why."

"Fine." She threw her hands up. "Then, let's come up with a plan to make sure he doesn't do anything stupid."

Felicity held the cards between her lips to sign, "I second the notion. Violetta, you shouldn't have to do this alone."

"And she won't have to." Dad slid off the bench and sat on the floor with a thunk, shaking the drink glasses we had beside our snack bowl. "I agree with Eleora: we're going to come up with a plan to save Bryce and keep you safe."

I nodded. I wanted their help, but I feared what Bryce might do. His tone and aggression grew tenfold from our last encounter. I feared he'd do something drastic.

I glanced in the mirror above the piano, hoping to see a ghostly reflection. Praying that you would appear to give me reassurance.

But you weren't there.

And you're not here now.

In Kayleigh's story, Little Ghost materializes and holds Bryce back from hurting her as best he could, but the police didn't get there in time. In my story, the police have no cause to arrive on scene because the Kazanskis called off the search, but we came up with a plan. My dad and Officer Budman should arrive moments after I get there. It's a safety precaution without "wasting police resources" as the detectives told me. But no matter how many times we rethink the plan, there is always one uncertainty:

I will be alone with Bryce.

And that terrifies me.

I pray you're there to save me.

Unable to sleep.
Violetta

August 2 – Morning

Second,
 It's 1 am. Bryce called me.
  He's at the abandoned train station.
  I'm begging you.
 "Please, please, please come back."
  I need you.

Yours aghast,
Violetta

August 2 - Day

Second,

Save me, please.

I drove far below the speed limit, dreading the moment I arrived. Trees streaked across my vision as I rode down the highway. The blazing sun hung high in a clear blue sky. The beautiful Sunday morning turned into a day of dread and horror. Every mile I feared what Bryce was doing. Would he be okay? Would I be okay? I felt confident in my family's plan, but lacked that assurance in myself.

The landscape grew eerily familiar as I slowed my car down a gravel road. Rocks flew up and smacked into my windshield. Each pebble sent a crack across my soul. The closer I got, the more I feared.

My ringtone rang through my car. Aunt Margot's name popped up on the screen. Mom and Dad hadn't told her anything. They begged me not to. My thumb hovered over the hang-up button on my steering wheel.

But a voice nagged at the back of my mind. Small, quiet, but there all the same. I answered the call. "Hello?"

"Violetta! Where are you? I had a horrible dream last night. Are you safe?" Her voice trembled. "You haven't spoken to me since you were hiding at Allura's. I tried talking to your parents, but they told me you needed time. Are you all right?"

"I am safe for now, but I don't know what will happen." I needed to be honest. I needed to tell the truth. "Frankly, I'm scared, but you'll be proud of me: I told my parents everything."

She gasped quietly. "You told them about the ghost?"

"Yes, they know about him. They know everything about Bryce." I took a shaky breath. "I finally did it, Aunt Margot."

"I am so proud of you." She quietly chuckled. "But you're not going to see him, are you?"

I hesitated.

"Violetta, he could kill you." Aunt Margot's words echoed through my car. They lingered between my ears until they shook my soul.

I didn't want to think about it. Fear clutched my heart.

I knew I could die.

My parents knew. My sisters knew.

But using me to draw him out was the only way to save him. To save me.

"I know," I replied, my voice small. My heart constricted as if cold chains ensnared it and the devil yanked it down. "But I don't think he will. Not yet. Despite me having a ghost like Kayleigh, I don't think he can. He calls me his future." My knuckles turned white as I gripped the steering wheel. "I have to play along a little longer."

"Oh, God, not again. Please Violetta. This is what happened to Kayleigh. Please." A sob cut off her words. "Stay far away from him."

"I am sorry, Aunt Margot." Fire caught in my throat. This is why I didn't tell her. I didn't want her to relive the same pain she experienced with Kayleigh's murder. It wasn't fair. "I can't let him hurt anyone else."

"You're just like Kayleigh. In the best and worst ways." She sniffled hard. "What are you planning to do when you see him?"

"Everything will turn out fine," I replied through a forced smile. The truth was? I didn't know that for sure. "My family and I have a plan. I'll update you once it's over."

A sigh of relief. "Thank goodness. Is your dad involved in this plan?"

"He came up with three of them," I replied with a chuckle.

"Ol' reliable, Finn." In a low voice, Aunt Margot continued, "Be safe, I'm praying for you. I hope Second helps you like he did Kayleigh."

"I pray so, too." I jabbed the hang-up button with my thumb and accelerated up the road, the station coming into view. Low-hanging trees draped leaves like blankets along the concrete building. Vines crawled up the sides like scurrying spiders. The musty rotten air rushed through my A/C vents and I coughed to clear my lungs.

I turned right and headed down the parking lot to find Bryce's car parked at the bottom. My heart hammered against my ribcage as I pulled up next to it.

Tremors shot down my limbs when I saw him.

Bryce stood in the doorway of the concrete station. His hair neatly combed, and a gray polo tucked into black jeans. A forced smile spread across his face. He looked clean and professional as if he was closing a deal on a business transaction.

I sucked in a deep breath. Five minutes. I only needed to keep him occupied for *five* minutes. Holding my phone below the window, I sent the message to my dad.

"There you are, Vi," Bryce greeted, jogging to my car. He flung the door open and extended his arm. "Come join me inside. We need to talk."

"Can't we talk out here?" I asked, eyes darting to the station.

He shook his head and reached out his hand. "I have something to show you."

My mouth went dry and I ignored his gesture. "I'd rather make our conversation quick."

Eyes darkening, he grabbed my arm and curled his fingers. "Come inside," he growled.

Nails dug into my bicep and heat bloomed where the tiny bruises would form. Sweat beaded on my forehead as I grabbed my bag with my other hand and stepped out into the August heat. Mosquitos swarmed around my legs, nibbling at my ankles. I'd rather be bitten a hundred times than spend another second with Bryce.

The plan was to keep him in the open with the station far behind him. When the time came, Dad and Officer Budman would surround him, and he'd have nowhere to run. I was never supposed to go inside.

But I had to. He was not going to take no for an answer. If I didn't comply, he'd know something was up. I needed to stall him for only five minutes. Anxiety trembled my body as he dragged me inside the station, messing up Plan A and jumping right to Plan B.

Hundreds of candles lit the dark hallway. Blankets lined the floor making a fabric red-carpet fit for a homeless princess. Boxes of canned food, water bottles, and paper products lined the back wall.

"Bryce, what is all this?" I asked, dumbfounded. My heavy footsteps echoed between the grimy walls as he continued to lead me down the path.

"You wanted to go camping, so we'll camp here. I've made adjustments to the style, but you'll love it," he said, his voice higher than usual. He let go of my arm. "I did some research on romance and took my findings for this date. I think I need to make some things up to you. "

This is a lie, this is a lie, this is a lie, I thought, clutching my bag. I couldn't fall for his manipulation. His constant flip-flop was why I stayed with him so long. He would be wretched for a week then nice for a day and I would convince myself he wasn't all bad.

But that's what Kayleigh had done. And she was dead.

I halted, straightened my spine, and leveled my tone as I said, "Bryce, I thought I made it clear on the phone I didn't want to see you anymore. Me being here, all this," I waved to the candles melting wax onto the mossy concrete, "does not change anything."

He stopped walking and looked over his shoulder. The candles on the floor darkened his expression. "You were upset, I can look past that," he stated. "Let's have this date and then we'll go back to how things should be." He continued down the hallway.

Again. Again he dismissed my feelings. Everything I said was wrong. He acted like I didn't know what I was talking about. He didn't accept how I actually *felt*. I should've played the part of the old Violetta. I should have simply gone along with him, pretending everything was all right until my dad arrived.

But my heart was finished.

"Bryce, enough," I spat through gritted teeth. "I don't want to be with you anymore."

His foot skidded across the long rug he placed along the platform, fabric bunched beneath his feet. Eyes glanced down at the mess he made. With a slow inhale, he bent down and smoothed it out. Without looking up, he quietly asked, "Is it because of him?"

"Of whom?" I was *not* a cheat.

Standing up straight, he took three steps forward. I held my breath and stood my ground, clutching my bag where a small pocket knife, mirror, and Kayleigh's notebook lay in wait. I never thought I'd be so scared around someone I called my boyfriend.

No. He was anything but my boyfriend.

"You know who I'm talking about," he sneered. "All the pieces add up. This is why you haven't wanted to spend time with me. There is another guy lying to you, making you think your future is brighter without me. Making you think you'll be happier without me."

"I am." The words flew out faster than I could think. Part of me wanted to reach out and grab them. To yank them back and shove them down my throat.

The other part of me was proud for saying them.

Bryce shattered whatever pride I felt. His eyes darkened and his lips formed a straight line. "You *what?*" he growled.

This was it. I had to say it. No one else would say it for me.

"I am happier without you," I stated. Straightening my back, I confessed, "You've hurt me more than you'll ever admit. The only reason I am here is because I'm worried about you. Just because I don't want to be your girlfriend, doesn't mean I want anything bad to happen to you. Just like—"

"The last time I was at a train station?" he asked, arms crossed. "Well, I have a secret I never told you."

My heart thumped in my chest. Every instinct told me to run. Logic told me to get out of there, but I had three minutes left.

And I needed to know the truth.

His eyes darkened as he stepped forward and whispered, "I have a secret you never figured out."

Breath caught in my throat as he kept coming forward. I was forced to back up. Five steps later, I backed against the wall. My grip loosened, dropping my bag to the ground. Cold tile scratched the skin beneath my thin shirt like nails clawing at my body. Goosebumps crawled along my stomach as he leaned his body against mine.

His hand shot out and pressed against the wall. The crack of his palm against the surface echoed down the platform. My cheek was inches away from his forearm.

Leaning forward, he pressed his lips to my ear. "My secret about that night last year?" Hot breath stung my face as he whispered, "I lied."

The weight of a boulder dropped from my head into the pit of my stomach. My body went rigid. Memories trampled the front of my mind. His cracked voice over the phone. The rush of the wind. The train horn blaring in the background. The threat to step onto the tracks.

That was an act?

"W-what?" I croaked.

His head tilted back. A smirk crossed his lips. "You are a people pleaser, Violetta. I knew you would help me. I knew you would be my rock."

Heat crawled up my neck.

He *played* me. He used me.

Water brimmed my eyes. "Why?"

"I don't like to be alone, but I'm picky. Melissa was too feisty. She can only handle me in small doses, and she complains and whines." He shrugged. "You're nicer than that. You're a good little girl that likes to serve so nobody else suffers. Your 'beliefs' are childish and preachy, but I am more understanding than anyone else."

I pinched my eyes shut. Bryce's past remarks swarmed my mind like a hoard of wasps. They stung every inch of my mind with their lies, manipulation, and passive aggressive insults. I uprooted everything I loved for him. I worked my ass off for him. "All this time…" I murmured. "You only want me because I give in easily?"

Bryce trailed his fingers down my arm. Goosebumps rose at his touch. "No, you don't give in easily," he said, "but you want to help. Look at you now? Here when you could've just let me go. You thought I would do something to hurt myself. You couldn't live with that on your conscience, could you? That's why we're the perfect pair." He leaned forward, dark eyes burning a hole through me. "Without me, you'd say yes to every person who asks you to help them cross the street. If you agree to stay, I'll lighten up on these 'insults' or 'remarks,' or whatever you call them. I can change."

I had enough. He insulted everything I stood for. Everything I am.

Everything I want to be.

He couldn't change. And if he could? It wouldn't be me by his side. He needed to find himself on his own. I would not suffer and be hurt day after day anymore.

I shouldn't have to stand up for myself in my relationship.

I was done.

I jammed my palms against his chest and shoved him away. A quiet gasp escaped his lips as he teetered back.

"How *dare* you?" I snarled. Red flickered at the edges of my vision. "I've been nothing but gracious toward you. I've given you countless chances with the hopes that I was helping you."

Unfazed, he straightened his gray polo and tousled his wiry hair. "Violetta, I told you these things so you'd understand. I did all these things for your own good. We're a perfect pair. I leave you alone and you say yes to everything else."

Bile crawled up my throat. My fists shook as the red crawled further across my vision. A *perfect* pair? How was making me shake every time I'm near him *perfect*? How was insulting how I want to live my life *perfect*? How was calling me a liar and a cheat *perfect*?

I had nothing more to say. I turned and began to storm out. I only had two minutes left. I didn't need to wait with him.

"Where are you going?" Bryce called.

"You're *insane*." Fury shook my voice. "I'm going to tell everyone the truth."

"The truth?" He chuckled. "The only truth is you cheated on me so we went to the train station to talk it out. The truth is I did all this to take care of our reputations. If we fix this now, I'll tell everyone I was mistaken."

I didn't stop walking. "I am going to tell everyone the only mistake was you."

Feet shuffled behind me against concrete. My body jerked backward as I reached for the door. A thick arm wrapped around my neck.

The red in my vision turned to stars as the air fought to enter my lungs. My feet lifted off the ground.

Bryce choked me.

I clawed at his arms until blood stained my fingertips. My body thrashed against his, kicking his shins but he wouldn't budge.

"I never wanted to hurt you, Violetta." His hot breath burned my ear. "But you can't go spreading more lies. If you agree not to tell anyone, we can keep going like nothing ever happened."

The final straw. I wouldn't let my end be like Kayleigh's. I wouldn't let anyone else have an end like Kayleigh's.

Bryce wouldn't hurt me or anyone else ever again.

With whatever strength I had left, I raised my leg and drove my feet backward, striking his groin.

Bryce exhaled and I fell forward. My body slipped on the rug. Heat shot through my shoulder as I smashed it against the concrete. I gasped, drinking in the musty air as quickly as possible. I glanced over my shoulder to see Bryce struggling to his feet.

I jumped up, snatched my bag, and ran forward, shoving my body into the double doors.

He locked them.

Stomach clenched, I spun around and bolted off the platform and down the tracks. There was an opening into the forest at the end of the building. I had remembered that from our first date. I wished I had used it to escape him then.

Crashing out the back door, I bolted into the woods.

I failed both Plan A and B. I couldn't survive five minutes.

Only two plans left.

The wind whipped through my ginger curls. The curls I loved but Bryce claimed were a nuisance and never looked right.

My heart wanted to burst out of my ribcage and splatter itself against the trees. The forest would drink it up, staining their leaves red.

Five words ran through my mind: Am I going to die?

Tears glinted against my cheeks in the afternoon sun. Sweat beaded on my skin and my shirt clung to my back. I clutched my bag to my chest.

"Violetta!" Bryce bellowed. Leaves crunched as he chased after me. He was bigger and faster. He'd catch up to me soon. "Where is there to run to? I'm the one who knows the way back from the station."

No, he didn't. He'd never been outside longer than a few hours. He knew the forest as much as he knew me: not at all.

My legs burned as I raced faster and faster through the woods. My sisters and a forest ranger waited for me at the base of the mountain. I only needed to get there. Then, I'd be safe. Then, I'd be free.

Bryce's voice melted away until I only heard the beating of my heart.

The terrain shifted from level to uneven and rocky. An unexpected dip in elevation ruined my pace. My legs gave way and I tumbled down the path, smacking against a fallen tree branch. My bag flew from my hands and I sprawled across the dirt. Stinging shot up my leg and my shoulder throbbed. I couldn't believe I succumbed to the classic maiden-running-away-in-the-woods cliché.

Red streaked down my right leg. A gash dug into my thigh. Thick blood pooled out.

Grimacing, I dragged myself over to my things. I grabbed my phone with shaking hands. The glass cracked and the screen glitched on the camera setting. The red circle blinked *RECORD* at the top, showing a time stamp of four minutes. An accidental video of blackness. I stopped it and tried to call my dad, but four words appeared on screen: *Call Failed. No Service.*

I choked back a sob.

I thrust my useless device back into my bag along with the once white notebook. I clenched the pocketknife in my fist and slashed at my shirt. I sloppily wrapped it around my leg and pulled it taut. With a wince, I tightened and tied it.

Bryce's screams bounced between the trees until it shook my soul. Rage laced every note.

I bit the knife between my teeth and grabbed onto the nearest tree, yanking myself to my feet. I couldn't stop. I needed to keep going.

"*Violetta!*" he bellowed.

Panic shot adrenaline through my limbs. I couldn't give up on Plan C yet. My sisters were so close. I feared shouting for them and giving away my location to Bryce. Dragging my foot, I hobbled through the forest until I reached a dangerous footpath. The side of the mountain tapered down to my left. If I slid, I'd tumble down into bushes far below. Teary eyes darted between the trees, trying to find a better way out. There wasn't. With the mountain at my back, I side-stepped across the path.

Fire shot up my limbs. Warm blood pooled down my leg. I wanted to sit, close my eyes, and rest, but I was almost there.

Footsteps closed in behind me. "You can't run," he snarled. Branches snapped as he ran forward. A hand snatched at my hair.

Squealing, I flung my left arm back, trying to strike him with the knife. He shoved my arm upward and I lost my footing, slipping off the path. Rocks scraped my back and fear powered my screams as I slid down the mountain. Digging my heels into the dirt, I slowed my descent until I reached the bottom.

Air escaped my lungs and I couldn't get it back. The world spun around me as my body succumbed to gravity. Stars flickered in front of my darkening vision. For an instant, I thought I saw a man between the trees. Dry lips parted, I whispered, "Second?"

The image disappeared instantly.

Tears cut through the dirt on my cheeks. Of course, it wasn't you, Second. I needed to do this myself. You couldn't help me.

"Stay there. I'm going to get you," Bryce shouted down the hill.

"Leave me alone!" I screamed. Flipping myself onto my stomach, I dragged myself along the ground. I needed to hide.

A few feet in front of me was a small cave carved into the cliffside. Dark, eerie. A place where monsters lie in wait for night to fall.

I'd rather be with monsters than a devil like Bryce.

I dragged my exhausted body into the cold hole no larger than a crawl space. Rocks and branches clawed at my stomach. Damp air pricked my skin. Something brushed against my ankles.

A scream caught in my throat when I heard him.

"This is a mistake, Vi," Bryce called. "I wasn't going to hurt you, I just wanted to knock some sense into you. When you woke up, you would've felt better."

I bit my lip until I tasted blood. I wanted to scream and swear and cry, but silence would be my saving grace.

Bryce shouted louder than the screams in my mind: "You are mine." Three wrong words break a heart. "The only one I'll love." Five wrong words consume a soul. "No man or forest will ever take you from me." Ten wrong words last eternity.

The moment he said the tenth word, my heart clenched.

This was it.

Plan A, B, and C failed.

The only one left was Z. The one I didn't tell anyone about. The one I kept tucked away in my heart. The one I never wanted to come to fruition.

Trembling hands fumbled into my bag and took out the mirror first. Praying, hoping, wishing for a miracle. I opened the case.

Only my reflection stared back.

Second wasn't with me. No ghost was there to stop Bryce from finding me. No ghost was there to give me advice or tell me it would be okay.

I was alone.

Sobs stuck in my throat as I pulled out the white notebook and black pen.

I wrote.

This letter is my Plan Z. My evidence. If Bryce finds me in this cave and kills me, let this be the evidence that locks him away.

Then, my story will end almost like Kayleigh's.

The difference? There was no ghost trying to save me.

At first, these letters were filled with hope and love. I wrote these letters to a man I thought would save me.

Then, I forgot I can't put my trust in people or magic or ghosts.

I can only trust two things:

God and myself.

I neglected both of them for a while.

So this letter isn't for Second anymore.

It's for me.

Violetta,

You're more amazing than you could ever know.

God created you in His image, blessing you with talents you should be proud of. Your fiery red hair was designed so you could set the world ablaze. Your big heart was meant to envelop those who needed it. But your mind is there to make sure you keep yourself safe.

Bryce was a fool for trying to take away who you are.

Second was a man who died due to a situation you could never have controlled. His ghost was meant to bring you joy, but never more than that. You weren't meant to fall in love with him. He showed you the kind of man you sought after. Second was meant to open your eyes to the devil lurking within Bryce. Second was never meant to save you.

Violetta, you're meant to save yourself even if that means asking for help.

You are so much more than what everyone thinks of you.

You are so much more than those past mistakes.

Violetta, I forgive you for not thinking of your safety sooner.

I forgive you for not caring for yourself as much as you should.

Violetta, I love you.

I love the fat rolls along your stomach. I love when you wear your favorite blue dress. I love the way the light speckles in your eyes when you look in the mirror. I love the way you sing off-key and draw wild creatures and fire arrows against the wind. I love the passion you have for your Faith and family, and how you would do anything for them.

Violetta, thank you for being you.

Sincerely,
Yourself

August 2 - Night

Second,

I am alive.

I passed out in the cave after finishing my letters, but they found me hours later. I am on my way to the hospital.

They found Bryce and have taken him into custody.

I get to live another day, but I'm handing off this notebook to someone I trust for now. I wanted to let you know although it doesn't matter. You won't answer me anyway.

I've given up on you, but now I know to never give up on myself.

Still breathing.

Violetta

August 5

Dear Kayleigh,

This is Margot. I hope you're here too, reading the letters in this white notebook. I know you roam the earth until a new girl writes.

Well, she wrote.

My beloved niece wrote for years and years. From the time she knew what love meant until the day her heart shattered into a million pieces.

She wrote. You answered through someone named Second, even though pain came as a price.

But her life is more valuable than the pain it will bear.

So, thank you.

You've done it. You've saved at least one from befalling the same fate as you. I know it was you who turned Violetta's camera on. It was you who captured the evidence of Bryce's manipulation and murderous intent.

You can go Home now, Kayleigh.

But I have one request before you go.

The ghost, Second. It seems like he and Violetta never had a chance to say goodbye. I know God granted you the grace to bring them together.

Kayleigh, grant my niece closure. When I visited her in the hospital, she wept for this man she never met. The man I claimed would save her.

I let her down. My broken heart only saw you in her that I was blind to seeing the true Violetta.

Let her speak to Second one final time: for my sake and hers. Her heart yearns for a man like him, but she feels he betrayed her. Surely it was not his intent, but Violetta's spirit shattered.

Please, Kayleigh, grant Violetta a final encounter with this soul.

Then, you may go in peace, glorifying God in your afterlife.

Until we meet again.

Your dear sister,
Margot

August 9

Second,

I didn't want to write to you anymore, because I don't need to.

Bryce is out of my life. I am alive.

No thanks to you.

My dad and Officer Budman found Bryce wandering around the woods, screaming and swearing. He was apprehended and will be charged for assault. My phone camera turned on miraculously and captured the audio of the entire exchange between Bryce and me. The video, my testimony, my family's witnesses, Officer Budman, and some excerpts of the letter I wrote in the cave were enough to convict him.

Aunt Margot believes God granted Kayleigh the ability to turn it on. However it happened, I would drop to my knees again and again before the cross, thanking Him for my life.

And I thank myself for not surrendering to Bryce. I thank myself for finally standing up.

I should've done it a long time ago, but I'm blessed to have it now. My freedom is sweeter than honey and my voice sings louder than the birds in the forest.

I left the hospital yesterday. The surgeons stitched up my thigh gash. It would be difficult to walk for a while, but it would heal in time. Under normal circumstances, I would've been released within 12 hours of receiving stitches. Night terrors tethered me to the hospital bed until I stopped screaming while I slept. The police and my new therapist visited my bedside several times a day before releasing me.

Now, I finally lay in my own bed, wounded leg elevated. I hold my notebook above my head and write to you because Margot asked me to. I doubt you'll reply.

So here it goes:

"Second, Second, Second."

> I'm here, please. I don't know how long it's been, but I promise you. It was only a day, and I have a good explanation.

My heart thumps in my chest. Aunt Margot keeps her promises.

Unlike you, but I'll never write these things in a way you will see. I remember you're dead, Second. I remember you're a ghost.

But that doesn't make it hurt any less.

"You promised."

> I know, I didn't mean it.

"You told me to do this! Then you leave me for almost a month."

You told me to break up with Bryce: solid advice. You also told me to call out for you when I needed you: you lied.

> I couldn't come visit you. I had to take care of a kid.

"You had to take care of a kid. He had to take care of his reputation. Men and their excuses."

My bitter heart scribbles the words faster than my brain can comprehend. I know you're a ghost. I know you're dead. But I'm not talking about the Second who died at a young age. My heart weeps for him and the life that was stolen.

I'm talking to the Second that made me a promise and broke it. No matter what, I will stand up for myself.

I wish you the best, but I will tell you the truth.

> What did he do to you?

A sentence I didn't think would wrap itself around my heart. In the back of my mind I hear sadness woven between the words of this sentence. A question so real I could reach out and feel it beneath my fingertips.

"He told everyone I was crazy and then went berserk. He thought I cheated on him."

Why would he think that?

"Because of you."

The truth. The short honest truth. My heart was elsewhere when it was with Bryce. My heart fluttered across planes of existence and settled with you, Second.

How is it my fault?

My heart clenches. Five wrong words consume a soul. There were so many ways to ask that question. So many ways to mend this broken relationship.

It hits me now.

That is what this is, isn't it?

I finally admitted it to myself. Now, I'll admit it to you.

"How is it *your* fault? You finally show up after ten years of writing to you. You tell me things I only prayed to hear. You give me the most honest advice I've heard. One that resonates with what my heart has been telling me."

Your list sounds like all good things I've done.

"They are, stupid. You don't get it, do you?"

Please, tell me what I don't get. Why do those things hurt you?

"You are an idiot. I've waited for years. And I've loved you since the beginning."

It was true. I fell for a ghost because he showed me what love can be.

Second, you showed me kindness, compassion, and care. I had never been treated like that.

But now I have to move on.

Y-you have?

"I told my boyfriend that I had found someone better. I couldn't tell him the truth… But withholding it didn't do me any good."

I can't say more. I can't tell you I was strangled. I can't tell you I ran for my life through a darkening forest until I took shelter in a snake infested cave.

I don't know what to say.

"How about an apology? Step off your high horse and apologize."

I am sorry.

Finally.

Tears stream down my face. This is all I ever wanted, wasn't it? I've only wanted someone to know how I feel. I've only wanted someone to look at me and say those three words.

Kayleigh wrote in this notebook that three words break a heart.

Well, three mend a heart as well.

Bryce never apologized. Those who hurt me because of their insecurities never apologized. Those who trampled my heart underfoot never apologized.

But Second did.

And I couldn't be more grateful.

Wait.

"I've been waiting long enough. Come find me."

September 10

To whom it may concern,

Today is my birthday. A day to rejoice for the life God breathed into my lungs. A day to reflect on years past and look ahead at what my future will hold.

I haven't written letters because I lost sight of who these were for. Words can mend hearts and break them. They can shatter souls and glue them back together with gold, making them brighter than ever. After that incident, I claimed I had written enough letters to last a lifetime.

But today, I've made an exception.

The Grand Little Lives charity gala finally arrived. The Senior Event Manager strode through the ballroom, directing vendors to set up.

And that person was me.

Lucio chose me for the role not only because of my past successes but because of the excitement and anticipation of what I'll accomplish next. I couldn't be more grateful.

Delicate blue tulle draped from the sparkling chandeliers until they fell like hair along the stone pillars. A sea of black and white shuffled along the polished dance floor as wait staff made final preparations. Round tables adorned with floral centerpieces made a U shape around the room.

Everything as I had planned.

Three claps erupted behind me. I looked back to see my boss, Lucio.

"Well done, Violetta." His grin reached his eyes. "We have a full house. I am sure Grand Little Lives will have thousands of donations tonight."

My cheeks warmed at his kudos. I couldn't be more grateful for a boss who believed in me even when there were moments I didn't believe in myself. "The small vendors helped bring the numbers up."

"All thanks to you and your practical thinking. Now, I must ask." He plucked small hors d'oeuvres from a shuffling waiter. "Chicken and waffles?"

I inhaled the scent of maple syrup, drinking every ounce of sweetness. My stomach growled and I held back the urge to snatch it from my boss and eat it myself.

"One of my favorite foods—besides french fries, of course."

"Well, we have potatoes too, I saw." He sniffed the bite-sized snack like a police dog sensing a threat. "You think these will be a hit? They're not very posh." He accented the last word like a snobby grandmother in a British drama.

I smirked. "Try it first. People don't want to eat snails, trust me."

"All right." He opened wide and popped the whole treat into his mouth. His pensive face relaxed and his eyes rolled back. "Delicious," he said with a slight moan. "I won't doubt you again."

"Good choice." I winked and left to finish preparations.

Not shortly after, guests pooled into the mansion like kids arriving for their first day of school. Their outfits were pressed and clean, ready to make a good first impression. They exchanged friendly glances and mingled slowly. Once I came around and introduced myself, their shoulders relaxed. Soon, the ballroom burst with conversation and energy.

The DJ played upbeat music during cocktail hour. Some donors tapped their feet or swayed to the rhythm of the music, eager to dance.

I walked by a group shuffling to the bassline. I recognized the man in the center as the representative for our local airline. He was a last minute connection, but I recalled he was a joy to chat with.

I slid into their group and copied their dance moves as the DJ turned the music up ever so slightly.

"Are we warming up for later?" I asked with a smile.

They chuckled and nodded as their moves became more dated featuring the sprinkler and charlie brown. I left them to their dancing as I floated about to ensure the evening ran smoothly.

"Hey, Violetta!"

I turned to see my cousin Brigid running up to me. She looked gorgeous in her peach wrap dress and her perfect curls.

I sucked in a breath to embrace her lightly. Her gentle touch sent a shockwave of danger signals to my brain. I had to repeat to myself that she was my cousin and I wasn't in danger. Cautiously, I gave her a brief hug. "I'm glad you made it."

She pulled away and mouthed, *Oh my gosh*. "I can't believe your boss gave us tickets to come to this event!"

"Well, technically your dad purchased them. My sisters are the only ones here for free." I looked around. "Speaking of, didn't they come with you?"

She chuckled. "They're already bombarding all the waiters." She pointed.

I followed her finger over my shoulder to see Aria and Eleora tag-teaming to gather the most amount of snacks off the wait staff's platters before they turned around. Felicity sat at the table with a notebook, clearly keeping score. Sage kept her head down; red flushed her cheeks. My parents had no knowledge of this while they chatted with a couple at the next table.

Joy sparked in my chest. My sisters enjoyed my work. This gala was something I planned. An event I created.

All I wanted was to see people happy.

I pointed to Aria who snatched a handful of grilled-cheese shooters off the platter of a distracted waiter. "You better head onto the floor, Brigid, before my sisters eat all the food."

"I told them to save some for me and my parents." She chuckled. "I can't say the same for my siblings, though."

I looked past her to see a group of four guys greeting each other in the doorway. It was hard to make out their faces and appearances with the flow of guests passing through. However, fiery ginger hair stuck out like a beacon on a foggy shore. My cousin, Riley: Brigid's older brother.

"Who are those guys with Riley?" I asked, jerking my chin to the door.

She didn't look over her shoulder. "Some super cute guys he doesn't want to introduce me to. He hates when I'm interested in any of his friends." Her hands clasped her cheeks. "It's *killing* me because he knows so many guys and he won't share."

I tried to hold back a chuckle but it slipped through my lips. A genuine laugh erupted from my belly. For the first time in a while, happy tears brimmed my eyes.

"Why are you laughing?" Brigid pouted.

"I am so sorry, I don't know." I wiped my eyes. "I think I just needed to laugh."

A smile crept across her lips. "I'm glad I could help." Before walking away, she added genuinely, "Also, in case no one will tell you tonight; you look absolutely beautiful."

I flattened the creases in my favorite blue floor length dress. The one where I felt like the Scottish princess. The one that fell around my body like it was sewn just for me. The one where I felt truly, absolutely, unapologetically Violetta. "Thank you, girlie." I leaned in and whispered, "I know."

Brigid chuckled and left to rejoin my family.

The night proceeded as planned. Donors ate and drank. Lucio walked up on stage. The DJ handed off the microphone and left to take a break.

My boss tapped the mic three times and began the official donation call. The current numbers projected on the walls beside him. Amidst his speech were videos of the charity at work, testimonies, and quotes from children it had helped that would make any Scrooge offer a plate of gold.

Pride coursed through my veins when the uplighting flashed a rainbow of colors and acclaims filled the ballroom. We met the goal. Grand Little Lives received over $30,000 in less than three hours. Applause thundered through the ballroom like during a rainstorm.

My parents appeared next to me with bright smiles spread across their faces.

Love flickered in my mom's eyes. "I am so proud of you,

Violetta," she signed.

Joy washed over me like a tidal wave, cleansing my soul. It took me a near-death experience to realize how a few words from my mother could heal a thousand cuts on my heart. I wouldn't take her for granted again.

My dad outstretched his arms, waiting for permission to give a hug. My heart fluttered a moment. His understanding knowing that I don't like to be squeezed tightly anymore shoved the painful memories away. I leaned forward and his hands gently pressed against my back.

His strong voice softened as he said, "We sure are proud, Little Sparkle. Our Braveheart."

"I hope the other Sparkles are just as proud," I half-teased. My sisters had never outwardly said the words, but I could tell by reading their faces. I looked over at the table to see three of them flashing smiles or giving thumbs-ups.

I waved and mouthed, "Save me extra dessert."

My mom looked over and pointed as she counted my siblings. "Where is Aria?" she signed.

Dad looked over his shoulder. "Oh, she must be with my brother or the cousins. Violetta, if you see her with him, please tell her to come back soon?"

I sighed. "You two are such worry warts, but yes, I will."

Mom pursed her lips. "You know the mischief she's capable of alone. She still needs close watch."

"Oh, I'm aware of her shenanigans," I replied with a small smile. Extending my arms, I sucked in a breath and gave them both one final hug before they left to return to their seats. The cheers started to dwindle, so I waved at the stage, giving Lucio the cue to leave.

But the DJ wasn't there to take over. He hadn't returned from his break.

My eyes widened and I frantically mouthed, "Keep it going. DJ is gone."

Perplexed, Lucio glanced over his shoulder. His eyebrows shot up and his lips formed an *o*. "Thank you all so much, I don't know how many times I can say this, but I will say it many times within the next few minutes."

I nodded and slipped out to find Kirk who was responsible for keeping tabs on the DJ.

I shut the ballroom doors behind me and shouted, "Where is the DJ?"

I heard murmurs in the hallway. A flash of ginger revealed Riley hung out in the foyer with his friends. I assumed they waited until the donation call was over. I didn't blame them. The donation goal is intimidating for a young adult. I wouldn't have been able to give much either.

I shuffled down the halls. "Kirk?" I couldn't run; my leg throbbed. I pushed away the pain and did my best to mask a limp, but I couldn't race through the mansion.

"Yeah, yeah, keep your skirt on Ms. Sparks," Kirk grumbled. "He just had to take a smoke break, all right?"

"Kirk, just go find him!" I snapped. I tried to quicken my pace, passing the door to the foyer. I didn't have time to say hi to Riley just yet. Things started to run off the timeline; I needed to fix it.

"Ugh, fine!" Kirk groaned and spun around to retrieve the DJ outside.

"Thank you!" I glanced down the halls and caught another glimpse of ginger. Giggles floated through the air. I assumed it was Riona and Niall. Aria must've been with them. That was another issue I didn't want to handle. With the DJ missing, I didn't want to deal with any mischief she may have been a part of with my cousins. I turned the corner to stop them, but they disappeared. "Ugh, now where is my sister? She was supposed to be with Uncle Rowan."

I spun around and peered down the corridor. Riona spotted me. I waved for her to stop so I could catch up, but she gasped and ducked around the corner, disappearing back into the corridor. Heat flushed my cheeks. "She was supposed to wait!"

I headed toward the ballroom, passing by where Riley and his friends hid. I could've sworn he called for me, but I wouldn't have known. My cousin never actually remembered my name. Our names get jumbled in his brain. I don't think he has ever gotten it right.

"Wait, Ms. Sparks!" someone called.

"I'm done waiting!" I shouted without thinking. I thought it was

Kirk, telling me to wait for the DJ to finish his pack of the day.

Five feet stood between me and the ballroom when that voice called again. This time, it stopped me. Three words ensnared my heart, yanking me backwards until I stood still.

"Please, I'm sorry!"

I exhaled and relaxed my shoulders. When I turned around, I didn't know who I would find.

My eyes fell upon the face of someone I never thought I'd see.

A tall lean man with a dark brown beard and neatly combed hair stood in the doorway. His crisp white button-up rolled to the elbows. A light blue tie hung from his neck. Thick lips parted, words desperately trying to escape.

My breath caught in my throat when I met his gaze. One blue eye sparkled. Darkness covered the other.

He wore an eyepatch.

Every step forward was like trudging through quicksand, but if I stood still I thought I'd sink. I stopped before him and looked up at his face. My eyes ran along every feature. The small scattered freckles on his forehead from days in the sunshine. Creases by his eye from grinning—whether they were real smiles or not. His breathing quickened and he bit his lip.

I couldn't fathom any of it. "Wh-what? Wh-who?" I grabbed my curls, entangling my fingers. I wanted to yank the strands out of my head. I couldn't comprehend the man standing in front of me. "A-Are you?" I glanced up at him again. His gaze never left my face. I felt him study me, trying to soak in my essence. My body acted before my mind could think. I raised a hand, fingers spread apart to touch him. To feel him. I needed to know this wasn't a dream. I needed to know the man standing before me was tangible.

I needed to know he *wasn't* a ghost.

My mind thought better of it and I stopped, inches away from his cheek.

The man gave a small smile. He took my hand, wrapping his fingers around my palm.

Electricity shot through my body. The jolt traveled from my fingers down to my toes. It warmed my belly and made my heart flutter. His hands were calloused, but his touch was soft and gentle. It was a support I didn't know I needed. A feeling I didn't realize I craved.

My breath hitched in my chest. I couldn't speak.

He squeezed my hand. "I-I'm sorry, Ms. Sparks." His breath smelled sweet of maple syrup and bourbon. Gently, he pressed my hand against his face.

A hundred volts shocked my heart. The scruff of his beard like soft wool beneath my hand. I couldn't believe I was caressing the cheek of a stranger. And yet, I felt like I knew him my whole life.

I drank in the scent and sight of him. It didn't feel real, and yet it felt more real than anything I had experienced the past summer. Was he what I prayed to be real as I wrote letters every day?

My heart thumped repeatedly against my ribcage when the word finally escaped my lips: "Second?"

His lips parted and his breath caught in his throat. Goosebumps trailed along his neck.

He was *alive*.

Peace flooded my soul. My anxieties and fear melted away like wax. The feeling was a fire that I wouldn't ever let extinguish.

"Nice to finally meet you, Second." I gently pressed my fingers against his cheek. Lightning crackled beneath my palm. "My name is Violetta Sparks."

Then, he said ten words that I prayed would last eternity:

"I'm Mason Piccirillo the Second. I've been waiting for you."

My breath caught in my chest. The air stilled and sparks flickered in the corners of my vision. I had nothing to say and so much all at once. I wanted to disappear in that moment with him.

But a voice snapped me back into the present. "Ms. Sparks!" Kirk hissed. "I found him. Go let Lucio know he's back."

I shook my head and pulled my hand away, sparks tingling my fingertips. Sadness hung in Second's/Mason's eye when I pulled away. "I-I'm so sorry," I apologized. "Are you in a rush to leave?"

He shook his head. "No, I'll wait for you."

Five words ignited my soul. My heart fluttered faster than a hundred butterflies. "I'll be right back." I spun on my heel and retreated to the ballroom.

A few donors started to nod off as Lucio dragged on and on about a story of him living in NYC and being chased by a dozen rats.

That story was not appropriate for this event, so I waved my arms and caught his attention.

His story trailed off and he glanced over his shoulder. "And those rats didn't know what hit 'em. But I've babbled long enough. Let's celebrate, shall we?"

Applause erupted as the DJ played a steady beat. A swarm of color invaded the dance floor as the volume increased. Hundreds of bodies converged and moved to the music.

A flash of color burst through the door as Aria, Riona, and Niall rushed into the crowd. Three teenagers mingled and danced with a sea of business professionals.

"Hey, Corporate Cousin!"

I turned around to see my cousin Riley walking back into the ballroom with three guys in tow.

My heart flipped when I saw Second/Mason behind him.

I crossed my arms. "Riley, do you actually know my name?"

"Uh, duh, of course I do." He brushed the ginger curls out of his eyes. "I just wanted to see if you would respond to my nickname."

"Yeah, okay." I looked past him and waved at the others. "Hi, I'm Violetta Sparks, in case he never told you my real name. Glad you could make it."

"Thank you for hosting." A tall man with smooth black skin extended his hand. After a moment, I shook it and he added, "You've done a wonderful job. My name is Jason Bancroft."

"Wow, so formal, thank you!" I elbowed my cousin. "You should learn from Jason."

"That's the most I've heard him speak in one sentence, so it takes a while for me to learn," Riley joked.

Jason Bancroft rolled his eyes but said nothing.

"I'm Theo, by the way." The other flashed a toothy smile. He had tan skin and curly hair that sat atop his head but faded into a close shave by his ears. "We all know your cousin from camp."

"Really?" My eyes darted to Second who gave a small smile. In our letters, he told me he worked at a Summer camp. He told me his co-captain's name was Anderson.

Second worked at camp with *my cousin*?

I cleared my throat. "Uh, Theo, your last name wouldn't happen to be Anderson, would it?"

His eyebrows shot up. "Yeah, it is! Has your cousin mentioned me before?" His back straightened and he fixed his appearance.

"Someone did, I'm pretty sure." My head swam with the memories of the ghostly letters. "Remind me of the camp's name again? Deerfoot?"

Second/Mason laughed. "Close. It's Southpaw."

His laugh made my face flush red. I hoped they didn't notice. "And I met you, Second—or Mason—however you'd like to be called."

"Mason?" Riley spun and looked at his friends. "That's your first name? Really?"

"What's that supposed to mean?" Second/Mason countered.

"You're just so cool, I thought it was something like Octavius or Gerard or something. Not 'Mason'." Riley made air quotes.

"Wow, you've known me for how long, Sparks, and you've never remembered my real first name?" Second/Mason crossed his arms. I tried to keep my eyes from darting to the muscles bulging beneath his rolled up sleeves. "Violetta, feel free to call me either," he said.

"I'll start with Second, if that works." I smiled, ignoring my fluttering heart and heated cheeks. "And if it makes you feel any better, I don't think he remembered which one I was until I introduced myself to you three." I waved my hand at the guys.

Riley was about to speak before Jason put a hand on his shoulder and shook his head. Knowing the meaning of the small gesture, Riley shut his trap.

I was impressed. It's hard to get him to stop talking.

I clapped my hands together. "Well, feel free to mingle with some of the others a bit and dance. We'll have the music playing for another forty-five minutes or so. I might go find something to eat while the guests are preoccupied."

They nodded and Riley tried to pat my shoulder on his way to the dance floor, but I shifted. I didn't mean to evade him, but I was still squeamish about people touching me.

Except Second, apparently.

Second walked past me, but paused. The muscles in his broad back tensed. After a moment, he turned around and came back. "Is it okay if I go get some snacks with you?"

My face beamed. "That sounds good to me."

We turned and walked—well, I limped—over to the bar where a few others sat chatting. There was only one stool left. Second stepped ahead of me and kindly asked if one of the guests could scoot over. Then, he pulled the barstool out and gestured for me to sit.

I paused, confused by the gentlemanly offer. My throbbing leg didn't want me to refuse. It had been about a month, but the pain lingered.

Second stood beside me and waved to the bartender. "I'll have a bourbon and cola. And…" He looked at me. "Would you like anything to drink?"

I smiled. He asked me what I'd like. He didn't decide for me. He didn't point out how much sugar was in a cocktail. He simply asked.

"Yes, I'd love a Vodka Cran please."

The bartender nodded and theatrically retrieved the glasses and began making the drinks.

"Ooh, good choice," Second said, resting his forearms on the counter. He stood to my right so I could see his beautiful blue eye.

I tried not to stare, but there was no way I couldn't. He was *here*. He was real.

And he was really hot.

We sat in silence for a moment as the bartender poured my red liquid from the shaker into a tall glass. I thanked him and held the cool drink between my sweating hands.

I needed to say something. In my letters, I was angry with him. I was emotional, stressed. I couldn't understand this miracle—if that's what I can call it—granted to me.

But I didn't want to think about the reason why. I couldn't tell him about Bryce. Even though I've felt like I've known him forever, I couldn't tell him the truth. Not now. Not here.

I cleared my throat. "Second, um, I'm so happy you're not—"

"A ghost?" he finished. He fidgeted with a paper napkin nervously.

I turned to face him. "Yes!" I glanced over his shoulder and whispered. "I thought you were dead."

He laughed. "I thought you were dead, too."

I never thought I'd exchange those words with a stranger. I rested my forehead in my hand. "Ugh, my brain hurts trying to think about it."

"Maybe, we shouldn't think about it just yet?" His face softened. "I wasn't there for you when I promised, and I don't understand it." He thanked the bartender and took his drink. "For *ducks* sake, I thought the alcohol messed with my head, but here you are."

I laughed at his fake-swear-word. "And here I am." I took a big sip. The sweetness of the cranberry coated my tongue. The bartender went a little heavy handed on the vodka. My stomach clenched at the thought of losing myself, but I felt safe here. I wasn't drinking to drown out sorrows or for liquid courage as the bartender at the bowling alley recommended. I enjoyed a cocktail with someone who I was excited to spend time with.

"So," Second started. "I think let's save the big questions for another day. Can you tell me about tonight? How has it been going?"

I smiled, grateful for the conversation pivot. I wasn't talking to someone I thought was dead. I wasn't talking to someone I poured my heart to over and over.

I was talking to a guy at a bar on my birthday.

And I was happy.

We had two drinks, snacked on leftover chicken and waffles, and laughed at memories from the night. I told him about how the food tasting was my favorite part, Second told me about his encounters with some of the guests, and he shared a bit more about his friends.

The DJ lowered the music to a soft steady beat. He did it a few times throughout the night to allow couples to dance as if it was a wedding. "This is the last one of the night," he announced. "So if you came here with someone, this is your last chance before going back to the kids at home."

I laughed and looked over as the guests moved two-by-two onto the floor. Dancing was something I always enjoyed, but Bryce hated it.

Upbeat, slowdance, none of it.

I shook my head. Bryce was gone. The trials were over. I didn't have to think about him anymore. He was locked away but will the painful memories ever leave me alone?

That was for me to decide now, I suppose.

Second cleared his throat. "Um, Violetta."

I turned to him, our faces a little closer than before. I could feel his breath on my lips. My body shaked as his gaze darted from my eyes to my mouth. An invisible string pulled me toward him.

With a steady gaze, he said five words: "Would you like to dance?" He offered his hand.

My heart fluttered and I replied with three: "I'd love to."

I put my fingers in his palm and my body tingled at our touch. He helped me down from the chair. If he noticed my limp, he didn't say anything. Gently, he wove us through the couples until we were in the center of the floor, away from the eyes of anyone we knew.

He lifted our clasped hands, hiding the scars scattered across my palm. "Is it okay if I–" His other palm hovered at my side.

A lump caught in my throat. After last month, my body has never been more sensitive to touch. I wanted him to touch me, to pull me close, but I was afraid of how my body would react. The image of Bryce flickered before my eyes, but I shoved it aside. It was time for new memories.

I took a deep breath. "Yes, gently please."

Concern flickered in Second's eye. "Of course." His palm pressed to my side and he gingerly pulled me closer.

Electricity crackled at his touch. My body lightened as we swayed back and forth. If you asked me last year how I would feel dancing with a stranger, I probably would've said "weird" or "awkward." But with Second? It wasn't. We weren't good, but we didn't care. We awkwardly shuffled, but his strength kept the weight off my bad leg, making me feel light as a cloud.

We chatted like old friends during the song, confessing neither of us had done this before. He laughed at my jokes, matched my sarcasm, and made me feel human.

He made me feel loved.

The world faded away. No guests danced beside us. No coworkers shuffled behind the scenes. No family members watched. No memories of Bryce tugged at the corners of my mind.

It was just me and Second in the ballroom.

I didn't want the moment to end, and he didn't either. His grip tightened on my waist as he pressed me closer to him. His strong body comforted my shaking frame.

He leaned over. His lips gently pressed against my ear as he whispered, "Is this okay?"

My stomach flipped and red crawled up my face as his strong body pressed against mine. "Y-yes, thank you."

We moved in a rhythm I couldn't explain. Our feet knew how to work in tandem like a duo that performed together for years. Not a very good dancing duo, but one all the same.

I studied his strong face. The scruffy beard. The lights sparkled in his eye as he looked at me intently. I couldn't break his gaze.

He sucked in a little breath. Gently, he brought our hands closer to his face. The hairs on my neck stood up as the heat of his cheek radiated against my fingers. We swayed back and forth for a moment before he closed his eye, and sweetly pressed his lips to my wrist.

My heart exploded. Electricity sparked down my veins until my soul was aflame. The softest, sweetest, gesture made me become a puddle at his feet. I wanted nothing more than to melt into him.

He smiled, pulling his lips away. "You've done a great job tonight."

My breath hitched. A gentle kiss, a proud compliment. My broken heart never held so much, but I craved even more. "Thank you so much."

The song crescendoed and the music morphed into something a little more upbeat. I didn't want to let go. I wanted to lean into him and become enveloped in his embrace, but my sisters would be back to dance any second. They never missed the last song. Reluctantly I stepped back but didn't let go of his hand just yet. His fingers were gentle against my skin. His nails didn't dig into my palm to keep me from escaping. Second's grasp made me feel safe.

He parted his lips to speak but Anderson crashed into his side. His hand slipped out of mine and my heart skipped, wanting to take it back.

"Heyyy, dude! There you are. You ditched usss." Anderson's words slurred and one of his eyes twitched. He didn't realize that he had interrupted our dance.

Second shrugged. "Well, you found me now."

I laughed away the quiet envy threatening to take over my mind. "I should probably go and finish up the night. You guys enjoy the last dance." I spun and took a step forward, but paused. Throwing a glance over my shoulder, I said, "Second, feel free to find me after. I have something for you."

His eyebrow raised and a smile spread across his face. "Of course! I'll be right there."

I disappeared down the hallway. My racing heart couldn't slow-down. Anxiety, joy, worry swirled in my body. I didn't know how to react to everything that just happened.

An employee in a shiny black tux stood behind the glossy coat check table. I approached and asked for my bag. He nodded and retrieved it after a few moments of searching through the back. Tossing the thin strap over my shoulder, I went down the hall to a bench beside a floor length mirror. I glanced at my reflection and smiled. I felt confident even though my cheeks were flushed and my fiery hair frizzed from a night of running back and forth.

I plopped my bag onto the seat and slid out the white notebook. I opened to the first page where Kayleigh's last words stared back:

Three wrong words break a heart.

Five wrong words consume a soul.

Ten wrong words last eternity.

"Thanks, Kayleigh. I hope you're safe now," I whispered. Paper flapped as I flipped to the very back. I tore out a page and scribbled my phone number on it.

"Violetta!" Second called.

My head snapped up to watch him jog over with the excitement of a golden retriever that found a bone. Adorable.

He quickly peered into the mirror and ran his fingers through his hair. I couldn't help but smile. Clearing his throat, he said, "Sorry, uh, you said you had something for me?"

"I do." I folded the paper and pushed myself off the bench to stand. My own reflection caught my eyes but I resisted the urge to fix my dress. "This is for you." I held the note between my first finger and thumb.

Eyebrows raised, he reached for it. As he touched it, a flash caught the corner of my eye. Chills ran up my spine. The hair on the back of my neck rose. Second must have felt it, too, because he sucked in a deep breath. We turned to look at the mirror.

I clamped my mouth shut to keep from screaming.

Two ghosts stared back at us.

I maintained my gaze as my heart thumped loud in my chest. Two full body phantoms stood in the mirror. Second and my reflections were muddled shadows through their golden transparent bodies. Tremors shot down my limbs as my brain tried to comprehend what we were seeing. The only ghostly image I'd ever seen was a man I *thought* was Second.

But as I studied one of the two ghosts standing, I realized the male looked similar, but not the same as Second. A tattered button up covered his broad torso. His strong jaw was clean shaven. Two soft eyes looked at me kindly. They were comforting, familiar. A beat passed before it clicked. They were the same eyes I saw in the mirrors at Peek-a-Brews and in my rearview. The same face I saw in the glossy bar counter. The same as the photograph Aunt Margot showed me.

The man was Little Ghost. The ghost bound to Kayleigh. The one destined to save her, but failed.

The one who never moved on.

I couldn't believe the dead man who tried to save Kayleigh stood in the mirror before me, holding hands with another apparition. When my gaze fell upon the female, I gasped.

She looked like me.

Slight differences in build, but curly hair floated around her round cheeks. White eyes brightened when her lips turned upward. A flowing dress swayed around her curvy frame.

One word escaped my lips: "Kayleigh?"

She smiled and nodded.

A crack of electricity popped between Second and myself and

I gasped. A burning scent tickled my nose. We looked down at the piece of paper between us. Smoke floated from its page, but no flame sparked. A crackle of bright electricity danced in the center like magic before quickly fading.

With trembling fingers, Second took the paper and opened it. His eye scanned it a few times before his jaw dropped. "Violetta, this is…" His voice trailed off and he handed me back the paper.

A lump formed in my throat as my eyes fell upon the page.

Beneath the phone number I scrawled were ten words that would live for an eternity in my mind:

```
We can't leave yet. There's one last thing
                  to do.
```

Second and I stared at each other for what felt like hours. Neither of us could comprehend the two sentences etched into the page between us. The two ghosts in the mirror faded away, leaving only our reflections.

Second cleared his throat and rubbed the back of his head. He composed himself faster than my shaking body could. "Well, Violetta Sparks, this is going to *ducking* haunt me until I figure it out."

I nodded, trying to be as collected as him. "Same here. I don't understand. We're both alive, Kayleigh saved me. Why can't she go home? And who is Little Ghost? I know he failed, but…"

"I'm not sure who either of those people are, so it sounds like you'll need to catch me up on some things. I only know the woman in the mirror: Ghost Girl." He shook his head. "I mean Kayleigh. She is the one who appeared to me in the woods." He cleared his throat. "She talked to me. She is the one who led me to you."

I blinked a few times. "She did? Is that how you were able to talk to me?"

He shrugged. "That's my guess. I don't know much about ghosts." Strong fingers ran through his thick hair. "I actually came here looking for the sister who loves paranormal stuff. I was hoping she knew the real ghost story and could maybe help me find Ghost Girl."

I cocked my head to the side. "You came with Riley to find my sister, Aria?"

"I guess so, but if that ghost is this girl you call Kayleigh, then, who was that other guy?" He jabbed a thumb toward the mirror. "Did you think he was me? I definitely thought Kayleigh was you."

Sparks flickered as I rubbed my fingers across the ghost's message. "I did think you were a ghost. I saw Little Ghost—that's what Kayleigh called him first before she died—in reflections a few times. But I *did* speak to you. I may have seen him, but I know in my heart I was the one speaking to you. You…" I hesitated, thinking of the right words. The truth? Magical text appearing on the pages of my notebook brought me closer to another person than I ever thought possible. In reality? He loved me through my letters, and I loved him.

But tonight, we were strangers. That's how our new relationship should start. "You talked to me through my letters. The text would appear in my journal." My trembling hands dropped my notebook before I could successfully show it to him.

He put up a hand as he bent over to retrieve it. Seeing the journal look small in his large hands made my lungs clench. My journal used to be the closest thing I had to him, but it's also evidence of a painful relationship. Second reading the entries was the same as seeing the scars of my patched up heart.

He returned the book and I sucked in a deep breath. Gingerly, I flipped through the notebook. I needed to show him. They were his words after all. My thumb stopped on one of our first exchanges. "This is how I would speak to you."

His eye widened and his mind seemed to wander as he re-read our conversations. I wondered what images flickered in front of his eyes. His breath hitched as he looked up at me and whispered, "I-it really is *you*, Ghost Girl."

I giggled and his face softened. Tears pricked my eyes. Smiling, I replied, "I guess I *am* your Ghost Girl."

A wave of relief, joy, and satisfaction washed over Second. The smile on his face was brighter than the stars in the heavens. Comforting, magical. Never had a man looked at me with such longing and happiness.

My stomach fluttered and I wanted to wrap my arms around his neck and hug him tightly. But I didn't. We didn't really know each other, but I wanted to. I wanted to start over. Second was someone I met at a gala and got to talk to at a bar. The ghostly ties that brought us together did their job.

Now, it's my turn to do the rest.

"So, what do we do now?" I asked with a smile. "Those ghosts seemed to have something else in store for us."

He laughed. "They do, and I think you need to tell me the whole Little Ghost and Kayleigh story. I'm a little lost, but I trust you." He stroked his beard and said, "I still can't believe I found *you*. My Ghost Girl. *Alive*."

Breath caught in my chest as he said *my*. My heart wanted to be his, but my mind needed healing. With my heart still beating, I have plenty of time. "I'm alive, and so are you."

Second beamed. "Well, then, Miss Violetta Sparks, now we've found each other alive and well, I have an important question to ask you." He clasped my hands as I clutched the notebook. Gently, he pulled me closer to him. My body pressed against him and my whole soul ignited.

Second cleared his throat and kept his eye locked on me as he asked, "Would you like to take me up on that adventure?"

I beamed. He truly was a man of his word. I brought his hands and the journal closer to my heart, remembering the letter in the forest.

"I would love nothing more."

TO BE CONTINUED

DON'T MISS THEIR STORY

Will We Adventure Always?

A NOTE FROM THE AUTHOR

This story wasn't supposed to be hard to write. My stories don't shy away from brokenness. They show cracks in humanity but also how we patch ourselves together. Each character has a small reflection of my soul.

But Violetta became a mirror. I saw more of myself than I was supposed to.

While *She Whispered through the Woods* started as a short story for my husband, *He Loved Me through My Letters* was only supposed to be Violetta's narrative. It wasn't supposed to be mine.

Violetta's weaknesses and desire for others' happiness caused my pen to falter as I wrote vulnerable moments. It was raw. Dark. On multiple occasions, I wanted to scrap the entire story.

Then, I realized this story wasn't about me.

It's about the kid who loved exploring but was told to get their head out of the clouds. It's the teen who was awkward, felt weird in their own skin, and wanted to fit in. It's the college student who struggled to balance studies and surviving. It's the new adult trying to find their place in the world while learning to love themselves.

This book is about you.

If you didn't like this story, that's okay. If it hit a little too hard at times, I want you to know it hit me, too. I believe this story will reach the person who needs it.

If that is you, know I am happy this book found you.

Love is four letters, but write even more. The end of your story is in your hands but don't make the journey alone. You have people who care about you. Bring them in. They'll be waiting for you.

With truth, hope, and strength,

Sara Francis

ACKNOWLEDGEMENTS

I continue to write because of my friends, family, and community. Without them, these stories wouldn't be on your shelves (or on your Kindle).

The Belletrists: R.C. Lloyd, Jenni Sauer, and Erin Forbes. You were there when I wrote the first draft. You were there when I cried saying I hated this story and wanted to throw my laptop out the window. You showed me that I can write what I want. I don't have to write for an agenda. I don't have to write something fake. If I wanted there to be a dancing ballroom scene in a book about ghosts, then *ducking bells* I'm going to write it. Moving forward, I'm only writing what I want. So, hope you're ready for a ghost road trip.

My beta readers: R.C. Lloyd, Emma Hill, and Stephanie Crachiolo. You read this story in its most vulnerable state. You saw it broken apart, ugly, and disgusting. Your love, support, and honest feedback guided me into publishing something I am proud of.

The HLMTML Street Team: The hype crew. The support group. Your enthusiasm, joy, and love for my story even before it was published got me through the hardest times of the publishing journey.

To my editor, Angela Watts: Your continuous support with editing this trilogy has brought a smile to my face. You're always quick to help and I couldn't be more grateful for you.

Bookstagram and Kickstarter Communities: Thank you for sticking with me throughout every crazy idea, viral video, new stretch goal, and late-night working session.

My family: Mom, Dad, Mary Grace, Therese, and Catherine, thanks for believing in me and inspiring the Sparks family in this story.

My husband, Paul (aka IV). My alpha reader. My unpaid intern. My salesman. Waking up to you everyday is the reason why I cannot wait to write the third book of this trilogy. Second and Violetta are going to go on as many crazy adventures as we have. I look forward to our next chapters.

I owe all my talents to the One True King. Let my work sing His praises and my words reflect His own.

And finally, thank you for reading. It's a raw story and not for everyone, but I appreciate you giving it a chance. Always remember you can craft your own story. Pick up the pen, and write that letter.

KICKSTARTER ACKNOWLEDGEMENTS

A special thanks to these amazing Kickstarter backers.
Their support truly brought this book to life.

@becksreadingbooks
Abigail Hawthorne
Adelaide Thorne
Alexandra Corrsin
Amanda Balter
Angela Miles
Angela R. Watts
Anna Cuccovia
Annarose Willhite
Aunt Bonnie
Bee
Benita J. Thompson
Bramwell AH Crocker
Brittany Mack
Cameron & Melissa Tidd
Catherine Holmes
Chandler Pope-Lewis
Charlotte Daaku
Cherelle H
Chloe Griffith
Chris Behrsin
Christina Tang-Bernas
Christy S
Claire
Connie Hendryx
Connie Webster

D.E. Carlson
Dana A. Caldwell
Danielle Harrington
Danielle Taebel
Deborah Raciti
Diego Riley
E. A. Hendryx
Elizabeth W.
Emerald Bruce
Emma Hill
Erin Lane
Eugénie
Felicitas Odemer
Fernanda Ortiz
Florentina
Franchesca Caram
Gina R. Briggs
Giselle
Greg Raciti
Hannah Pennington
Haven Bahr
Iqra Shafi
Irene Sylvan
Isabel K
Jen Woodrum
Jess Micklethwaite

Josh Baron
Jules Dyrud
Julia Priest
June C. Cali
K Werntz
K.L. Smith
K.Q. Kimler
Katherine
Katherine Crowe
Katherine Shipman
Kayla De La O
Keric
Kimberly Byrd
Kira Chandra
Kristen Schleif
Laura Linker
Lauren Raciti
Lindsey
Lindsey Petrucci
Liza Czahlo
Maggi W
Maria Zavala
Mark Edelson
Meagan
Michaela Bush
MichelleG
Midnightmare
Morgan G.
Morgan Hagar
Natalie Colburn

Nicholas Stephenson
Nicole Folsom
Nicole Wright
R. M. Everhart
Rachel Simpson
Rébecca Boileau
Samantha Mendell
Samantha N Newberry
Samantha Tucker
Simone Perry
Stephanie Crachiolo
Stephanie De Luna
Svenja Kristina Beck
Terri Raciti
Tetiana Kocherhan
The Horn Family
Valerie Anne
Vickie Grider

ABOUT THE AUTHOR

Sara Francis has over 12 fiction publications. Her writing career started with The Terra Testimonies, a YA Dystopian trilogy for fans of The Hunger Games, X-Men, and Ender's Game. From there, her writing career evolved into writing children's books, poetry, short stories, and contemporary fiction. She hopes to make souls brighter and lives lighter through her stories. Her books are meant to inspire you to seek what is true, good, and beautiful, remembering you're loved and valued beyond measure.

When Francis isn't writing or working with UGC clients through SF Publishing & Media, she's going on adventures with her husband, or making fun reels for her bookstagram page. She loves coffee and may end up drinking too much and staying up late, playing games or chatting with friends. Sweet potato fries are her favorite food and she believes some problems can be solved with a sweet treat.

Her favorite story tropes are found family, slow burn romance, "Who did this to you?", secret identity, stupid humor, and love triangles (I know, controversial).

At the end of the day, she wants to inspire others to become the best version of themselves, enjoying this life to the fullest until it's time for the next.

KEEP IN TOUCH WITH SARA FRANCIS ON
SOCIAL MEDIA

☉ SaraFrancis_Author

ⓕ SaraFrancisAuthor

♪ SaraFrancisAuthor

PLEASE SUBSCRIBE TO HER NEWSLETTER
TO STAY UP TO DATE

WWW.SARA-FRANCIS.COM/SUBSCRIBE

CONSIDER LEAVING A REVIEW ON GOODREADS
AND AMAZON TO SPREAD THE WORD ABOUT
HE LOVED ME THROUGH MY LETTERS

SCAN FOR QUICK LINKS!

STORMY NIGHT MOCHA

INGREDIENTS

- ¾ cup milk of choice
- 2 tablespoon hazelnut spread
- 2 shots of espresso OR 5 teaspoons instant coffee
- Dark chocolate syrup
- 1 tablespoon heavy cream
- Cocoa powder (optional)

INSTRUCTIONS

- Place your milk and hazelnut spread in a small saucepan over medium heat until the spread dissolves and the milk is simmering.
- If you do not have an espresso maker, whisk together 5 teaspoons of instant coffee and 1/4 cup of hot water until the coffee is completely dissolved.
- Add your desired amount of dark chocolate syrup to the bottom of the mug. Pour in half of the espresso and stir. Stir in the remaining espresso.
- Froth the hot milk using a handheld milk frother. Slowly pour the frothed milk into your mug.
- Whip your cream in a small bowl or cup with the milk frother until it's softly whipped. Spoon over your caffé mocha.
- Sprinkle with cocoa powder and more dark chocolate syrup if desired.

Drown out the World mix

my theme song

when the tears pour down...

- It's Raining, It's Pouring - Anson Seabra
- Better Than This - Set It Off
- Don't Tell My Mom - Renee Rap
- can't find the words - senses
- Happy - NF
- making the bed - Olivia Rodrigo

... but Second replies

- Invisible - Knox
- Wildflowers - Maddie Poppe
- Sugar Rush - Addison Grace
- Enchanted - Taylor Swift
- Oxygen - Hometown Losers

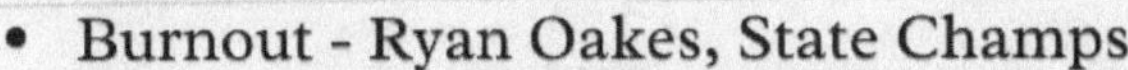

working 9 to 5

- Burnout - Ryan Oakes, State Champs
- Overwhelmed - Sweet Ascent
- Surface Pressure - Our Last Night Cover (obvi)
- better than this - senses
- Quitting - Ian McConnell

getting rid of bryce

- Narcissist - Avery Anna
- enough for you - Olivia Rodrigo
- Time Machine - Knox
- You're Just A Boy - Maisie Peters

finding me again

- Head in Her Heart - Nico Callins
- Keep Your Head Up Princess - Anson Seabra
- Might Not Like Me - Brynn Elliott
- Just Begun - WILD
- Something That I Want - Grace Potter